PENGUIN C

PUZZLE F

Patrick Quentin is the pen-name of Hugh Callingham Wheeler, born in Hampstead in 1912. He was educated at Clayesmore School and at the universities of both London and Berlin. In 1934 he went to the United States, where he has lived ever since; he is an American citizen. Apart from a period in the U.S. Army Medical Corps his work has been writing. He spends six months of the year in his eighteenth-century farmhouse in New England and his New York apartment, the other six in his house on the island of St Kitts in the Caribbean. His interests, apart from writing, include music, modern painting and gardening.

Until 1952, 'Patrick Quentin' was a collaboration, also involving Richard Wilson Webb. Wheeler and Webb also wrote under the pseudonyms 'Q Patrick' and 'Jonathan Stagge'.

Several of Patrick Quentin's books have been published in Penguin, including *The Wife of Ronald Sheldon* and *The Follower*. His final mystery story was *Family Skeletons*, published in 1963. Following this he totally changed his career and turned to playwrighting under his own name. His Broadway plays include *Big Fish, Little Fish* and *Look We've Come Through*, as well as several musicals including *A Little Night Music* and *Sweeney Todd* in collaboration with Stephen Sondheim, and *Candide* in collaboration with Leonard Bernstein. He has also written the opera *Silverlake* with Kurt Weill, and an *Impresario* with the music of Mozart. He has won many awards for his plays including three Tony Awards, four Drama Critic's Circle Awards and several *Evening Standard* awards.

PATRICK QUENTIN

PUZZLE FOR FIENDS

A Peter Duluth Mystery

PENGUIN BOOKS

PENGUIN BOOKS
Viking Penguin Inc., 40 West 23rd Street,
New York, New York 10010, U.S.A.
Penguin Books Ltd, Harmondsworth,
Middlesex, England
Penguin Books Australia Ltd, Ringwood,
Victoria, Australia
Penguin Books Canada Limited, 2801 John Street,
Markham, Ontario, Canada L3R 1B4
Penguin Books (N.Z.) Ltd, 182–190 Wairau Road,
Auckland 10, New Zealand

First published in the United States of America by
Simon and Schuster 1946
First published in Great Britain by Victor Gollancz 1946
Published in Penguin Books 1955
Reissued 1986

CIP data available
ISBN 0 14 00.8082 1

Printed in the United States of America by
R. R. Donnelley & Sons Company, Harrisonburg, Virginia
Set in Garamond

Prologue

BEHIND us the bomber's propellers were roaring. The Burbank Airfield stretched endlessly. Iris looked small and rather frightened. It was that horrible just-before-saying-good-bye moment.

'Take care of yourself, baby,' I said, being jaunty. 'Give my love to Tokyo.'

'Peter, it's crazy. I'd never have signed up if I'd known the Navy'd discharge you so soon.' My wife's lips were unsteady. 'It's such a waste. Me going away – you staying home.'

'It's only three months, baby. And think of that Occupation Army panting to see its favourite Hollywood cookie in the flesh.'

'I don't want to be seen in the flesh except by you.'

The studio had sent photographers to immortalize the occasion. Camera shutters clicked.

Iris asked anxiously: 'You're sure you've got to drive straight back to San Diego?'

''Fraid so. Promised the boys I'd show up for a last fling. They want to see me as a civilian.'

'You in your fancy palm beach suit and gent's haberdashery. I still hardly believe it's you.' Iris sneaked her hand into mine. 'Do be careful driving, Peter. All that champagne we drank at the hotel. You know what champagne does to you.'

'Don't forget your rubbers and button up your overcoat,' I mocked her, trying to kid myself I didn't feel forlorn. 'Baby, you sound the way Mother used to sound.'

'I wish your mother were still alive so there'd be someone sensible to watch out for you when I'm gone. You're such a goon.' Iris clung to me. 'Don't have accidents, Peter. Don't drink too much. Don't whistle after sultry brunettes.'

'Not even small ones?'

'Not even small ones. Oh, Peter darling, miss me.'

'Miss you, baby? Miss you?'

The co-pilot came out of the plane. 'Sorry, Mrs Duluth, we're set to take off.'

I slipped my arms around my wife and kissed her. It was a long kiss. It had to last me ninety lonely days. She twisted away from me and hurried into the plane without looking back.

I wasn't going to turn the knife in the wound by sticking around any longer. I headed back through the wire fence to the airport building and found my way to my car. As I opened the door, I felt a hand on my arm.

I turned to see one of the boys I'd noticed hanging around the plane, a rather unprepossessing boy with a thin, narrow face, close-set eyes and an untidy mane of black hair.

'Going to San Diego, mister?'

'Yes.'

'Gimme a ride?'

The champagne had made me expansive. 'Sure. Jump in.'

As we drove away, I caught a glimpse of Iris's plane zooming down the runway.

The boy was scrutinizing me out of the corner of his eyes. 'Say, ain't you the husband of that movie star just went off? Iris Duluth?'

'Yes,' I said.

He gave a low wolfish whistle. 'Lucky guy.'

'Lucky guy is right,' I said.

Lucky guy!

That's what I thought....

Chapter 1

I WAS awake, but something was wrong. That was the first thought I had. This wasn't the proper way to wake up. My ominous dreams had faded. The whirring of propellers was scarcely louder now than the murmur of a sea-shell in your ear. But nothing came to take the place of the dreams – nothing but a sense of warmth, a dull ache in my head and the knowledge that I could open my eyes if I wanted to.

I didn't want to open my eyes. The consciousness of my closed lids, screening me from whatever there was around me, was comforting. I was confusedly convinced that I had awakened like this – blankly – several times before. A few tenuous memories stirred, a memory of whiteness, of corridors, of the hostile smell of ether, of stretchers and a jogging ambulance. The mental image of the ambulance started the propellers roaring again. I lay passive waiting for them to whir themselves out.

When they had droned down to a mosquito whine, I made a terrific effort of will. In my mind I managed to form the sentence.

I am in a bed.

The effort exhausted me. I lay still, receptive. There was sunlight. I could feel it, half see it, on my lids. There was a smell too. Not ether. A sweet, summer smell. The smell of roses.

I was lying on my back. I knew that. I knew too that I was uncomfortable. I tried to roll over on my right side. I couldn't. My right elbow seemed huge and unyielding as a boulder. I felt down my right forearm with the fingers of my left hand. I didn't feel flesh. I felt something hard, cold, and rough. It was too difficult to try to understand. I forgot it and made an attempt to shift onto my left side. Once again I made no progress. This time it was my left leg that obstructed me. It was twice as big as a cow. I groped down to touch it. No flesh there either, just hardness, coldness, roughness.

I was annoyed. Distinctly and out loud I said:
'Twice as big as a cow.'

A rustling sound came, very close to me – the sort of dry rustling, of someone fumbling through a box of candy at the movies. Its closeness, its vague implication of danger, made me open my eyes.

I was staring straight at a woman, and she was staring back placidly. She sat very near my bed in a shimmering pool of sunlight. A bowl of pink roses stood on a table next to her. She had a large, beribboned box of chocolate candy on her knee. She was putting a piece in her mouth.

'What's twice as big as a cow, dear?' she asked. 'Me?'

I knew perfectly well that something was twice as big as a cow, but I was almost sure that it wasn't she. And yet it might have been. I studied her gravely. She was big – a large comfortable woman with lovely skin and thick auburn hair piled on top of her head in a slapdash attempt at a fashionable upsweep. She wasn't young. She must have been almost fifty. But she was still beautiful in a rich, overblown way – the way the pink roses would look just before their petals started to drop. She was wearing unrelieved mourning black that didn't belong with her ripe, autumnal sensuality. My bemused and unpredictable thought processes decided that she was posing as a widow.

Of course, I thought. Here is a woman posing as a widow.

For a moment this deduction seemed to explain the entire situation to my complete satisfaction.

Uneasily, however, I began to remember that she had asked me a question. I knew it was impolite not to answer questions. But I no longer had the slightest idea what the question was. Behind her, broad windows, draped in voluptuous cream brocade, opened onto an unknown, sunny garden. All I could see of the room was light and luxurious as meringue. The woman was eating another chocolate. Had she offered me one? Yes, that was it, of course.

'No thank you,' I said.

'No thank you for what, dear?' she asked soothingly.

'I don't think I want any candy.'

Her eyes, large and liquid brown, stared. 'My darling boy, I don't imagine you would – not with all that ether and the drugs and things inside you.' She stretched out a smooth, white hand and caressed my cheek. 'How do you feel? Terrible?'

'Terrible,' I said promptly.

'Of course. But there's nothing to worry about. You'll be all right.' Her hand groped for a piece of candy and then hesitated. 'Does watching me eat this turn your stomach? I'll stop if you really want me to only it's such divine candy. Selena bought it for you down at that little candy place that's just opened on the Coast Boulevard. That's so like Selena, isn't it – thinking you'd want candy at a time like this.'

The conversation had become too complicated for me. I just lay watching the woman, listening for the faint whir of the propellers, waiting warily for them to come back. I hadn't any idea who the woman was. I was sure of that. But I liked looking at her, liked the precarious pile of glossy auburn hair and the full, satiny bosom which thrust so unashamedly out of the square-necked widow dress. I wanted to lay my head against it and go to sleep. Vaguely I started to wonder who she was. I thought of asking her. But wouldn't that be rude? Disconnected fragments of what she had said were drifting in the haze of my thoughts. *Ether, drugs.* I considered those two words for a long time and finally decided upon a question that seemed both clever and subtle.

'Ether,' I said, 'drugs. What's the matter with me?'

The woman put the box of candy down by the roses and leaned towards me, taking my hand.

'Don't worry, dear. It'll all come back soon.'

I felt testy, frustrated. 'But what...?'

She sighed, a full, chesty sigh. 'All right, dear. If you really want to know. Feel your head.'

I put up my left hand. I felt bandages.

'Bandages,' I said.

'Good boy.' She smiled showing vivid teeth. 'Now try your right arm.'

I reached my left hand over and touched my right forearm. It was still the way it had been – hard, rough, cold. I turned my head to look. There was a sling and under the sling a cast.

'A cast,' I said.

'Go to the head of the class, darling.' She leaned across the bed and patted a hump that pushed up the grey and gold spread. 'That's a cast too. On your left leg.' She turned. Her face, grave and gentle, was close to mine, curved up on a white throat that was only a little thickened. She was wearing an exotic, unwidowish perfume. Its headiness and the warmth of her nearness confused me. 'What's a cast for?'

I thought, and felt suddenly brilliant. 'When you break something.'

'Exactly.'

'Then I've broken something.' I was pleased with myself. I also felt fond of her for letting me prove how intelligent I was.

'Yes, darling. You've broken your right arm and your left leg. And you've also been hit on that poor old head of yours. An accident.'

'An accident?'

'An automobile accident. You were out in the Buick by yourself. You smashed head on into a eucalyptus grove.' A smile played around the fresh lips. 'Really, darling, you are a naughty boy. You know how dangerous it is to drive when you've been drinking.'

I was struggling hard to keep abreast of her. An automobile accident. I had been in a car. I had run into a tree. I had broken my leg and my arm. Those were facts, the sort of things I should be able to check in my mind. Did I, perhaps, have some recollection, dim as the date on a worn dime, of a car lunging forward out of control?

She was sitting very still now by the bowl of pink roses, watching me with patient curiosity.

'Accidents and hospitals,' I said. 'I'm not in a hospital, I...' I broke in on myself. 'I was in a hospital. I remember I was in a hospital. But I'm not in a hospital now.'

'No, dear. You were in the hospital for two weeks but you've been out two days now. Dr Croft's been keeping you under sedatives. I don't quite know why, something to do with the hit on the head.'

A fuzzy pattern was beginning to form. I had been in a hospital. Now I was out. Out? Where was out?

I stared at the woman and beyond her at the rich, unfamiliar cream drapes screening the long, sunny windows. 'Where am I now?' I asked.

She leaned towards me again, her lips almost touching my cheek. Vague anxiety seemed to be rippling her monumental passivity. 'Dearest, you know where you are. Look around.'

Her face and the mass of hair blocked almost all of my view. But dutifully I looked at what I could see – an area of deeply piled corn-coloured carpet, a fantastic vanity all white bows and perfume bottles, and, beyond the woman, another bed like mine, a large, voluptuous bed covered with a gleaming grey and gold striped spread.

'It's nice,' I said. 'But I've never seen it before in my life.'

'But, darling, really, you must know.'

I felt rather apologetic because I could tell I was somehow worrying her. I said: 'I'm sorry. I'm really trying. Where am I?'

'You're home,' she said.

'Home?'

'Home, dear. In your own bed in your own room in your own house in Lona Beach, South California.'

My slight ability to keep a coherent thought track was weakening. I knew she said I was home. I also knew that home was a place you were meant to know and that I didn't know this place. Something, I felt dimly, was a little unusual about all this. But the bed was warm and I liked the smell of roses. The propellers hadn't come back either. I nestled my head back against the pillows and smiled. She was such a nice, pillowy woman. It was so pleasant having her there. If only she wouldn't talk so much, this would be wonderful.

'Darling, don't smile like that. It's worrying. It's such a

stupid smile – like a chimpanzee.' The anxiety was in her eyes now. 'Dearest, please try and remember. I'm sure you can if you try.' She paused and added abruptly: 'Who am I?'

With a sinking sensation, I knew I was going to flunk that question too. I felt awkward. I wanted very much to know who she was, but I didn't want her to think I was stupid, like a chimpanzee. Craftily, I thought, I said: 'You're not a nurse.'

'Of course I'm not a nurse.' She made a rather agitated stab at her untidy back hair. 'Who do I look like, dear?'

Suddenly I knew. 'A barmaid,' I said. 'A glamorous English barmaid in a book.'

For a second she seemed staggered. Then her whole face flushed from a delightful smile.

'Dear, that's the sweetest thing you've ever said to me.' A far-away, dreamy look came into her eyes. 'I serve a haunch of venison to a dark stranger in the back parlour of the tavern. He pinches my behind, turns out to be Charles the Second travelling incognito. I am installed in a small, discreet palace on the Thames.'

The conversation was hopelessly running away from me.

'I am the toast of the town, gorgeous négligés, young bucks, handpicked from the peerage, drink champagne from my slippers. But only the King can snap my garters.' She shook her head in sad return from fantasy. 'No, dear, I'm not a barmaid.'

'Then who are you?' I said, too muddled to try any longer to be subtle.

'This is awfully disturbing, dear. I do hope Dr Croft will be able to do something about it. After all, it's not much to ask you to recognize your own mother.'

'My mother.'

'Of course. Who else could I be?' She looked slightly pained. 'And a good mother I've been to you too – even if I do say it myself.'

The knowledge that I was convalescent and still legitimately confused in the head cushioned me from the shock. But it was still a shock to hear a perfectly unknown woman with auburn hair announce that she was my mother. Mothers were things you were supposed to recognize without having to be told. I thought about saying something rather stiff like: *Absolutely absurd. You my mother – nonsense!* But when I tried to cling on to the actual words to say them, they slid away from me like wet trout through your fingers. I felt weak again and my head was aching. I gave up trying to communicate with the woman and struggled with the problem in silence.

Someone was my mother. I couldn't get around that. If this woman wasn't my mother, who was? That's easy, I said to myself. My mother is ... Then the sentence stuck. I hadn't any idea who my mother was. The realization seemed infinitely pathetic. So pathetic that I was able to say it out loud.

'I don't know,' I said wistfully, 'who my mother is.'

The woman had been looking at the roses. She turned sharply.

'Darling, do please try not to be too complicated. I'm supposed to be nursing you. I thought it would be nicer having your mother nurse you instead of one of those cold pillars of starch from the hospital. But I'm not very much of a nurse. I mean, I did a little in the last war and I've taken a Red Cross Refresher Course. But if you start having weird symptoms, I'll have to get one of those professionals after all and she'll keep giving you bed pans and plumping out your pillows and breathing down your neck.' She smiled and patted my hand. 'You wouldn't like that, would you?'

I didn't know whether I would like it or not. I was lost now in self pity. Her smooth, warm fingers had curled around my left hand again.

'Darling, tell me. Just how much do you remember?'

'I remember the hospital. I remember white ...'

'No, dear. I don't mean about the hospital. I mean the real things – the things about you.' She turned her head, indicating the second bed beyond her. 'Who sleeps in that bed?'

'I – I don't know.'

'Who's Selena? Who's Marny?' She must have seen the blank expression on my face because she didn't wait for me to attempt an answer. She added quickly: 'What's your name?'

'My name is ...' I began, then panic wormed through me. Since my return to consciousness, I had never actually thought about my name. You don't think about your name. I knew I was me, that my personal identity was inviolable. But what was my name? I stared at her as if her big, curving body would act as an anchor, steadying me.

'You don't remember even that, do you?' she said.

I shook my head. 'It's crazy. When I try to think there's nothing. There's ...'

'Don't worry, my baby.' Her voice was rich, soothing. 'It's just the hit on the head. That often happens. I know it does. You'll soon be well again, Gordy.'

'Gordy?'

'Yes, dear. That's your name. Gordy Friend. Gordon Renton Friend the Third.'

There was a gentle tap on the door. The woman called: 'Who is it?' The door opened a crack and the head of a uniformed maid peered around it. I noticed that her eyes, greedy with curiosity, flashed instantly to my bed.

'What is it, Netti?'

'Dr Croft, Mrs Friend. He's just arrived. Shall I send him up?'

'Thank heavens. No, Netti. I'll come down.' The woman rose. She stared down at me and then bent over me, kissing me on the forehead. Loose strands of the auburn hair tickled my cheek. The perfume wreathed into my nostrils. 'Just lie there calmly while I'm away, dear. Don't be frightened. Don't try to force yourself. Just say it over and over again. Say "I'm Gordy Friend". Do that – for me.'

She moved out of the room, large and majestically voluptuous in spite of the drab widow's weeds. After she had gone, I did what she said, I lay in that luxurious bed in that great sunsplashed room, marshalling my pathetically small array of facts. I had been in an accident; I had broken my left leg and my right arm. I had been hit on the head. I was home in my own room in my own house in Lona Beach, South California. My name was Gordy Friend. I said that over and over:

I am Gordy Friend. I am Gordy Friend. I am Gordon Renton Friend the Third.

But the words just remained words. I presumed that was my name. After all, my mother had told me it was.

My mother? My name?

The propellers started to whir again. And, although I hated them and feared them, somehow they had more reality than everything that had happened or been said in this room.

If only I could remember what the propellers meant.

Propellers – a plane ... seeing someone off on a plane ...

Was that it?

Had I seen someone off on a plane?

Chapter 2

SEEING *someone off on a plane*. Those few words, linked together, seemed to have terrific significance. For a moment I felt I was teetering on the brink of an ultimate revelation. Then the words and the image they almost conjured up blurred and dissipated in my mind. I felt spent from the effort of concentration. Like a torpedoed sailor clinging to a floating board, I clung for security to the one established fact of my life.

I am Gordy Friend.

Curiosity, without much motive behind it, made me raise my bandaged head so that I could survey the whole room. It was as luxurious as I had imagined it to be from the part of it that had already come into my field of vision. Beyond the fantastic, rococo vanity, stood a chaise longue upholstered in pale green satin. On it, thrown in a careless tumble, was a shimmering white négligé. There was sunlight everywhere and the colours of the room brought their own sunlight too. The pink roses by the bed were only partly responsible for the perfume. There were vases of flowers everywhere – more roses, massed yellow tulips, tall irises and spikes of white stock.

Slowly my gaze moved from object to object and returned to the white négligé on the chaise longue. I stared at it as if it had some secret which had to be puzzled out. A woman's négligé. The whole feeling of the room was feminine too – frivolous, vivid, individual. Was that the secret? That my room was disguised as a woman's room?

I couldn't make much headway with this thought. The harder I struggled with it the more elusive it became.

'Gordy Friend,' I said out loud. 'Gordon Renton Friend the Third.'

The door opened. My mother came in. I could feel her without even turning my head – feel that presence, mellow as ripened wheat, intrude upon the spring freshness of the room.

She was at my bed. Her tranquil hand was on my forehead. 'I've brought Dr Croft, dear. He says we're not to worry. It's the result of the concussion. It's something he expected.'

A man moved into my field of vision. He was in the early thirties, very dark. He was dressed in tweeds that were expensive and casual. He was standing casually too, his hands in his pockets. My sensibilities, as unnaturally sharpened in some particulars as they were dulled in others felt that it was more important to him than anything else in the world to look like any one of a hundred impeccable young members of the most exclusive country club of his neighbourhood.

I've just dropped in after a round of golf, his stance said. Quite a good workout today.

But in spite of the conforming camouflage, he didn't look average at all. His dusky face was far too handsome to be unobtrusive, and his black eyes, beautiful and long-lashed as a Turkish dancing girl's, gave the lie to the successful-broker tweeds.

'Hi, Gordy,' he said. 'How d'you feel?'

I looked up into his white smile, feeling faintly hostile.

I said: 'Are you someone I'm supposed to know too?'

His hands still in his pockets, he rocked gently back and forth on his heels, studying me. 'You honestly don't recognize your mother?'

'No,' I said.

'Well, well. What a state of affairs. We must fix this up.'

'He thought I was a barmaid.' My mother smiled a shy, girl's smile that brought rose pink to her cheeks. 'I never realized it before but that's always been my secret desire. A pint o' bitter,' she called in a hoarse, cockney voice. ''Urry up with that 'alf and 'alf.'

A certain rigidity in the young man indicated that this vulgar pleasantry made him uncomfortable. A new personality was forming in him. He was the serious young doctor getting down to business.

'Well, let's see what we can do, shall we?' He turned a professional brisk look on my mother. 'Perhaps I should be left alone with the patient for a while, Mrs Friend.'

'Why, of course.' My mother threw me a coaxing smile. 'Do try to be good and helpful, Gordy. Dr Croft's such a sweet man and I know you'll be remembering everything if you just do what he says.'

She started for the door, turned, came back for the be-ribboned box of candy and, rather guiltily, carried it away with her.

As soon as we were alone, the young man became affable efficiency personified. He brought a chair to the bedside, swung it around and sat on it back to front. I was feeling clearer in the head now and something in me, without conscious identity, was putting me on my guard.

'Okay, Gordy.' I got a head-on smile. 'In the first place, I'm Nate Croft. You'll remember that soon. You'll also remember that I'm quite a pal of yours and Selena's and Marny's.'

Adrift as I was, I was stubbornly sure that I could never have been 'quite a pal' of this man with the soft, dusky skin and the vamping, dancing girl eyes. I didn't tell him that, though, I just lay there, waiting.

He lit a cigarette from an expensive case with a 'Sorry I can't offer you one, old man.' Then, watching me brightly through smoke, he asked: 'Tell me, Gordy, just how much can you remember?'

'I can remember whirring propellers,' I said. 'I think I can remember an airfield, and a plane, and seeing someone off on a plane.'

'Anyone in particular?'

I strained to recapture some vanished half image. 'No. Not exactly. Except that it seems terribly important.'

'The propellers come first?'

'Yes. They always seem to be almost there, if you see what I mean. Even if I can't hear them, I ...'

'Yes, yes,' he broke in, very much the professional interpreter of amateur information. 'I'm afraid that isn't going to be very helpful to us.'

I felt inexplicably depressed. 'You mean there wasn't anyone going away on a plane?'

'A common ether reaction.' Dr Nate Croft held his cigarette poised between us. 'The loss of consciousness visualizing itself as a whirring propeller. This person you imagine you were seeing off, was it a man or a woman?'

Suddenly I knew, and I felt a rush of excitement. 'A woman.'

Dr Croft nodded. 'The nurse in the operating room. We get that frequently. A patient clings to the nurse's image in exact proportion to his reluctance to lose consciousness. She is the image of reality that the patient feels he is saying good-bye to before the journey into unconsciousness.'

I couldn't understand why that rather pompous medical explanation brought a strange despair. He went on:

'Forget the propellers, Gordy. Anything else?'

I said listlessly: 'There's a hospital, various snatches of things in a hospital.'

'Of course.' Dr Nate Croft studied his clean hands. 'You recovered consciousness several times in the hospital. Is that all?'

I nodded: 'All except what happened after I woke up here.'

'Well, well, we won't let it worry us, will we?' The teeth flashed again. 'How about I bring you up to date a bit, Gordy. Your mother's told you about the accident?'

'Yes,' I said.

'It happened down the Coast Boulevard. In the evening. You know, that deserted stretch on the way to San Diego.'

'San Diego?' I tried to sit up .

'Yes. Why? Does San Diego mean anything to you?'

'San Diego.' I added uncertainly: 'Am I in the Navy?'

'The Navy?' Nate Croft laughed. 'What strange little things cling on in the mind. A couple of months ago, you went to San Diego, tried to enlist. They turned you down. Remember?'

The bed was very comfortable and the effort to remain suspicious was becoming too taxing. Dr Croft seemed quite a nice guy now, kind, considerate. Too pretty but quite a nice guy.

'Funny,' I said, wanting to confide in him. 'I don't remember it that way. But San Diego means something. And the Navy. I feel as if I'd been in the Navy a long time. Isn't that dopey?'

'No, it's perfectly natural. A wish-fulfilment changed into a false memory by the concussion. You wanted to get into the Navy badly, you know. Now your mind's trying to pretend that you did. But enough of this flossy medico talk.'

He patted my shoulder. His hand was brown and warm. 'Okay. Let's get on with the story. I guess you don't remember, but I run a small private sanatorium up in the mountains. Some people passing in another car found you. They asked for the nearest hospital and brought you up to me. A lucky coincidence – with me being something of a pal.'

'I was conscious?' I asked, listening as if it was a tale about someone else.

'You came to pretty soon after they brought you in. You were in quite bad shape. They had to operate right away on the arm and the leg. We got you in time, however, to prevent any compound fractures.'

He went on: 'It was always the blow on the head that had me the most worried about you, Gordy. Your arm and leg are fine. You won't have any pain from them. But, after we'd got the casts on and you came to from the ether, you were pretty vague, hadn't much idea about what anything was. I kept you under sedatives. I was giving your mind a rest. After you'd come to a couple more times and still weren't clicking, I was sure you had a temporary amnesia. I kept up the sedative treatment for two weeks. Then I thought our best bet might be to bring you home. I was hoping the familiar associations would help you.' His smile was self-deprecatory. 'Seems like I was too optimistic.'

Once again the brown hand, intimate as a woman's, caressed my shoulder. 'But don't you worry yourself about anything, Gordy, old man. You never can tell with these concussion cases. There's no gauging the duration of the amnesia. Things will come back gradually. Maybe in a couple of days, a couple of hours even ...'

'Or a couple of years?' I asked gloomily.

'Now, don't let's get depressed about it, Gordy.' Behind the silky lashes, his harem eyes were watching me. 'Frankly, I'm optimistic. We've nothing to worry about with the arm and the leg. In fact, tomorrow I think I'll let you play around in a wheel chair. You'll be meeting people you know, pushing yourself around places you know. Yes, I'm optimistic all right.'

Although I knew all this was bedside manner, it soothed me. I was beginning to feel a delightful sense of passivity. Here was my mother and this friendly doctor. They were both doing all they could for me. After all, what was there to worry about? I was in a beautiful room. I was cared for. People were nice to me. I was Gordy Friend. Gordon Renton Friend the Third. Soon I would remember just what being Gordy Friend entailed and take up my old life.

I glanced around the sunswept gold and grey room. If this was any indication, being Gordy Friend was pretty painless.

I said, pleased: 'I own this place?'

'Of course, Gordy. The house has been yours since your father died.'

'My father?'

20

'You don't remember your father?' Dr Croft looked amused. 'It seems impossible that anyone could ever forget Gordon Renton Friend the Second.'

'He was famous?'

'Famous? In a way, yes. He'd moved here from St Paul only a couple of years before he died. But he certainly managed to make himself felt in that time.'

'By what?'

'By his personality and ... oh, well, I think you'd better let the family explain about your father.'

'But he's dead?'

'Yes. He died about a month ago.'

'So that's why my mother's in mourning.'

I lay still considering these bare outlines. I tried to stir up a memory picture of Gordon Renton Friend the Second who had certainly made himself felt. Nothing came. My glow of contentment increasing I asked: 'Then I suppose I'm rich?'

'Oh, yes,' said Dr Croft. 'I'd say you were very rich – very rich indeed.'

My mother came in then. She patted Dr Croft's shoulder as she passed him and sat down by my bed next to the pink roses.

'Well, Doctor?'

Nate Croft shrugged the tweed shoulders. 'Nothing very much yet, Mrs Friend.'

'Darling boy.' My mother took my hand and placed it on her large lap. 'Feel better?'

'At least I know now who my father was,' I said.

'I told him a little,' said Dr Croft.

'Only a little, I hope. Poor Gordy, I'm sure he's not strong enough yet to have to start remembering his father.'

I said: 'What was wrong with him? Was he a skeleton in our closet?'

My mother laughed her rich, syrup laugh. 'Good heavens, no. We, darling, were the skeletons. But don't fuss yourself. You just lie quiet while I ask the doctor intelligent questions about what should be done with you.'

'I've nothing much new to say, Mrs Friend.' Dr Croft was glancing very discreetly at his wrist watch. 'Keep on with the same treatment for the time being. As for this miserable temporary amnesia, the best therapy's to keep him in constant contact with familiar objects. That's how we're going to bring him back to normal.'

My mother looked at me and then looked at the doctor and blinked. 'Talking about familiar objects, shouldn't we try Selena on him now?'

Dr Croft shot a swift look down at the hump in the bedspread made by my cast. 'I was just going to suggest it.'

'Selena,' I said. 'You keep talking about Selena. Who is Selena?'

My mother still had my hand in her lap. She squeezed it. 'Darling, you really are sweet. Perhaps I even prefer you without your memory.' She pointed at the second bed. 'Selena is the person who sleeps in that bed. Selena's your wife.'

The white négligé. The feminine room. My wife.

Dr Croft was saying: 'Is she somewhere around, Mrs Friend?'

'I think she's in the patio with Jan.'

'Then I'll send her up. Have to be running, I'm afraid.' Doctor Croft patted my shoulder again. 'I'll be in tomorrow and I'll try to bring you a wheel chair. Chin up, Gordy, old boy. We'll have you back with us before you know. So long, Mrs Friend.'

He left. My mother rose.

'Well, darling, with Selena coming, I think I should beat a tactful retreat.' She scooped up untidy strands of hair. 'If anything's going to bring your memory back, it'll be Selena.'

She moved towards the door and then paused.

'Really, all these flowers. I told Selena she was crazy to bring so many. This room smells like a tomb.'

She crossed to a corner table and picked up two vases. One was full of red roses. The other held a large bunch of white and blue iris.

'I'll take these roses and the iris to Marny's room.'

Carrying the flowers, she looked splendid as an Earth Fertility goddess of some ancient cult. I watched her admiringly as she went to the door. Then a sudden sensation of inconsolable loss swept over me and I called:

'Don't take the iris. Leave the iris.'

She turned, staring at me through the bright flowers. 'Whyever not, Gordy, dear? They're depressing flowers. You know you've never liked iris.'

'I want them,' I said with a vehemence out of all proportion. 'Please leave the iris.'

'Very well, dear. Since you're so passionate about them.'

She put the vase of iris back on the table and went out with the roses.

I lay staring at the slender blue and white flowers. The propellers had started up again in my brain. I told myself that my wife was coming. I had a wife. Her name was Selena. I tried to remember what Selena was going to look like. Nothing came. Always the image of the flowers rose up blotting out the vague image of a wife. I had no control over my thoughts. There were the propellers, and that one word reiterating itself pointlessly.

Iris.... Iris.... Iris.... Iris....

Chapter 3

AFTER a few moments the violence of the iris reaction subsided. But it was still there. Even when I wasn't looking at them, I was conscious of the tall blue and white flowers on the table, and the word stuck in the back of my mind, firmly implanted as a bullet in a dead man's chest.

I was still poor at gauging time. For an indefinite period I lay in bed and gradually the smug sensation of well-being returned. The run-of-the-mill amnesiac didn't come back to such an ideal existence as this. I had a charming mother and a beautiful house. I was rich and they were sending my wife up to me. I had passed through that first, unphysical phase of returning to consciousness. In spite of the faint ache in my head and the cramping casts, I could feel the blood running in my veins again. And the thought of my wife excited my blood.

Selena. I played with the name speculatively. It was one of those tantalizing names. Selena could be tall and slinky with cool green eyes. Selena could be prissy too, bony, spinsterish, with a tight mouth. I was caught up in a sudden unease. Things had been too good to be true so far. There had to be a hitch. What if Selena was the hitch? A bony, spinsterish wife with a tight mouth.

The suspense was almost unendurable now. To combat that cold, elbowy image, I conjured up a host of voluptuous fancies. Selena had to be a brunette, I told myself. Wasn't there a certain type of brunette I was crazy about? What was the word? It was on the tip of my tongue.

Sultry. That was it. Selena had to be a sultry brunette.

The door was kicked open. A young girl crossed the threshold. In one hand she carried a small cocktail shaker full of drinks. In the other she held a single empty glass. For a moment she stood there, quite still, by the door, staring at me.

I stared back, feeling wonderful. She was about twenty-two. She was wearing a dashingly cut black suit with broad shoulders and a skirt that stopped just below the knee showing long straight legs. She had one of those figures that fit under the arm. Her hair, blue-black as tar, fell glossily around her shoulders. She had a face like a chic French doll with a red painted cupid's bow mouth and brown, uninhibited eyes.

She crossed to the bed and sat down next to the roses. My mother was an overblown rose. This girl was a cool, red bud. She still clung on to the shaker and the glass, still stared at me appraisingly. Suddenly she smiled.

'Hello, Gordy, you dreary object.'

She put the shaker and the glass down, and she moved over onto the spread close to me and kissed me on the mouth. Her lips were soft and fragrant. Her young breasts pressed lightly against my pyjamas. I brought my one good arm up and slipped it around her, bringing her closer. I went on kissing her. She squirmed away.

'Hey, Gordy. A sister's a sister.'

'Sister?'

She shook back her hair and sat watching me broodingly. 'Of course I'm your sister. Who d'you think I am? Your brother?'

I felt dejected. 'The doctor said he was sending my wife up.'

'Oh, Selena.' She shrugged. 'She's off somewhere with Jan. Nate couldn't find her.' She twisted around and poured herself a Manhattan. She held the glass by its stem, still watching me. 'Mother said you'd lost your memory. Boy, you certainly have.' She laughed, a deep, rich laugh, my mother's laugh, young. 'If I had your memories, I guess I'd lose them too.'

Her skin was white and soft as my mother's. Against it, the red mouth was fascinating. I knew it wasn't in the book to feel about your sister the way I was feeling. I put it down to the amnesia.

'Okay, sister,' I said. 'Who are you?'

'I'm Marny.' She crossed her legs, the skirt slipping back from her knees. 'Really, this is quite intriguing. Let's talk about me. What shall I give with?'

I reached out for her drink. 'You could give with that cocktail.'

She pushed my hand away, shaking her head. 'Uhuh.'

'Why not?'

'My dear Gordy, one of the things you're so conveniently forgetting is that we're making a good boy of you.'

'I'm a bad boy then?'

'Terrifically. Didn't you know?'

'I don't know anything. Remember? What's wrong with me? Drink too much?'

Marny's impervious young eyes stared. 'My dear, you've been potted off and on since you were sixteen. You were stinking the night you had your accident. Now the word's gone forth. No drink for Gordy. Nate says so.'

I suppose I should have been discouraged to hear that about myself, but I wasn't. I couldn't remember any especial interest in liquor and I didn't have any particular desire for her drink. I'd only asked to be sociable.

I said: 'Tell me more about myself. What am I except a drunk?'

'I guess the police word for you's playboy. But to me, darling, you're just a lush. A sweet one for those who like lushes. Selena likes lushes.'

'Selena? Oh yes, my wife.' I paused. 'Do you like me?'

Marny swallowed half her drink. 'I've always thought you were quite a louse.'

'Why?'

She grinned a sudden, spontaneous grin. 'Wait till your memory comes back, dear. Then you won't have to be told.'

Her hand moved to tug her skirt down. It made me conscious of her knees. I said:

'If you're my sister, I wish you'd go sit somewhere else. You – you unnerve me.'

'Really, Gordy.' Marny twisted back onto the chair by the roses. 'Nate says I'm to try to refresh your memory. Shall I tell your tales from your childhood?'

'Tell me anything you like.'

'Check if I strike a chord.' She paused, reflecting. 'Remember the time when …? No, we'd better not go into that. Remember the Winter Ball at Miss Churchill's dancing school in St Paul when you spiked the fruit punch with gin and started an orgy in the men's cloak room?'

I grinned. 'What an enterprising lad I was. No. I'm afraid I don't remember.'

Marny wrinkled her nose. 'How about the time when Father took us to the Aurora Clean Living League Summer Camp up in the Lakes? You bet me you could stir up an unclean thought in Mr Heber and switched clothes with me and had him proposition you in the canoe?'

26

'I see what you mean about the advantages of amnesia,' I said uneasily. 'No. I don't remember a thing. What the hell is the Aurora Clean Living League?'

She put her glass down. 'Gordy, you can't have forgotten the Aurora Clean Living League. It's the most important thing in our lives.'

'What is it?'

Marny shook her head. 'Skip it. Have a few more easy moments, while you may, darling.' She leaned forward. 'We're not getting anywhere with this system. Tell me. What do you remember?'

I'd almost forgotten that I was not myself. Somehow Marny had made my forgetfulness seem like an amusing, frivolous game. That question brought back the old disturbing sensation of something being hidden behind something, of everything being wrong and faintly menacing.

'I remember iris,' I said.

'Iris?' Marny's alert eyes moved to the vase on the table. 'What sort of an iris?'

'I don't know.' My disquiet was almost fear now. 'Just the word. Iris. I know it's important if only I could pin it down.'

'Iris.' Marny's lashes flickered over the candid eyes and for a moment they did not seem quite so candid. 'Probably some hideous Freudian image. There's nothing else?'

I shook my head. 'A plane, maybe. Someone ... Oh, what's the use?'

'Gordy, don't get depressed, darling.' She was back on the bed again, holding my hand. 'Think what a snazzy life you've got. All the money in the world. No worries. No work. All of Southern California to play around in. Us – and Selena.'

'Selena?' My doubts about Selena started to stir again. 'Tell me about Selena. What's she like?'

'If you've forgotten Selena,' said Marny, finishing her cocktail and pouring another, 'you're in for a shock.'

I asked anxiously: 'Thin and sharp nosed with steel rimmed spectacles?'

'Selena?' Marny wiped a smudge of lipstick off her glass. 'My dear, Selena's probably the most gorgeous thing in California.'

I was feeling contented again, and smug. 'A nice temperament too?'

'Angelic. She just adores everything and everyone.'

'And a fine, sterling character?' I asked enthusiastically. 'Would the Aurora Clean Living League endorse her?'

Marny gave me that straight, uninhibited stare. 'The Aurora Clean Living League would not endorse Selena.'

'Why not?'

Marny put her drink down. 'That,' she said, 'is something you might as well find out for yourself.'

Chapter 4

I HADN'T said anything in reply when the door opened. A girl came in, a girl in a brief white cotton dress with no sleeves. The first sight of her dazzled me. She was the blondest girl I had ever seen. Her hair, cut loose to her shoulders like Marny's, was fair as fresh country cream. Her skin too was cream, a deeper shade of cream darkened by the sun. Her body, her bare arms and legs had the moulded quality of sculpture. Looking at her, I felt I was touching her. And, although she was full bosomed and thighed, she moved to the bed with a grace that was liquid as milk.

'Gordy, baby.'

Her lips were natural dark red; her eyes were blue as summer in the sky. She sat down on the bed, studying me, the cream hair spilling forward.

'Scram, Marny,' she said.

Marny was staring at this new, breath-taking girl, her brown eyes stubborn with antagonism. She seemed small, now, artificial, rather metallic.

'Really, Selena,' she drawled, 'do you have to be in that much of a hurry? His leg's in a cast, you know.'

'Scram.' Selina turned to Marny then and her face relaxed into a swift smile that would have coaxed a platoon of mules. 'Please, darling, be a sweet baby. You can be sweet if you try.'

Marny's long black lashes flickered. 'All right, I suppose.' She got up and, with a sudden rough movement, pushed past her sister-in-law and kissed me aggressively on the mouth. 'If things get too hot for you, brother, ring an SOS on the buzzer, I'll be up.'

She mussed Selena's hair. 'Take it easy, Snowwhite.'

She picked up her cocktail shaker and her glass and strolled out of the room, kicking the door shut behind her.

'That Marny. Such a sordid infant. Sweet, though.' Selena's sunwarm fingers curled into mine. 'How do you feel, baby?'

I grinned. 'Better by the minute.'

Her smile drooped swooningly. 'I'm your wife, Gordy. You don't remember me, do you?'

This settled it, I was thinking. Being Gordy Friend exceeded the dreams of the most ambitious amnesiac. 'I can't imagine getting hit that hard on the head, but I guess I was.'

'Poor baby. What's it matter anyway? Remembering things is usually so embarrassing.'

Selena leaned over me, pressing her mouth quickly against mine. Her lips were warm and liquid as her walk. They seemed to melt into mine. It was a kiss that blotted out the memory of other kisses. Dimly I thought: *Didn't I say something about brunettes? Sultry brunettes? I must have been out of my mind.*

'I loathe sitting on beds.'

Impulsively Selena tumbled back on the grey and gold spread next to me, her hair foaming over the pillow.

'Ah.' She sighed in satisfaction and twisted around to take a cigarette from the bedside table. As she lit it, she murmured: 'What happened to that divine candy I got for you? I bet your mother ate it.' She gazed around the room through half-shut lashes, blue-grey as the cigarette smoke. 'She's taken half the flowers out too. How boring, I wanted to make your return to consciousness a real production.'

'As returns to consciousness go, I'd call this colossal,' I said.

'You would, baby?' She turned her head so that her face was almost touching mine on the pillow. 'Darling, with those bandages you look different, kind of tough. Isn't this exciting? It's almost like having a new man.'

It's hard to say what Selena was doing to me. She probably was the most gorgeous thing in California. Marny was right about that. But she was more than that. It wasn't that part of me remembered her. It didn't. But there was none of the awkwardness of a completely strange girl lying on my bed. It was exciting, yes, but it was somehow natural too. Selena made it that way. Some easy, ungrudging thing about her made her sensuality clean and spontaneous as a pagan Greek's.

With my good hand I caught up some of the soft, shining hair, letting it slide through my fingers.

'My wife,' I said. 'How long have I been married to you?'

'Two years, darling. Two years and a bit.'

'Where in heaven's name did I find you?'

'Those bandages, they do something to me.' She arched her head up on her neck, kissing me. 'Pittsburg, dear.'

'I bet you were the Pride of Pittsburg.'

'I was. They were crazy about me in Pittsburg. In the Junior League poll I was voted the girl most likely to exceed.'

'Honest?'

'Honest.' She nestled against me, bringing my hand down from her hair and holding it against her dress. 'Darling, Nate's awfully worried about you. Nate's so sweet. Do try and get your memory back. It would do such things to his professional pride.'

'To hell with Nate.' I studied the gentle line of her nose in profile. 'Tell me more about myself. Do I love you?'

The blue, blue eyes went solemn. 'I don't know. I really don't know, Gordy. Do you?'

'On a snap judgement, I'd say yes.' I kissed her before she kissed me. 'How about you? Love me?'

She moved away slightly, stretching contentedly. 'You're awfully sweet, Gordy. I simply adore you. I really do.'

'But I'm an ornery character, aren't I? Good for nothing. Drink too much.'

'That Marny.' For a moment her face was almost savage. 'The mean little limb of Satan. What's she been telling you?'

'Just that. That I'm an amiable heel and a lush.'

'Really, she makes me sick. What if you do drink too much? How can anyone be nice without drinking too much?'

'Do you drink too much?'

She smiled and then laughed, a frank, husky laugh. 'Darling, I do everything too much.'

She sat up again suddenly, straightening her skirt, stubbing her cigarette on an ashtray.

'Baby, this is all gay, but I'm supposed to help make you remember.'

'That's what you've been doing, isn't it?'

'I haven't been doing anything. I've just been being pleased at having my husband conscious again. You can't imagine how dreary it's been sleeping with a husband as unconscious as a corpse.'

'You've been sleeping here?'

Her eyes opened wide. 'But, of course. Ever since you came back from the hospital.' She pointed at the other bed. 'Where d'you suppose I'd been sleeping?'

'I'd only just started thinking about it,' I said.

'Really, darling, and you all plaster of Paris.' Selena grinned and took another cigarette, inhaling smoke deeply. 'But seriously, I mean, let's talk about something – anything. Just something you're supposed to remember.'

I said: 'Okay. I'll take the Aurora Clean Living League.'

'The Aurora Clean Living League? Really, I mean, do we have to talk about that?'

'I'm supposed to know about it, aren't I? It's important, isn't it?'

'It's terribly, terribly important, of course, but it's terribly, terribly dismal.'

'Even so – give with the Aurora Clean Living League.'

Her full mouth drooped sulkily. 'All right. Well, it all

begins with your father. I suppose you don't remember your father, either?'

I shook my head. 'They tell me he was called Gordon Renton Friend the Second and that he died a month ago. That's all.'

'Your father,' Selena brooded. 'How to describe your father? He was a lawyer in St Paul. He was terrifically rich. That was the nice thing about him. But the important thing about your father was that he was godly.' Absently she had picked my hand up again and was stroking it. 'Incredibly godly. Against things, you know. Against tobacco and dancing and lipstick and liquor and sex.'

'Uhuh. Go on.'

'What nice hands you have, darling. So square and firm. Like a sailor's hands.'

'A sailor.' Something stirred faintly deep down in my consciousness. 'Selena, I wondered....'

'Oh, yes, your father.' Selena's glance had moved from my face and she was talking rather quickly. 'What else about him? Well, as you can imagine, he was awfully dismal to live with. And then, ten years ago, when you all thought things were just about as lugubrious as they could be, your father met the Aurora Clean Living League and fell in love with it.'

The disquiet had gone again. I had almost forgotten it. 'Did he have sex with it?' I asked.

'Gordy, don't be frivolous.' Selena was smiling down at me again. She had tucked my hand into her lap. 'The Aurora Clean Living League is a nationwide organization to make America pure. It publishes dozens of pamphlets called: *Dance, Little Lady – to Hell* and *Satan Has a Deposit on Every Beer Bottle* and things like that. It runs jolly summer camps where youth can be hearty and clean-living. And, of course, they're frightfully against ...'

' ... lipstick, tobacco and dancing and liquor and sex,' I said.

'Exactly, baby. Well, the head of all this gloomy business was a repulsive man called Mr Heber. Mr Heber *was* the Aurora Clean Living League in St Paul. And Mr Heber loved your father at first sight and your father loved Mr Heber at first sight. Your father started deluging the League with money and made St Paul cleaner and cleaner and cleaner by the minute. And all the time, he made all of you cleaner and cleaner too.'

She fell back again on to the pillows, her fair hair shimmering close to my cheek. 'Darling, you can't imagine what life was like. I mean, I suppose you will imagine when you get your memory back. Every morning you all inspected for seemliness of attire. Your father scrubbed powder off Marny's nose himself in the bathroom. You weren't allowed to go to the theatre or the movies. You spent long, crushing evenings at home listening to your father recite pure poems and quote from Mr Heber's nauseating pamphlets. And as for sex – well, your father was particularly against sex.' She sighed, a deep, reminiscent sigh. 'Baby, if you knew how pent-up you all got.'

'I can imagine,' I said. 'But how did I, the drunken heel, fit into that picture?'

'You didn't, baby.' She had picked up my hand again. It seemed to fascinate her. 'That's the whole point. The more clean living your father got, the more dirty living you went in for. At college, you did the most shameless things....'

'Like switching clothes with Marny and having Mr Heber proposition me in a canoe?'

Selena sat up, amazed. 'Darling, you remember?'

'Sorry,' I said. 'Marny told me.'

'Oh.' She sank back. 'Well, yes, things like that – and worse. Mr Heber pronounced you permanently unclean. Father would have loved to throw you out for good. But there he was in a cleft stick. You see, The Family is one of the things the Clean Living League has a passion for. And one of your father's favourite compositions was a long poem about your son is your son and you forgive him seven times seven, nay seventy times seven. You know – all that.'

'I know,' I said.

'But after college he tried to keep you away from home as

much as possible. He got you a job in Pittsburg. Somenow you managed not to be fired. But, boy, the things you did to Pittsburg.' She looked dreamy. 'That's where you met me. Darling, what a night.' She snuggled against me cosily. 'Gordy, how long is the cast going to be on?'

'Don't know. You'll have to ask your buddy Nate.'

She frowned. 'Oh, well.... Where was I? Oh, yes, you met me. We were married. I wasn't at all the sort of thing your father relished, of course. But we scrubbed my face and I bought a perfectly hideous brown dress like a missionary in China and you brought me home and I was wonderful and your father adored me and I wrote a poem against sex myself and drank ginger ale and then, after we'd gone to bed, we used to get potted on stingers in the bedroom. Darling, don't you remember?'

I shook my head disconsolately. 'No, baby, I'm afraid I don't. Not yet.'

Selena lay a moment, quite still, holding my hand against her dress. I could feel the strong, healthy pulse of her heart.

'All this,' I asked, 'was in St Paul?'

She nodded.

'And then a couple of years ago we moved to California?'

'We didn't, darling. Not you and I. We stayed in Pittsburg. But the others did.'

'Why?'

'Mr Moffat,' said Selena. 'Mr Moffat's the head of the California branch of the Clean Living League. He was visiting Mr Heber and your father fell even more in love with him than with Mr Heber. Mr Moffat is even cleaner, you see. So your father sold everything and trailed out here. Fairly soon, he developed a bad heart. I guess all that purity preyed on his organs. A couple of months ago he had an attack of some sort addressing the local chapter. He was supposed to be getting better. Then, suddenly, he died.'

'And we came out here because of his sickness?'

Selena shook her head. 'No, darling, we came a couple of months ago because we had nowhere else to go.'

34

'You mean, Pittsburg was through with us?'

'With you, dear. You lost your job. We had one hundred and twelve dollars in the bank. Darling, you must remember.'

I tried very hard. Nothing came. 'I'm afraid I don't,' I said.

'Oh, dear,' she pushed her hands under her hair to support her head. 'Well, baby, I guess that's all about the Aurora Clean Living League – except Jan, of course.'

'Jan? Marny talked about him. Who's Jan?'

'Nobody knows, but he's the only gay thing your father ever did. He hired him as a kind of man of all work around the house. Mr Moffat produced him. He's Dutch, from Sumatra, wherever that is. Somehow he was in the Dutch Army and then somehow he wasn't. He's about eight feet tall and built like something on the cover of one of those health magazines – you know, the ones that are not quite under the counter. He grins all the time and never wears anything but swimming trunks. Father and Mr Moffat had a passion for him because he doesn't drink or smoke.'

'Or have sex?' I asked.

'That,' said Selena thoughtfully, 'we don't know. You see, he's kind of simple-minded, in a nice way, of course, and he either can't or won't learn a word of English so there's no point in asking him.' A flat, speculative look came into her eyes. 'One day I'm going to find out – with gestures.' She moved her face closer, kissing me almost abstractedly. 'Darling, there's your whole life in a nutshell. Don't you really remember anything?'

The shadowy image of a sailor and of an iris spun pointlessly in my mind. I thought the propellers were coming back. But they didn't. For a moment, the nearness of Selena, the liveness of her bare skin against my hand lost their magic. I felt bleak, uneasy.

'No,' I said. 'I don't remember a thing – not a solitary thing.'

'Never mind, baby.' Her voice was low, soothing. 'No one really expected you to remember anything yet. Don't bother about it. Let's forget it. Let's relax.'

We were still relaxing when the door opened. My mother came majestically in, carrying a tray with medicine bottles. She paused, surveying Selena lying on the bed from placid brown eyes.

'Selena, dear,' she said mildly, 'I don't think we should overtire Gordy, do you?'

Selena grinned up at her. 'I'm not tiring him, Mother. We're just relaxing ...'

'Relaxing,' said my mother, putting the tray down on the bedside table, 'is all very well. But I don't know that you are quite the relaxing type. Run along now, dear.'

'But Mimsey, sweet ...' Selena pushed herself up on the bed and flashed one of her blonde, sunshine smiles. 'Please.'

'Darling, you've been here long enough.'

Reluctantly Selena rose, smoothing down her skirt. As she did so, there was a scuffling sound from the open door and a small black spaniel dashed into the room, bounded onto the bed and pranced towards my face, waving fat, feathery paws.

'Peter,' called my mother sharply. 'Peter, get down.'

The dog was licking my face and batting at me enthusiastically. Suddenly, as my mother called out, I felt a tingle on the surface of my skin. A sensation, like the one that had come with the word 'Iris', stirred in me, only this time it was stronger. It was half excitement, half dread of something ominous just beyond my comprehension.

'Peter?' I asked. 'He's called Peter?'

'Why, yes, darling,' said Selena. 'He's your dog. He remembers you. Don't you remember him?'

'Peter. Yes, yes. I think I do. For the first time I think I really remember.'

The spaniel had rolled over on its back and was kicking flirtatious feet in the air.

Peter ...

The crawling of my skin made me shiver. The propellers came, whirring with a deafening roar. I felt dizzy. I hardly knew what I was saying but I blurted:

'The dog's not called Peter. I'm called Peter. I'm not Gordy Friend. I'm Peter.'

A change started to spread like a shadow over that lovely, sunny room. It was one of those indefinable nightmare changes where the very blandness and security of a scene seems to cloak some lurking horror.

The change infected the two women. They were both standing by the bed, looking down at me. Both, in their way, were as beautiful as women could be – Selena golden as summer, my mother splendid as autumn. But their faces seemed suddenly marred with an expression that was hostile, ruthless.

A quick glance passed between them. I was sure of that. Then, slowly, they both moved forward and sat down on the bed. I could feel the warmth from their bodies. Their soft, feminine nearness was almost suffocating.

My mother took my hand. Selena's smooth fingers rested on my arm. My mother was smiling a smile so serene and gentle that it was almost impossible to believe in the expression I had caught a moment before.

'Darling boy.' Her voice was rich, cooing. 'Of course you're Gordy Friend. What foolish ideas you have! We tell you you're Gordy Friend, dear. And who could know better who you are than – your mother and your wife?'

Chapter 5

SELENA left, taking the dog with her. My mother continued to sit on my bed. Her friendly bosom, framed by the neck of her austere widow dress, was very close to me. Her thick, hot-house perfume overpowered the scent of the roses. She was still holding my hand and smiling that 'everything's-going-to-be-all-right' smile.

'My poor baby,' she said. 'So miserable it must be – not remembering.'

My outburst of a moment before was becoming confused in my mind. I couldn't remember what I had said. It had been something to do with the dog. Something had flashed in and out of my mind, leaving a residue of uneasiness. Somehow, far back in my consciousness, I was still suspicious of this woman sitting at my side. But I could no longer track down the source of my suspicion.

She was stroking my head now, letting her cool hand move softly over the bandages.

'Head ache, darling?'

The white bosom, the tranquil face on the stately neck, the very untidiness of the piled auburn hair all conspired to soothe me. It seemed silly to be suspicious unless I could remember a reason.

'Yes.' I said. 'My head does ache a bit. What happened just now with the dog? What did I say?'

My mother laughed. 'Nothing, dear. Nothing at all.'

'But it was something – something about the dog's name.'

'Don't worry yourself, sweet. Please don't worry.' She leaned forward, kissing me on the forehead just under the bandages. Ever since my return to consciousness, I seemed to have been smothered in kisses. 'You'll have funny little quirkish illusions, dear. Nate said you would. Things getting tied together in your mind, making patterns that seem real to you but aren't. That's all.'

She patted my hand and rose, moving to the tray of medicine bottles on the bedside table.

'Now, it's time for your pill. A nice rest. That's what you need. You've had a fearfully taxing first afternoon, haven't you? Me, Marny, Selena. I'm afraid we are a trifle overwhelming.'

She turned, a capsule in one hand, a glass of water in the other. She sat down, smiling.

'Open your mouth, dear.'

I felt an impulse to refuse the proffered capsule, but it was a feeble one, for I could think of no valid excuse for not taking it. There was something too about this woman that tempted me to invalidism. Her breadth, her quietness made me want to forget my problems – what were my problems? – and yield to the voluptuous lure of the pillows.

I let her slip the capsule into my mouth and tilt some of the water after it. I swallowed.

She patted my hand. 'That's a good boy, Gordy. Now, smile for Mother.'

I smiled. Somehow she had made us conspirators together.

'Darling boy.' She kissed me again. 'Now, before you know it, you'll be off to bye-byes.'

And it happened almost exactly that way. One moment I was watching her idly rearranging the pink roses in the bowl. The next moment unconsciousness, heavy as an eiderdown quilt, engulfed me.

When I awakened, I was alone. There was no more sunshine. A grey-green evening light from the windows gave the room a submarine quietness. My headache had gone. My thoughts seemed exceptionally clear. I remembered all the people who had come into the room that day. I remembered everything they said.

I'm Gordy Friend, I said. *I've had an accident and I've lost my memory.*

I lay still in the bed. Gradually I became conscious of the rigidity of the casts on my arm and my leg. For the first time, I thought of them not merely as props in my role as a patient. I thought of them as the restrictions they were.

I'm here in this bed with a cast on my arm and a cast on my leg, I thought. *I'm helpless. I couldn't get away.*

There was nothing to have to get away from, of course. I was Gordy Friend. I was in my own home. I was surrounded by love and care. But the realization of my helplessness seemed, perversely, to bring a sensation of impending danger.

My gaze, moving uneasily around the room, settled on the side table. On it stood a vase of stock, white and sulky purple in the fading light. Before I went to sleep hadn't there been a vase of irises there? Iris. I was gropingly aware that irises had some significance and that their absence had significance too. My sense of uneasiness grew, stretching almost to the borders of panic.

What if I'm not Gordy Friend? I thought suddenly and with no conscious reason.

I knew instantly that the thought was preposterous. My mother, my sister, my wife, my doctor had all told me I was Gordy Friend. Only a plot, too insane or too fiendish to imagine, could give all four of them motive to deceive me.

But the thought, with all the force of commonsense marshalled against it, persisted, nagging like a boil almost come to a head.

What if I'm not Gordy Friend?

The door opened a crack and Marny peered around it. Her young face wore that hushed expression of someone looking at a sleeper.

'Hello,' I said.

'So you're awake.'

She pushed the door open and walked to the bed. As before, she carried a small shaker of Manhattans and a single glass. She tossed back her glossy black hair and sat down by the roses, watching me brightly.

'Hello,' she said.

Her young, oval face, with its cool eyes and splashed scarlet mouth, was both appraising and friendly. I found her brittleness reassuring ... more reassuring than my mother's lushness or Selena's animal vitality would have been.

'Still drinking?' I asked.

'Don't be silly! That was lunch. This is dinner. They're just going to bring you yours.' She poured a Manhattan into the glass. 'I thought you might like a cocktail so I sneaked one up.'

My half-lulled suspicions grew alert again. 'I thought you said I wasn't supposed to drink?'

'Of course you're not, darling.' She laughed, showing small white teeth and the glimpse of a pink tongue. She leaned towards me almost wantonly, stretching the glass out. 'But what's a little veto between sister and brother?'

'The woman tempted me,' I said, and took the drink. Its stinging taste on the roof of my mouth was good.

Marny, her legs crossed, was still watching me carefully. 'Selena,' she said suddenly. 'Like her?'

The false stimulant of the liquor made me even more alert. I was definitely on my guard now – on my guard against something I didn't know for a motive I did not understand. 'Do you?' I parried.

Marny shrugged. 'What difference does it make what I feel? Selena's not my wife. She's yours.'

'Is she?' Something made me ask that question quickly.

'What do you mean – is she?' Marny's thick, curled lashes batted, and she snatched the half-full glass from me. 'Really, Gordy, has half a Manhattan made you pie-eyed?'

The door opened and my mother came in. Her gaze settled on Marny.

'Marny, I hope you haven't been giving Gordy a drink.'

Marny stared back blandly. 'Of course not, Mimsey.'

'I'm sure Nate wouldn't like that at all.' My mother crossed to my side and smiled. 'Hungry, dear? They're bringing your dinner up.'

'I guess I can eat,' I said.

'Good. Have a nice rest?'

'Fine. I feel fine.'

I kept my mother under unobtrusive observation, trying to catch some trace of falseness in her expression. She was smiling at me, half humorously as if she had guessed my vague suspicions and was trying to emphasize their absurdity. 'No more troubles, I'll be bound,' she said. 'No more foolish fancies.'

'That I'm not Gordy Friend, you mean?'

Marny's lashes flickered again. She half turned to glance at her mother and then seemed to change her mind. My mother patted the girl's head. 'Run along, dear. Dinner's ready downstairs.' As Marny left, she turned back to me. 'Don't you remember anything at all yet? Not even me?'

'Not yet,' I said.

The maid, who had looked in before to announce the doctor, entered carrying a tray. 'Ah, here's your dinner, dear,' said my mother. 'When you're through I'll send Jan up. He can take care of all those unfeminine bedroom things.' Almost as if relieved at the arrival of dinner as an excuse for going, she murmured one of her 'darling boys' and departed.

The maid slid an invalid bed-table from a corner and arranged the tray on it in front of me. She was in uniform and obviously trying to maintain the colourless discretion of a well-trained domestic. She wasn't very successful. She was too plump and her hair, peroxide blonde and tightly waved, suggested hot-dogs and dates in bars with sailors. I remembered my mother had called her Netti.

'Thanks, Netti,' I said. 'That looks fine.'

She giggled. 'It's nice having you eating again, Mr Friend.'

Dinner, on beautiful blue and white Spode, looking inviting. Here, I thought, was an easy way for dispelling my foolish doubts once and for all. If there was some crazy conspiracy, surely the maid would not be party to it.

Casually I asked: 'Well, Netti, has my accident improved my looks?'

She giggled again, patting at the prim cap on the far from prim hair. 'Oh, Mr Friend, don't ask me. I wouldn't know.'

'Wouldn't know?'

'You have lost your memory, haven't you?' Her refinement was slipping by the second. 'Cook told me about it in the kitchen. My, that's too bad.'

'What's losing my memory got to do with it?'

'Asking me if the accident improved your looks, Mr Friend.' She was grinning. The grin showed pink gums veined with red. 'Why, I never even saw you. Not before they brought you back from the hospital.'

'You're new?'

'Sure, I'm new. They hired me right the day after the old – after Mr Friend died. They fired all the servants then. Except Jan. Mr Friend fired him the very last day. Then they took him on again.'

I stared. 'But my father died a month ago. My accident was only two weeks ago. You had a couple of weeks to see me in.'

'Not you, Mr Friend.' A suggestive titter had crept into her giggle. 'You wasn't around, sir – not ever, after your father died.'

'Where was I then?'

She hesitated. Then she blurted:

'You, Mr Friend! The old cook told me just before she left. They said you'd gone off on a visit. But you never even showed up for the funeral. The old cook, she said ... Well, she said as it was more likely you'd gone off on one of your ...'

She broke off. I felt for a moment that she was going to put her hand over her mouth – a gesture which had surely gone out with the invention of the vacuum cleaner.

'One of my – what?' I said.

She squirmed. 'Oh, sir, I really shouldn't have ...'

'One of my – what?'

'Your toots.' She grinned again and, as if this admission had forged a bond of intimacy between us, she moved a trifle nearer. 'You're quite a one for the ...' She bent her elbow significantly.

'So I understand,' I said. 'So I was off on a blind drunk for two weeks before I had the accident. Why did I pick the day my father died to leave?'

She giggled again. 'That old cook. With her imagination, she ought to write stories. The things she hinted at!'

'What things?'

Netti looked suddenly uncomfortable. 'Oh, nothing.' The discomfort had become genuine anxiety. 'Don't ever tell them I said anything about you being away and everything. Promise. I didn't ought to have ...'

'Forget it, Netti.'

I didn't press the point further. I knew she wasn't going to tell me any more anyway.

She was staring at me uncertainly, as if she was plucking up her courage. Then, with a glance over her shoulder at the

43

door, she whispered: 'I suppose you wouldn't have just a little snort? Carrying that heavy tray from the kitchen and ...'

'Sorry,' I said. 'They put me on the wagon.'

'That's too bad.' She leaned towards me and breathed: 'There's times when I get the liquor closet if it's a sherry dessert or something. Sometimes I sneak maybe a pint of gin. Next time, I'll slip you some up – okay?'

'Okay.'

I got the gums again. 'I like a drop myself once in a while. I know how it is, Mr Friend.'

She patted at the cap and left the room with a lot of hip-rolling.

I'd made a buddy. And was I glad. You never know when you need a buddy.

But somehow the chicken breast in wine sauce didn't seem so inviting now. They'd fired all the servants after my father died. Why? And they'd kept it from me that I'd been off on a blind drunk for two weeks before the accident. Why?

'I.' I was beginning to think quite naturally in terms of 'I' whenever Gordy's past was discussed. Did that mean that my identity as Gordy Friend was coming back? Or was it just a new habit forming?

I wished I knew more about amnesia. I wished I could be more sure that the stubborn conviction of something wrong was just a normal symptom.

Netti had never seen me. That meant none of the servants had ever seen me. For all they knew, I could be King Tiglath-Pileser the Third.

The dog. The iris. The propellers. Seeing someone off on a plane. San Diego. The Navy.

Why had they fired all the servants after my father's death? And what were the things at which the former cook with the literary imagination had hinted?

Chapter 6

I HAD finished my dinner. My mother had turned on the lights and drawn the curtains. In the artificial light, the room had lost some of its frivolous gaiety and seemed almost oppressively luxurious. The cream drapes over the windows were cloying as a fancy dessert. The green chaise longue gleamed richly. The roses seemed larger, pinker than real roses and more heavily perfumed. I tried moving the cast on my left leg. With a great effort, I shifted its position a couple of inches. That was all.

I wanted a cigarette. Selena had smoked all that were in the pack by the bedside. I thought about ringing, but for some reason I shirked another meeting with a member of the family. My thoughts weren't straight enough yet. I didn't know whether I trusted them or whether they were enemies. *Of course they can't be enemies*, I said.

There was a loud knock on the door.

I called: 'Come in.'

The door opened on a giant. It was quite a startling experience. Before when the door opened, I had always caught a glimpse of the passage beyond. Now there was nothing but man.

He came in, shutting the door behind him. He must have been close on six foot five. He was dressed only in brief navy swimming trunks and a sleeveless blue polo shirt. His hair, shining and fair as Selena's, fell forward over his forehead. His bare legs and arms were solid muscle and burnt by the sun to a light apricot. All I noticed of his face was a broad expanse of teeth bared in a dazzling smile.

It took him about two steps to reach the bed. He looked down at me. His eyes were the blue of denim faded in the sun. His nose was short, almost snub. His mouth, curled at the corners in a friendly smile, seemed amused by everything and by me in particular.

'Jan,' he said, stretching the smile even further.

I knew from Selena that old Mr Friend's 'only gay thing' spoke no English. I certainly spoke no Dutch. But I tried: 'Hiyah, Jan. How's tricks?'

He shook his head, making his blond forelock slip down over his eyes. He tossed the hair back again into place and shrugged, indicating that it wasn't worth my time to try to converse. And certainly, simple-minded or no, he seemed to know what to do without being told. Efficiently, he performed all the tasks which my mother had described as 'those unfeminine bedroom things'. And all the time he was grinning as if I was an uproarious joke.

When he was through, he suddenly tugged all the bedclothes off me. The great arms slipped under me and, laughing out loud, he picked me up, casts and all, as if I was a bag of popovers, carried me across the room and laid me down on the green chaise longue. He brought a corn-coloured quilt from a closet and spread it over me. In spite of his immense strength, he was gentle, almost tender. He made me feel like an elderly dowager with a lot of money to leave.

He crossed back to the bed, and, whistling some monotonous and presumably Sumatran melody, started to remake the bed. He was very careful about hospital corners, making them neat as if for inspection.

When the bed was ready, he came back to me, picked up the quilt, folded it meticulously, and took it back to a closet. He moved to a chest of drawers, selected a pair of opulent red and grey silk pyjamas and came back to me. He sat down at my side and started unbuttoning my pyjama coat. I protested, but he only laughed his big gusty laugh and stripped the jacket off. He eased the pants off too and then began to slip as much of me as the casts permitted into the clean pyjamas.

It should have been pleasant to have such efficient valet service. But I disliked it. It made me so conscious of my own helplessness. As Jan bent over me, his fair hair tickling my chest, I knew that by slipping one arm around me, he could crush me as easily as a python crushes a deer. With only my left arm to protect myself, I would be completely at his mercy, or anyone else's mercy.

Having tied the cord on my pants in a neat bow, he picked me up again and put me back in the freshly made bed. He tucked the clothes around me and stood, grinning. I resented being thought so funny.

'Jah?' he asked questioningly.

I assumed he was asking me if there was anything else I wanted.

'A cigarette,' I said.

He looked blank.

'Smoke.' I lifted my left hand to my lips and puffed an imaginary cigarette.

His face instantly darkened. He shook his head vigorously. He was mad all of a sudden. I remembered then that Selena had told me he neither smoked nor drank. That's what Mr Moffat and my father had liked about him.

On a sudden impulse, I said: 'I am Gordy Friend, aren't I?'

'Jah?'

I pointed at myself. 'Gordy Friend?'

He grinned. It was a deliberately foolish grin, indicating that he didn't understand.

'Let it go,' I said.

He stood a moment, his eyes sliding up and down me, checking up, making sure everything was okay. Then, tossing the blond lock back again, he put a huge hand on my shoulder, nodded and went away.

I had started to brood again over Netti's admissions when my mother came in, followed by the lounging figure of Dr Croft.

My mother came up to the bed and smiled. 'Well, darling, Jan *has* fixed you up. Those pyjamas. You always looked so attractive in them. Doesn't he look attractive, Doctor Croft?'

The young doctor had strolled by her side. He was looking down at me from his liquid, caressing eyes.

'Hi, Gordy. I was passing, thought I'd drop in and say

hello. I got the wheel chair, by the way. It'll show up to-morrow. How're we coming?'

I noticed a certain tenseness in my mother. I was almost sure that the doctor's visit was not as casual as he made out. Quickly, my mother put in:

'He had a funny feeling this afternoon, doctor, a feeling that he wasn't himself, if you see what I mean. That he wasn't my Gordy.' She patted my hand. 'Tell the doctor about it, darling.'

Her frankness in bringing that out should have disarmed me, but it didn't. For some reason, my suspicions flared up again. Almost psychopathically sensitive, I seemed to feel a falseness in my mother and in the quiet unconcern of the doctor.

'It's nothing,' I said evasively.

'No, tell me, Gordy,' said Dr Croft.

'Okay,' I said. 'I felt I wasn't Gordy Friend. I still feel it.'

My mother sat down on the edge of the bed. 'You mean, dear, that you think we're lying to you?' She laughed. 'Really, baby, isn't that rather strange? That your mother and your wife and your sister and ...'

Dr Croft raised his hand. He was staring at me steadily. 'No, Mrs Friend, don't laugh. It's perfectly understandable. Perfectly normal.' He smiled at me vividly. 'Listen, Gordy, there's a certain split in your mind. The result of the con-cussion. Now maybe there's a lot of memories that you sub-consciously don't want to have back. I guess that would apply to all of us. Part of your mind is fighting against remembering. A mind can be a pretty sly thing, Gordy. One of its ways of fighting is by trying to invent other plausible memories. A scrap maybe from here, a scrap from there – ingeniously the mind links them together and tries to present you with a com-pletely false identity.... Say your dog's called – Peter. Say you had a vivid recollection of – oh, a town where you had a good time, a boy maybe who you palled around with at school. Your mind can suddenly forge them into something and seem to give it an immense significance. It's worrying to you, of course, but I can assure you it's all an illusion.'

48

He moistened his lips with the tip of a sharp pink tongue. 'Get it, old man?'

'I guess so,' I said.

'No, Gordy. Come clean. If you don't get it, tell me.'

My mother was watching me anxiously. What Nate said was plausible. What Nate said always was. Maybe I was convinced.

'Sure I get it,' I said. I turned to my mother. 'Where was I for the weeks before I had the accident?'

'Where were you?' My mother looked at her most serene. 'Why, you were here, of course, darling.'

'I stayed on right here after my father died? I went out in the Buick from here when I had the accident?'

'Why, of course, Gordy. You ...' My mother broke off suddenly, a flush spreading her cheeks. 'Marny hasn't been telling you things, has she?'

I had promised Netti not to give her away, but since my mother assumed I'd got the information from Marny I had no scruples.

'I heard,' I said, 'that I disappeared the day my father died and that I never showed up again until I was found in the wrecked car. I heard,' I added, 'that I was on a prolonged and colossal bat.'

My mother's smooth white fingers were tapping agitatedly on her lap. I caught a flash of anger blazing in her eyes. She wasn't the sort of person I had thought of as getting angry. But she controlled herself superbly. Almost immediately the old soothing smile was in command.

'Darling, whoever told you that was awfully naughty. Yes, I'm afraid I lied. You were off on one of your – er – jaunts.' She glanced swiftly at Dr Croft. 'Nate and I decided it was best to keep quiet about it for a while. After all, it's not a very nice memory and it does you no good to be told.'

'Don't worry, Gordy, old man.' Dr Nate Croft was smiling his reassuring smile. 'We all of us go on a bender once in a while.' His face was serious. 'Maybe that's the memory you're trying to suppress, Gordy. Getting tight, missing your

49

father's funeral... You know, it the sort of thing a guy wishes he hadn't done.'

I asked the question to which Netti had given me so darkly cryptic an answer. 'Why did I pick the day Father died to go off on a bat?'

Mrs Friend was in entire control of herself now. She watched me serenely. 'Really, dear, I wouldn't know, would I? I expect you were depressed about your poor father being sick. Or' – she shrugged – 'you never were particularly reasonable about the times you chose, you know.'

'But I walked out while he was actually dying.'

Mrs Friend patted my hand. 'Darling boy, don't start nagging yourself about it. After all, it wasn't as if you knew he was dying. It happened after you left.'

'Suddenly?'

'Yes, dear, quite suddenly – with no warning.'

Dr Croft's lips were stretched again, but this time the reassuring smile looked a bit sickly. 'Even the doctor wasn't prepared for it, Gordy. So you see you can't blame yourself.' He turned to my mother. 'Well, Mrs Friend, this is a lot of fun, but a doctor's a doctor. There's a pile of work ahead of me still.' He took my left hand in his, letting his warm, smooth fingers linger there. 'I think we've got you straightened out now, eh, Gordy?'

'I guess,' I said.

A shadow of annoyance passed across his face as if he felt I wasn't convinced and it wounded his professional pride.

'If the feeling keeps up,' he said stiffly, 'we'll get a second opinion. There's no reason why you should have confidence in me.'

He made me feel I had been pointlessly crass. I said: 'Sure I have confidence in you, Nate.'

'You do? After all, it's kind of silly thinking of us as enemies. We're your friends, you know.'

He smiled. So did my mother.

'We're your friends, aren't we, darling?' she repeated.

'Sure,' I said. 'Sure, you're my friends.'

Chapter 7

'TAKE it easy, Gordy. Don't force anything. You'll be all right. 'Night now. 'Night, Mrs Friend.'

Nate Croft moved to the door. My mother looked down at me and then, as if suddenly remembering something, she rose hurriedly and followed the doctor out of the room.

Although she was supposed to be nursing me, she didn't come back. No one came for a long time. I started feeling sleepy. The little gold travelling clock on the bedside table eventually said eleven o'clock. I thought of leaning over and turning out the light but I felt too lazy to make the effort.

Dr Croft's words, in retrospect, were reassuring. He had suggested a second opinion. No phony doctor would have done that. I was forgetting my doubts. The pillows were soft. I shut my eyes. I was drifting off into some fanciful half dream when I realized the door was opening. Lifting my lids the fraction of an inch, I looked through my lashes.

Selena had tiptoed in. She moved toward my bed. I don't know why I feigned sleep, but I did. She paused at my side and looked down at me, studying my features with a long, speculative stare.

Squinting as I was, her image was blurred. I could see the cream hair gleaming in the subdued light, hear her light breathing and smell her perfume, warm and faint, a summer meadow perfume that seemed to catch the very essence of her free, country beauty.

Satisfied that I was asleep, she stretched voluptuously, her breasts sprouting upward. She half turned away, reached behind her back for buttons and pulled the white dress off over her head. She tossed the dress carelessly onto the chaise longue, and kicked off her shoes.

Humming very softly, she moved to the french windows, tugged back the heavy drapes and stood staring out. The glittering California moonlight, streaming around her, turned her hair silver and gave her skin the bluish delicacy of milk. The picture she made was so entrancing that I forgot I was supposed to be asleep.

'Hello, Selena,' I said.

She turned, the hair swirling around her bare shoulders. She came to my bed, sat down and took my hand, quite unembarrassed. She smiled her vivid smile.

'Baby, I thought you were asleep.'

She leaned over me, kissing me on the lips, relaxing against me. Once again, her nearness brought summer images. Hay-fields. Soft, warm sand with the faint murmur of waves. When Selena was near, only the thoughts she conjured up existed. Everything else dissolved.

'Where've you been all evening?' I asked.

She shifted her head on my chest. Her face was so close that I could feel her lashes fluttering against mine. 'Miss me, baby?'

'Sure I missed you. What were you doing?'

'Oh, nothing,' she shrugged. 'Nothing delirious. Just bridge. Mimsey adores it and she's only just been able to play again. It was far too sinful for your father. Just the four of us. Mimsey, Marny, me and Nate.'

'Nate? I thought he had to go to another patient. That's what he said.'

Her laugh was rich, husky. 'I know, darling, but Mimsey wanted a fourth so I persuaded him to stay. Didn't Mimsey give you a sleeping thing?'

I shook my head.

She kissed me. 'Mimsey fancies herself as a nurse. Person-ally I'd think twice about letting her loose on a sick baboon. Never mind, baby. I'll be here for the rest of the night. If you want anything – shout.'

'Anything?' I let my hand stray over her glossy shoulder.

'In time, baby. In time.' She grinned and fell back on the bed, staring up at the ceiling. 'Oh, life is such fun. Why do people have complexes and things? Why don't they do what they want when they want and wallow in life instead of glooming around in Clean Living Leagues, with warts on their noses and smelly breath? Sleepy, baby?'

'No.'

'Want to start remembering things?'

'No.'

'What do you want to do?'

'Just this.'

'Baby!' She took my head between both her hands. 'You,' she said studying me. 'Your jaw's right. You smell nice. You've got real arms. Your lips are so – serviceable. You and your plaster of Paris.'

She kissed me again, pressing herself almost fiercely against me. The spell of her was like a drug. I had seen her only twice to remember and yet I was already feeling as if I must always have wanted her in my life. It was a strange, rather frightening sensation – not like remembered love, rougher than that, a sort of hunger and a simultaneous desire to resist. Because something in me, something very weak, was still trying to warn me.

Steady, it said. *You don't know who your friends are.*

I didn't pay it much attention. All my thoughts were with Selena.

'I'm crazy about you, baby,' I said, hardly realizing I had spoken the words out loud.

'I know you are.' She gave a soft laugh in which there was a faint ring of triumph. 'Of course you are, Gordy. You always were.'

Abruptly she pulled herself away from me. She picked up the empty pack of cigarettes, said 'damn' and, crossing to her tumbled dress, pulled a thin platinum case out of the deep side pocket. She came back to the bed, lit two cigarettes at once and handed me one.

'Like in the movies,' she said. She puffed smoke, enjoying it. 'Baby, I've got an idea. A wonderful idea. About your memory.'

'To hell with my memory,' I said.

'No, baby. Listen. Please. Your father's poems. For years

and years, ever since you started to drink and heaven knows how long that's been – whenever you went on a toot, your father made you learn by heart and recite one of his poems against drink. I'll make you learn one again. Don't you see? Association and things. It's bound to be frightfully, frightfully therapeutical.'

'I don't want to learn a poem against drink,' I said.

'Darling, don't be dreary.' She got up again, fumbled in a bureau drawer and brought out a drab grey volume with gilt lettering. Casually, as if it didn't matter one way or the other, she pulled an oyster white négligé from a closet and slipped into it. She sat down on the green chaise longue.

'All published privately. At terrific expense.' She leafed through the book. 'Ah, here's my favourite. *The Ode to Aurora*. It's divine. Disinfected Swinburne. Baby, you've learned this one fifty times. It must be needlepointed on your heart.' She looked up laughing. 'Darling, I'm much smarter than Nate. You see.'

I was bored. I wanted her to come back to the bed.

'Ready?' she said. 'I'll read the first verse. Then you learn it.'

'Okay,' I said. 'Give with the disinfected Swinburne.'

In a voice croaky with mock evangelical fervour, she recited:

> '"Seven sins led our sons to Perdition,
> Seven sins that lure youth like a whore.
> And the first of them all – (Prohibition
> Alas can repress it no more) –
> Is alcohol, weevil-like borer,
> Only one can combat its foul stealth.
> That's sober and saintly Aurora,
> Clean Lady of Health."'

She looked up. 'Isn't it heaven, darling? He doesn't mean the Greek Aurora, of course. She was a frightful cut-up, sleeping with shepherds on mountains and things. This is all written to the Aurora Clean Living League of St Paul, Minnesota.' Her eyes clouded earnestly. 'Don't you remember any of it, baby?'

'No,' I said. 'Fortunately.'

'Oh, baby.' She grimaced. 'Really, you're awfully tiresome. Never mind. Learn it. Maybe that'll help.'

She reread the first two lines. I repeated them. The rhythm made it easy to learn by heart. But it brought absolutely no recollection.

'How did we ever recite it without laughing out loud?' I asked.

'Laughing?' Selena looked horrified. 'My dear, you wouldn't ask that if you remembered your father. He was simply terrifying. You were more scared of him than any of us – except maybe Marny. That's why you got drunk really. It was the only way you could feel brave. Want to try the next verse?'

'No,' I said.

She leaned forward coaxingly. 'Gordy, baby, please – just one more.'

'Okay.'

'This is really my pet verse.'

She started to read:

> '"In the taverns where young people mingle
> To sway their lascivious hips,
> The youths with sin's wages to jingle
> At the maidens with stains on their lips.
> Smoke rises like fumes from Baal's altar,
> Ragtime drums like a plague in their blood.
> Oh, come and rend off its lewd halter,
> Our Lady of Good."'

I learned that verse too. Selena made me repeat both verses together. But nothing happened. Discouraged, Selena gave up and soon she was lying in the other bed.

''Night, baby.'

She leaned toward me, turning out the light between the beds. Her hand came through the moonlight, touching my cheek and caressing it. I kissed the soft, blue-white fingers.

''Night, Selena.'

'Won't be long, will it?'

'What won't be long?'

'The cast, baby.'

'I hope not, Selena.'

As I lay alone, drowsy but not really tired, the magic Selena cast began to fade and my old disquiet returned. I didn't remember my father's poems. I didn't really remember Selena. I didn't remember anything. A vision of Netti's pink, red-veined gums swam in front of me. Somehow that peroxide maid with her weakness for gin-nipping and her giggled hints seemed the only normal, real person in the house. All the servants had been fired on the day my father died. Suddenly that one fact seemed to be the focus of everything that was wrong.

'Selena?' I called.

Her voice, thickened by sleepiness, murmured: 'Yes, baby?'

'Why did you fire all the servants when father died?'

'What?' Her voice was alert now.

'Why did you fire all the servants when father died?'

'My dear, what weird questions you ask.'

I had an absurd sensation that she was stalling.

'Please, baby. I want to know. It's one of those things that stick in your mind,' I lied. 'Maybe, if you tell it'll help me remember.'

She laughed softly and her hand, stretched across again, rested on my pillow. I didn't touch it. Somehow I didn't want to.

'Baby, that's frightfully simple. In the old days Father hired all the servants. My dear, you can't imagine how spectral and dismal they were, creaking around in elastic boots and sniffing in drawers for contraband cigarettes. Your father paid them to spy on us. Firing them was our first act of emancipation. Mimsey did it. She was wonderful. She just swept them out like dead leaves.'

It was a soothing explanation. It fitted so well with the set-up. I reached for her hand and squeezed it.

'Thanks, Selena.'

'Help you remember anything?'

''Fraid not.'

'Damn.' Selena drew her hand back. ''Night, baby.' After a moment she gave a little chuckle.

'What's so funny?'

'I was just picturing how you'd look swinging lascivious hips in that plaster cast.'

Now that Selena had told me there was nothing sinister about the firing of the servants, the last lingering fumes of my suspicions were dispersed. For the first time that evening I felt an unqualified sense of well-being. There was no pain in my leg or my arm. My head didn't ache. Sleep stole deliciously through me. My last conscious thought was:

I'm Gordy Friend. Selena's my wife.

My last conscious act was to turn my head and look at her. She was lying with her back to me, the long line of her hip visible under the humped bedclothes. Her hair gleamed metallic on the pillow.

I dreamed of her hair. It should have been a wonderful dream but it wasn't. The cream hair was tumbling over me, curling around my throat, smothering me.

I was awake suddenly. I knew I was awake because a hand was touching my cheek. My mind was quite clear. Selena, I thought. The touch was light, just the tips of the fingers moving gently across my skin. There was a faint perfume too. What was it? Lavender.

I didn't open my eyes. Contentedly I raised my arm and imprisoned the hand in mine. The fingers weren't smooth and soft like Selena's. It was an old, old hand, bony, coarse and wrinkled like a lizard's skin.

With a chill of disgust and horror, I dropped it. I opened my eyes wide. I stared up.

A figure was bending over me. The bright moonlight made its reality unquestionable. It was a female figure, short and dumpily shapeless in some black trailing garment.

Its face was less than a foot from mine. Lines splayed over cheeks dry as parchment. Eyes, round and luminous, in puckered sockets stared straight into mine. There was an odour of old age and lavender.

It had happened too quickly. I wasn't ready for it. My skin started to crawl.

'Gordy.' The name was whispered in a subdued, croaking whine. 'Gordy. My Gordy.'

'I'm Gordy,' I said.

'You!' The peering eyes looked closer. The voice trembled with ancient, impotent rage. 'You're not Gordy. They said my Gordy'd come back. They lied to me. They always lie to me. You're not Gordy. You're just another of Selena's ...'

She broke off with a whimper.

I sat up, quivering. 'What d'you mean? Who are you? Tell me.'

Something white – a handkerchief – fluttered across the face. The smell of lavender flew from it like moths.

'Gordy,' she moaned. 'Where's my Gordy?'

She turned from the bed.

'Come back,' I breathed.

She didn't seem to notice. She started away. I could hear the shamble of her bedroom slippers across the carpet.

'Hey,' I called in an urgent whisper. 'Come back. Please come back.'

But the bedroom slippers shambled on. I heard the faint squeak of the door opening and closing.

She was gone.

For a moment I lay back against the pillows, my heart racing.

You're not Gordy Friend. They lied to me.

Now that she was gone, I could hardly believe in that unknown old hag. She seemed like the materialization of my own amorphous suspicions.

They said my Gordy'd come back. They lied to me. You're just one of Selena's ...

I turned to the other bed. Selena's hair gleamed motionless in the moonlight.

'Selena,' I called. 'Selena.'

She stirred slightly.

'Selena.'

'Yes, darling.' The words were burred, reluctant, coming from half sleep.

'Selena.'

'Yes, yes, I hear you, baby.'

'Selena, wake up.'

She started into a sitting position, rubbing her eyes, tossing back her hair.

'What ... Who ... Oh, Gordy, Gordy, baby, yes. What is it?'

'That woman,' I said. 'That old, old woman. Who is she?'

'Old woman?' She yawned. 'What old woman, dear?'

'The old woman. She just came in here. I woke up. I found her bending over me. Who is she?'

Selena sat for a moment saying nothing. Then she murmured: 'Baby, I haven't the slightest idea what you're talking about.'

'An old woman,' I persisted. 'Who's the old woman who lives in this house?'

'Mimsey? Really, I don't think anyone would call her an old woman.'

'I don't mean her. Of course I don't.'

'Then you don't mean anyone, baby. There's no old woman in this house.'

'But there must be. She was wearing bedroom slippers. She ...'

Selena suddenly burst out laughing. It was a deep, pulsing laugh. 'You poor baby, you've been dreaming. Dreaming of old hags in bedroom slippers. What a depressing mind you must have.'

'I wasn't dreaming,' I said. 'I saw her as plainly as I see you.'

'Baby. Don't worry your poor head. It's only the drugs and things. You're simply stuffed full of drugs, darling. Probably, if you tried, you could see a moose.'

She pushed back the covers and slipped out of her bed, coming to mine. She sat close to me, warm from sleep. She slid her arms around me and kissed my forehead, drawing my head down to her breast.

59

'There, baby. Selena will protect you from predatory old women in bedroom slippers.'

Nothing could have been more restful, more to be trusted than those smooth arms and the soft hair brushing my cheek. But the hair seemed like the hair in my dreams, suffocating me.

'Over?' she asked at length. 'Is the old woman over and done with, baby?'

'I guess so,' I lied. 'Thanks, Selena. Sorry I woke you up.'

'Darling.'

She patted my hand and slipped off my bed. Before she got into her own, she gave a little laugh, pulled open the drawer of the table by her bedside and took out a revolver. She dangled it for me to see.

'There, darling, your own gun. Next time you see an old hag, scream and I'll shoot.'

She threw the gun back in the drawer and slid into bed, yawning: ' 'Night, Gordy.'

' 'Night, Selena.'

She had confused me. After she had left, I lay trying to think. I was sick. I was full of drugs. It was just possible that the whole scene had been some bizarre illusion. I forced myself to remember every detail of that moment when I had awakened and seen the face looming over mine. I knew just how terrifically important it was to decide once and for all whether there had or hadn't been an old woman.

If there had been an old woman, the old woman had said I was not Gordy Friend. If there had been an old woman, Selena had deliberately lied to me. And if Selena had lied to me, then the whole situation surrounding me was a monstrous tissue of lies.

The faintest scent of lavender trailed up to me. I glanced down. Something white was gleaming on the spread. I picked it up.

It was a woman's handkerchief, a small, plain, old woman's handkerchief.

And it smelt of lavender.

Chapter 8

I PUT the handkerchief in the pocket of my pyjama jacket, hiding it under the big one Jan had brought me. I knew I had to keep steady. That was about the only definite thought I had at that moment.

You – whoever you are – keep steady.

The room, washed in moonlight, seemed particularly beautiful. Selena, blonde and insidious as the moonlight, was lying in the next bed, asleep or pretending to be asleep. Part of me was rash and yearned to call her name, to have her come over again, to feel the warmth of her bare arms around me. But I fought against it. I didn't even look at the other bed. Because I knew now that Selena was false.

That was how this new, huge anxiety first came to me. The old woman had existed. Selena had tried to make her into a dream. Selena had lied. Selena had lied because if she had admitted the existence of the old woman then I would have demanded to see her and the old woman would say again what she had already said:

You are not Gordy Friend.

I repeated those words in my mind. With the ominous clarity that comes to the wakeful invalid at night, I knew then quite definitely that I was not Gordy Friend. My instincts had always known it. But there had been nothing tangible to support them until the arrival of this flimsy, lavender-scented handkerchief.

I was not Gordy Friend.

Strangely calm, I faced this preposterous truth. I was lying in a beautiful room in a luxurious house which I had been told was my own. It was not my own. I was nursed and petted by a woman who said she was my mother. She was not my mother. I was treated to reminiscences from an imaginary childhood by a girl who said she was my sister. She was not my sister. I was lured and made love to by a girl who said she

61

was my wife. She was not my wife. My vague suspicions had been lulled whenever I voiced them by the plausible psychiatric pretences of a doctor who said he was my friend.

Friend. In that calm, moonlit room, the word seemed illimitably sinister. They called themselves Friend. They called me Friend. They were constantly soothing me with the sickly sweet sedative of their sentence: *We're your friends*.

They weren't my friends. They were my enemies. This wasn't a calm, moonlit room. It was a prison.

I was sure of that because there could be no other explanation. At least four people were banded together to persuade me that I was Gordy Friend. Mothers, sisters and wives do not embrace an impostor as a son, brother and husband, doctors do not risk their reputations on a lie – except for some desperately important reason. The Friends had some desperate motive for wanting to produce a make-believe Gordy Friend. And I was their victim.

Victim. The word, falling on my mind, was chilling as the touch of the unknown old woman's hand on my cheek.

For all their cloying kindliness, I was the Friends' victim, the sacrificial lamb being petted and pampered in preparation for – what sacrifice?

Selena's voice, low and cautious, sounded through the extreme quiet of the room.

'Gordy. Gordy, baby.'

I lay still, I did not answer.

'Gordy, are you awake?'

I could feel the pulses in my temples throbbing against the bandages.

'Gordy.'

I heard her bedclothes being softly pulled back. I heard the faint scuffle of her feet pushing into slippers, then her tiptoeing footsteps. For a moment she came into the range of my vision, slender, graceful, her hair gleaming. She was bending over my bed, staring down at me. There was something purposeful, calculating about her. It was a bitter sensation being half in love with an enemy.

After a long moment she turned and moved away from the bed. I heard the door open and close carefully behind her.

I couldn't follow her to find out where she was going. It was that one little fact which brought home to me my extreme helplessness. I was more than a victim, I was an immobilized victim with a broken leg and arm, a victim without a sporting chance to escape.

I was a victim with a broken mind too. As I took stock of my predicament, that fact loomed above all the others. I knew I was not Gordy Friend, but I had not the faintest idea of who I was. I struggled to make something of the few, feeble hints that drifted in my mind like dead flies in a jar of water. The irises, a sailor, propellers, Peter, the dog ... Peter ... For a second, I seemed on the brink of something. Then it was over. I felt dizzy from the effort of concentration. There was no help from memory. I had nothing to help me except my own wits.

I was really on my own.

Not quite on my own. For I realized that I had two potential allies. The old woman knew I was not Gordy Friend and was ready to admit it. If somehow I could contact the old woman, I might at least find out who I was. It would be difficult, of course, because the Friends were obviously keeping her from me. But there was someone to whom I did have access – Netti with the red-veined gums. I would have to move warily. If I let the Friends know that my suspicions were anything more than an invalid's hazy vagaries, I would have played and lost my only trump card. But perhaps, carefully, through Netti....

My mind, so recently free from the influence of sedatives, was easily tired. I felt spent, incapable of coping with the situation any more. Netti's white maid's cap started to spin around in my mind like a pin-wheel.

I was asleep before Selena came back.

I awakened, as I had awakened the morning before, with warm sunlight splashing across my face. I opened my eyes. The gay luxury of the room betrayed me. Selena was lying asleep in the next bed. I could just see the curve of her cheek on the pillow behind the shimmering fair hair. She was as warm and desirable in the sunlight as she had been cool and insidious in the moonlight. I wanted her to be my real wife, I wanted to pretend everything was all right.

For a moment, because I wanted it to so much, the elaborate edifice of logic that I had built up in the night seemed a morbid fantasy. It was true that Selena had lied about the old woman. But, even if Selena was trying to prove she didn't exist, why should I take the old woman's word that I was not Gordy Friend? Perhaps she was crazy and Selena was keeping her existence from me out of consideration for an invalid. Or perhaps her old eyes were dim and in the moonlight she had made an honest mistake. The bandages alone might easily have confused her.

How pleasant it would be to forget my doubts and relax. How pleasant to be Gordon Renton Friend the Third.

The faint odour of lavender drifted up from my pyjama pocket. Its effect was tonic as a cold shower. Selena had lied. Until I could explain that away, I had to be on my guard. I would have to start to plan too. There was no time to lose. For all I knew, time might be a crucial factor in this battle of wits against the Friends.

The door opened. I was hoping it would be Netti with my breakfast. But it was Marny. She was wearing Chinese pyjamas and her feet were bare. Her glossy black hair was tousled from sleep. She strolled to the bed and sat down cross-legged at the foot by my cast.

''lo, Gordy. Anything good in the Amnesiac's Gazette this morning?'

She grinned, watching me from insolent brown eyes. She was so young that she was attractive even though she was obviously straight from bed and had made no attempt to fix herself up. In spite of what I now knew, it seemed almost impossible to suspect the disarming candour of her gaze.

She glanced scornfully at Selena. 'Selena. She sleeps like a cow.'

She stretched over me, picked up Selena's cigarette case

from the bedside table and lit a cigarette. She stayed half across me supporting herself with one hand.

'Well, Gordy, how did the night treat you?'

'Roughly.' It was a risk but I took it. 'An old woman burst in on me. By the way, who is she? My grandmother?'

Selena was suddenly awake, so suddenly that I wondered if she had really been asleep. She sat up in bed, smiling at us dazzlingly.

'Hi, Marny. Morning, Gordy, baby. Still fiddling around with that old woman?'

She slid out of her bed and came to mine, sitting down on the spread across from Marny. Lazily she kissed me on the cheek. I wanted desperately not to be excited by her nearness.

'You didn't really believe me last night, did you, baby?' She glanced at Marny. 'Poor Gordy had a frightful dream about a hag with a stringy neck. He's sure she really exists. Tell him we don't have any old crones locked up in the attic.'

'Old crones?' Marny puffed smoke at me. 'I'm sorry, Gordy. No crones.'

She spoke casually but I caught an almost imperceptible flicker of understanding in the glance she exchanged with Selena. With a sinking heart, I was sure then that she had been primed. That must have been one of the things Selena did last night when she slipped out of the room. It had been so important to keep me from knowing about the old woman that Selena had woken the others up and warned them.

Just as I couldn't stop being excited by Selena, I couldn't kid myself any longer, either. She was my enemy. They were all my enemies.

'What did she say to you?' Marny looked down at her knee, brushing idly at a piece of lint on the red silk. 'The old hag in the dream, I mean?'

I wasn't falling into that trap.

'Nothing,' I lied. 'She just seemed to be there and then floated away. You know how it is with dreams.'

'So you realize she was a dream now?' asked Selena.

'Sure.'

'Darling.'

She leaned toward me, kissing me again. I was scared she would smell lavender and realize that I had in my pocket definite evidence that the old woman wasn't a dream.

But she didn't seem to notice anything. In fact, she seemed exhilarated as if she had scored a victory.

Knowing she would lie, I said: 'And how did you sleep, Selena?'

'Me, baby? You know me. Five seconds after I said goodnight I was dead to the world.'

She pushed the hair up from the nape of her neck. 'Oh, Marny, I had a divine idea last night. I made Gordy learn two verses of your father's poem against drink. To help him remember.'

'Do any good?'

'No.'

'But it's a super idea.' Marny's enthusiasm was a shade too well-trained. 'Absolutely super. Where's the book? Let's make him learn some more.'

She saw the book on the bedside table, grabbed it up and started to leaf through it. Crazy as it seemed, I started to feel that there was something important about that poem. They seemed unnecessarily eager for me to learn it.

To test them I said: 'No more poem, Marny. I'm suffering enough as it is.'

'You've got to, Gordy.'

'Yes, baby,' Selena was snuggling against me. 'Please, don't be dismal. Even if it doesn't help, it's such fun.'

'First,' said Marny, 'repeat the verses you already know.'

'I've forgotten them,' I lied.

A momentary but a very real alarm showed in Selena's eyes. I knew then that I'd been right. My learning the poem was part of their plan. I considered carrying on with my pretended forgetfulness. Then I abandoned the idea, I still knew so little. It was dangerous to force an issue at this early date. I grumbled, made a few false starts and then recited the verses.

66

Their satisfaction was obvious. Marny read a third verse. When I learned that, they were positively purring.

All the time that I was playing this only dimly understood game with them, I was hoping that they would leave before Netti brought my breakfast tray. My plans were no more than half formed, but I knew that my way out of the trap could only come through Netti.

> '"Oh, haunt of the Lost and the Losing,
> Vile Saloon of Squalorous Sin,
> Satan sits there, the wine list perusing,
> Luring lads to Damnation with gin."'

Marny was reciting this fourth and even more lugubrious verse when the door opened. Mrs Friend – I didn't call her mother in my mind any more – came in. A faint chill settled on me as I saw that she was carrying my breakfast tray.

Gently chiding the girls off my bed, she set the tray down in front of me and kissed me.

'Good morning, darling boy. I hope the girls aren't worrying you.' She surveyed me with serene affection. 'You look better, dear. More rested. Any memories yet?'

'No,' I said.

'We've been teaching him Father's Ode to Aurora, though,' put in Marny. 'He's wonderful, Mimsey. He's learned four verses.'

If this information was of any importance to her, Mrs Friend was completely successful in concealing it. She smiled and started to straighten the things on the breakfast tray.

'How very clever of him. He can recite the poem to Mr Moffat tomorrow. It would be a charming gesture.'

'Mr Moffat?' I queried.

'A very old friend of your father's, dear.'

'You know, darling,' said Selena. 'The Aurora Clean Living League. I told you.'

'He's coming tomorrow?' I asked.

Mrs Friend sat down on the bed, patting at refractory wisps of hair. 'It's the anniversary of your father's death, Gordy.

67

Just exactly thirty days. Mr Moffat is making a sort of cere-monial visit of respect. I'm afraid it'll be on the dismal side, but the least we can do for your poor dear father is to show Mr Moffat a decent courtesy.'

Both the girls were standing at her side. Mrs Friend sur-veyed Marny's tousled red pyjamas and Selena's white frothy négligé.

'My dears, don't forget. Plain black tomorrow, mourning black. And no lipstick. I don't want you denounced as harlots.'

She laughed her deep, amused laugh.

'And Gordy will recite your father's poems. Yes, that would be delightful, most delightful.'

Selena twisted away, picked up the book of poems and opened it at random.

She chanted:

> ''"Whether weary or woeful, Aurora
> With her amber Olympian arms
> Will charm and caress ..."

'Listen, isn't that wonderful? He's lusting after Aurora now.' She giggled suddenly. 'And he can't even spell. He spells whether W-H-E-T-H- instead of W-E-A-T-H. Really....'

'Really, indeed,' broke in Mrs Friend with a sigh. 'Some-times I am gravely disturbed by your lack of education, Selena.'

Selena's face fell. 'You mean he spells it right?'

'Of course, dear.'

'Oh, God, I can never remember.' Selena moved to me, grinning. 'Darling, do you mind having an illiterate wife?'

I was hardly listening because a plan had come – a small one. The vase of irises had meant something. The vase of irises had been removed when I was asleep. The spaniel, Peter, had meant something too. Where was Peter now?

I grinned at Mrs Friend. 'I'm kind of lonesome for my dog. How about sending him up?'

Mrs Friend's expression changed to one of gentle concern. 'Oh, dear, I was so hoping you wouldn't ask about him.'

'What's happened?'

'A fever, dear. In the night. The poor little mite, he was shivering like a leaf. And such a hot nose. I do hope it isn't distemper.' Her steady glance moved from one to the other of the girls. 'I had Jan take him in to the vet this morning.' She patted my hand and smiled. 'But don't you worry, dear. The vet's wonderful. I'm sure he'll be back with us right as rain in a day or two.'

She rose from the bed. She could even invest the undignified act of getting up with a stately beauty.

'Now, girls, let's leave poor Gordy to his breakfast. Ours is being brought up to my room so you needn't bother to dress.'

Ritualistically, one after the other, they gave me a Judas kiss. Mrs Friend slipped her smooth heavy arms around the two girls' waists. The three of them, lovingly embracing, moved out of the room.

Alone with my orange juice, coffee, scrambled eggs, and carefully cut squares of toast, I tried to piece together the scraps of information I had obtained. They were so eager to keep me from remembering my real identity that they had removed the irises and disposed of the dog the moment they seemed to provide me with a clue. They were lying to me about the old woman. They wanted me to learn the late Mr Friend's ludicrous poem. I was to recite it to Mr Moffat. Mr Moffat was arriving tomorrow. My father had died thirty days before – suddenly without warning.

I felt a dim but sinister pattern was there if I only could find it.

I was recovering from the initial shock now and wild schemes started to form. A citizen in a jam calls the police. But how could I call the police, when I was in bed, unable to move without the assistance of the people who were my enemies. No. It would have to be something more practical than that.

As I toyed listlessly with my breakfast, I thought of Netti again. I couldn't be entirely sure of Netti. She might be as much part of the plot as the others. I had nothing but a hunch and I would have to move cautiously. But Netti had known the old cook, the cook who had been working here when my father died, who had known Gordy Friend and who had hinted dark hints. Selena had said that all the fired servants had been paid by Mr Friend to spy on them. That meant the fired servants would be against the Friends and potential allies for me. If only Netti knew where the old cook was now and somehow could get in touch with her....

I finished my breakfast and lay back in bed smoking a cigarette from Selena's platinum case. It seemed a threadbare hope, that deliverance could come from an unknown, fired cook, but ... with growing impatience I waited for the sound of footsteps outside which would herald Netti's arrival to remove the tray.

Because it had to be Netti who would come for the tray.

After a while I heard footsteps outside. The door opened. My hopes were dashed. It was Jan.

The huge Dutchman wore the same navy swimming trunks and blue polo shirt that he had worn the day before. He looked even larger, if possible, and even more amiable. His unruly straw hair tumbled over his forehead. His lips stretched in a smile.

'Hi,' he said.

He gave me the works that morning, carrying me into the bathroom, sponging me all over with warm water and generally tidying me up. The almost loving tenderness with which he ministered to me seemed more ominous than it had the night before. The victim image was in my mind now. As he sprinkled lilac talcum powder over me and rubbed it gently into my skin, he seemed like some priest's giant slave preparing the Chosen One for sacrifice.

At length I was back again in the smoothed bed with its meticulous hospital corners. He laughed and asked his questioning: 'Jah?'

I shook my head. I could think of nothing I could ask Jan with safety.

He tossed back his hair and strode towards the door. He

70

had almost reached it when he turned and, crossing to a side table, picked up the breakfast tray.

'No,' I called.

He turned his head, watching me guardedly over his massive shoulder.

'No,' I said. 'The tray. Leave the tray.'

His tanned forehead wrinkled with concentration. He looked at the tray and then at me. Suddenly a grin of understanding came. He brought the tray over to me and pointed down to an unfinished piece of toast.

' Jah?'

'That's it,' I said.

He continued to stand by the bed. I realized he was planning to wait till I had eaten the toast and then to take the tray.

I shook my head again. 'No,' I said. 'Leave it. Scram.'

He looked sulky.

'Scram,' I said. I pointed at the door.

He followed the direction of my pointing finger. He seemed to get it then. With a vague shrug, he went out, shutting the door behind him.

It was my first victory. That tray gave me one more chance of Netti.

And my feeble stratagem worked. A few minutes later there was a tap on the door and Netti slipped into the room. Her white maid's cap was slightly askew on the peroxide hair. In spite of the formal, frilly uniform there was a distinctly blowsy air to her plump figure. Over her left hand and forearm hung a napkin as if she were trying to caricature a headwaiter.

' Jan forgot your tray, Mr Friend. They sent me up.'

She glanced over her shoulder and then moved conspiratorially to the bed. The gums stretched in an intimate, rather leering smile which, at that moment, was far more welcome to me than Selena's most alluring blandishments.

Suddenly she whipped the napkin from her left hand, revealing a jigger of liquor clutched between thumb and first finger. She held it out to me.

'Gin,' she said. 'Cook sent me to the liquor closet. Had a snort myself. Then you was the first I thought of.'

'Thank you, Netti.'

I took the jigger. She stood watching me with the satisfaction of a mother robin who had just presented her baby with a particularly juicy worm.

The Friends didn't want me to drink. I was pretty sure of that. I was pretty sure too that even they could not be devious enough to have sent Netti up to tempt me to do something against their own interests. I felt I had Netti summed up then. She was a rummy and she thought I was. The bond between two rummies is a very real one – and exploitable.

I swallowed the gin at one gulp and then winked at her appreciably. She liked that. Giggling, she said:

'Goes down good, don't it?'

'Sure does.' I stared down into the glass, stalling, forming the right approach.

'I sneaked out a whole tumbler full,' she said suddenly. 'I was saving it for my afternoon. But if you could go for another....'

'No, Netti. This'll hold me.' I looked up at her then. 'Know something? Everyone in this house is trying to get my memory back but you're the only one that helped me so far.'

'Me, Mr Friend?' She was rubbing her hands up and down the front of the frivolous apron as if they were wet and she was expecting me to shake hands. She giggled. 'Why me?'

'Remember yesterday you told me about the old cook? The cook that was fired the day you came here?'

Her face fell. 'Oh,' she said, 'that old Emma.'

'Emma!' I repeated. 'That's just it, Netti. After you'd gone I suddenly remembered the cook's name was Emma, and you didn't tell me. You just talked about the old cook. See?'

She didn't seem interested.

'Yes,' I said. 'That's very important. That's the first thing I've remembered.' I paused. 'Emma was the one who told you about me going off on that toot, wasn't she?'

'Sure.'

'Guess she didn't think much of me, did she?'

Netti grimaced. 'Oh, her. Church wasn't holy enough for her. She didn't go for you at all.' She grinned. 'You were sinful.'

'And the rest of the family were sinful too?'

'Your mother? Selena? Marny?' She laughed. 'Scarlet women, she called them. No better than street walkers.' She winked. 'Gee, I was glad she left. What'd she of called me if she'd stuck around for a couple of days?'

I took her sticky hand and squeezed it. 'You're my pal, aren't you, Netti?'

She squirmed. 'Your pal? Sure I'm your pal, Mr Friend. You and me's got things in common.'

'Then maybe you'd do something for me?'

'You bet your life. Want another slug of gin after all?'

I shook my head. 'Just tell me what she hinted about me. After all, if she made accusations, I've got a right to prove they're wrong, haven't I?'

She looked nervous. 'What Emma hinted at?'

'You told me yesterday she'd hinted at something about my going off after Father died.'

She laughed suddenly. 'Oh, that. That wasn't nothing. Nothing real. Just crazy foolishness.'

'Even so...'

'It wasn't nothing. Really.' She patted her back hair and giggled. 'I was laughing myself silly inside while she was talking. She said –' she paused, '– she said with you going off real quick like that and your father dying sudden – well, it just looked very funny to her. Maybe you bumped him off. Or if you didn't, one of the others did.'

She yawned. 'That Emma, she couldn't think of nothing but your father. Thought he was Jesus Christ himself, she did ... Jesus Christ with a lot of Satans ganging up on him. If you ask me, she was stuck on him, the dirty old thing.'

I suppose it was my invalid weakness, but I felt as if my fancy pyjamas were wet and clammy, clinging to my skin.

Netti had been laughing herself silly when Emma had told her that. I wished I could laugh myself silly. But I couldn't, for here at last was a pattern – a pattern based on the slenderest evidence of servants' gossip but one which could explain with sinister logic my presence in the household.

What if the Friends *had* killed the old man? What if that was my function? To wait here, trapped in my casts, until the police came to arrest me as Gordy, the patricide? To kill a man and afterwards groom a helpless and unsuspecting amnesiac to play the role of murderer – wasn't that the diabolically intricate type of plan the Friends might well evolve?

Trying with a great effort to be casual, I said: 'Guess you don't know where she's working now, Netti?'

'Emma?' She jutted a hip to one side and balanced a cupped hand against it. 'Why, sure. Ran into her only maybe a couple of weeks ago down to the Supermarket on the Boulevard. She's working for some folks called Curtis up on Temple Drive. Crabby old thing. Why, she's so old she ought to be dead, Mr Friend. I only hope I die young.' The gums showed again. 'Over sixty? No more fun? Not me.'

It was desperately important now to get Emma here. If only I could invent a plausible enough story to have Netti bring her around and smuggle her up....

I started to speak but Netti got in ahead of me. Her eyes gleaming with a sudden, knowing light, she leaned a little closer. I could smell the sourness of gin on her breath.

'Quite a night you had last night, Mr Friend.'

'Me?' I was still casual.

She leaned nearer. There was spite in her eyes too now – spite that was not directed at me. Maybe she didn't like the Friend woman any more than Emma had. 'I heard all about it. You being woke like that and all scared. Mrs Friend made me promise, but you and me being pals....'

She broke off. I could tell she had been able to see how her words affected me. She was on the verge of telling me about the old woman and she wanted me to coax her so that she could extract every ounce of satisfaction from this indiscreet confidence.

'Oh, you mean the visitor I had last night?' I said, playing up to her.

'Visitor,' Netti grimaced. 'I don't call that no visitor. Waking up, seeing her bending over you with them big, shivery eyes. Ugh. It's a shame. That's what it is. Saying you wasn't to be told about her just because you're sick and all.'

'I'm not meant to know about her?'

'No.' Netti stared anxiously as if she was afraid her thunder had been stolen. 'You mean you *do* know?'

This was the moment.

'Matter of fact,' I said. 'I don't.'

'What don't you know, dear?'

That sentence, mild as a gentle spring breeze, wafted from the door.

I looked over Netti's head.

Mrs Friend was moving into the room, large, comfortable, smiling her mellow smile.

Chapter 9

NETTI grabbed the empty jigger from my hand and hid it clumsily under the napkin. Embarrassment blotched her cheeks with red. Mrs Friend progressed to the bed, took my hand and smiled at both of us.

'Netti, you'd better be running along. I'm sure cook will be wanting you.'

With a flustered 'Yes, Mrs Friend', Netti poked her cap straight, made a dive at the tray and scurried out.

It seemed almost impossible that Mrs Friend had failed to notice Netti's awkward juggling with the empty glass. But she made no comment. She was carrying a small brown paper sack. As she sat down on my bed, she took a flat disc of chocolate-covered peppermint from the sack and popped it in her mouth. She produced another piece for me.

'There, darling, I don't think candy'll hurt you today.'

Suspecting what I now suspected, her affectionate sweetness was almost more than I could bear. I had been on the very brink of success with Netti, too. Now everything was gone and Mrs Friend was feeding me peppermint candy.

'That Netti,' she mused. 'Marny swears she sneaks sailors in after we've gone to bed. I wouldn't get too friendly with her, dear.'

'In this cast?' I said.

She laughed her resonant, infectious laugh. Then her face grew grave. 'Gordy dear, I do wish you wouldn't go on being hostile.'

'Hostile?'

'It's just the amnesia. I realize that. But if only you'd stop being suspicious.' She ate another piece of candy. 'We're awfully harmless, you know. Think of the unattractive mothers and wives and sisters you might have come back to.'

She sighed. 'But it's no use arguing, is it? You feel the way you feel and it's up to us to help you. By the way, Nate's arrived. He's brought the wheel chair. He's instructing Jan how to work it – with gestures. So that Jan can push you around. He'll be up in a moment – Nate.'

Sitting there in her square-necked widow dress munching candy, Mrs Friend was terrifically plausible in her role of understanding mother. I tried to think of her as a husband-murderer and the leader of a giant conspiracy to deliver me to the police. The effort was almost impossible. But only almost.

I was tempted to pull the lavender-scented handkerchief out of my pocket and say: *Look at this. It proves you're all lying. It proves an old woman exists who knows I'm not Gordy Friend.*

I didn't say it, of course. It would be absurdly dangerous to let them know I had evidence to support my suspicions. It was dangerous enough that they sensed I was suspicious at all.

To reassure myself, however, I did feel in my pyjama pocket. My own handkerchief seemed smoother and starchier than I had remembered it. When Mrs Friend turned from me

76

to toy with the pink roses, I glanced down at the pocket. The handkerchief, neatly thrusting out of it, was brand new. I pulled it out and, with unsteady fingers felt for the lavender-scented handkerchief which should have been beneath it.

It was not there.

By then I was so impressed by the almost superhuman cleverness of the Friends that I thought Mrs Friend must somehow have guessed its existence and slipped it out of my pocket herself. Then I remembered Jan. Jan had taken off my pyjamas to bathe me. Jan, with his passion for the detail of tidiness, had probably changed my handkerchief and pulled out the old woman's one with it.

I felt a mixture of exasperation at myself and despair. The handkerchief had been my only tangible clue to convince the outside world, if I ever reached it, that the Friends were my enemies. Now it was gone.

Mrs Friend had lost interest in the roses and, leaning forward, started unnecessarily to plump the pillows behind my head.

'I'm not being a very good nurse, am I, dear? I'm always that way about everything, I'm afraid. I'm thrilled to begin with and then I get bored. Too bad you were unconscious when you first came home. I was such an impressive nurse then. I took your temperature and your pulse and sat with you and gave you all the right medicine at the right times. By the way, aren't you supposed to be having something now?'

On principle I was on my guard against any of Mrs Friend's medicines. 'I feel fine,' I said.

'I am glad, darling. But we'll ask Nate when he comes. See what he says.'

Nate came then. The young doctor strolled into the room. That morning he was in a formal grey suit but the general tweedy effect remained. He was carrying a green book which looked like a telephone book. He tossed it down on a table.

'Hello, Nate,' said Mrs Friend. 'I hope Jan was able to understand how to work the chair.'

'Sure. For someone who's meant to be simple-minded, he's

a bright lad. If you ask me, he doesn't learn English just because he can't be bothered, not because he's too stupid.' Dr Croft was at the bedside giving me a long, serious look. 'Well, Gordy, how do you feel?'

'He still doesn't quite trust us, Doctor,' said Mrs Friend. 'He's being polite, but I can tell.'

The tip of Dr Croft's tongue appeared between his white teeth. As a gesture, it was meant to indicate brisk, professional reflection. He succeeded only in looking seductive – the Sultan's favourite inviting me to slip with him behind a Persian arras.

'I've been thinking, Gordy. You've got this bug in your brain. I'm not worried. It's perfectly natural for you to rebel against your identity. But we've got to clear it up, and the only way I can think of is to get in another doctor.'

He grabbed a chair and, spinning it around, sat down on it back to front.

'I know plenty of doctors with experience in matters like this, Gordy. I could bring my pick of three or four excellent men and they would all tell you the same thing. But,' – he examined his own dusky-skinned hand – 'that wouldn't do. Just because I'd selected a man, you'd suspect he was in cahoots with me, wouldn't you? It's crazy, of course, imagining a reputable doctor would risk his professional career trying to make you believe you're someone you're not. But that's the way you'd react. Don't feel bad about it, old man. You can't help it. That's just the way these things go.'

Dr Croft's talent for candour was as disarming as Mrs Friend's.

'So.' He smiled suddenly, got up and, crossing the room for the green book, brought it to the bedside. 'Here's what we do.' He handed me the book. 'Here's the telephone book. Look up the physicians in the classified selection. Pick any one at random. And we'll let you call him yourself.' He patted my arm. 'No chance at collusion there. That's the way to do it, my boy. That'll clear up this psychological block. Then we'll have a free hand and your memory'll be back before you can spell Aesculapius.'

I took the telephone book. I looked at Dr Croft and then at Mrs Friend. They were both smiling affectionately. For a moment I was almost forced to believe that I had grotesquely exaggerated the implications of a sour servant's scandalous gossip, a doddering old woman's fancies, and my own amnesiac's whimsies. Surely no conspirators, however daring, could make their victim so frank an offer as this.

I found the Physician column in the Classified section. Dr Frank Graber, I saw. Dr Joseph Green, Dr Decius Griddlecook.

Griddlecook. The name fascinated me. For a moment I toyed with the idea of calling Dr Griddlecook. Then, it began to dawn on me how ingenious this latest ruse of the Friends' was.

If I did call Dr Griddlecook, I would have to telephone as an invalid who was not satisfied with the services of his own personal physician. That, from the start, would make me an eccentric in Dr Griddlecook's eyes. Then he would have to come to the house. He would be greeted by Dr Croft, Mrs Friend, Selena, and Marny. Sweetly, attractively, they would represent themselves as an anxious family eager to settle the morbid doubts of a beloved son. Long before Dr Griddlecook reached my bedside, he would be prejudiced. And once I talked to him, what could I say? That an old woman, whose existence was denied, had told me I was not Gordy Friend and had dropped a handkerchief which was subsequently taken from me. And that I had a wild idea Mr Friend had been murdered and I was being groomed to take the rap.

Dr Croft and Mrs Friend were still watching me intently waiting for my answer.

'Well, dear?' asked Mrs Friend. 'Don't you think Nate's got a terribly good idea?'

Dr Griddlecook, as a potential saviour, faded in my mind. All I'd achieve by calling him would be to put the Friends more on their guard, and I had no chance of outwitting them until they were convinced that I was one hundred per cent duped. Here was my opportunity to bluff.

I let the telephone book drop. I gave them what I hoped was my blandest smile.

'You're taking this too seriously,' I said. 'I don't want another doctor's opinion. Yesterday I did have some crazy feeling about not being Gordy. But it's gone today.'

'Darling boy,' beamed Mrs Friend.

Dr Croft was still watching me. 'You really mean that?'

'Sure.'

'Honest? This is important, you know – important for your recovery.'

'Cross my heart and hope to die.' I grinned up at Nate. 'After all, you took care of my father and you're taking care of me. I'd be a dope not to trust the old family physician.'

I had said that partly to discover just what Nate Croft had had to do with Mr Friend's last illness. I got a rise out of Mrs Friend.

Gazing gravely at the pink roses, she murmured: 'Nate wasn't your father's doctor, dear. Old Dr Leland was. A most reputable old duck. But just a little stuffy.' She turned her illuminated smile on me. 'You could have him to see you, if you like. But I'm sure you'll find that Nate's a lot more fun.'

'Uhuh,' I shook my head. 'I'm sticking to Nate.'

So Mr Friend's death-bed had been attended by old reputable Dr Leland. Presumably, too, old reputable Dr Leland had signed the death certificate. And the fact that the Friends were ready to have me see Dr Leland proved they weren't bluffing. I felt a lot easier in my mind. They might have Nate Croft sewed up. But surely they couldn't have made a conspirator out of old reputable Dr Leland too.

I glanced at Nate to see how the question had affected him. It didn't seem to have affected him at all.

'So you're ready to tag along with me, eh, Gordy? Swell and dandy.' His voice was hearty as a country-club locker-room. 'That's our last obstacle gone. Now we'll go ahead like a house afire.'

'Lovely.' Mrs Friend held the paper sack out to Dr Croft. 'Have some candy to celebrate.'

'Thank you.'

Dr Croft took a piece and nibbled at it daintily.

'Okay, Gordy. Now listen, old man. I've brought the wheel chair. This afternoon I want to try you out in it. You'll get more liberty that way. I think you'll enjoy getting out of this boring old bedroom and I think you're up to it. But first' – he glanced at his watch – 'I think you ought to have a little sleep now. To freshen you up, marshal your strength.'

'I was wondering whether I should have given him a pill,' murmured Mrs Friend. She moved towards the tray of medicine.

'Don't bother. I've got one here. It'll work fast and wear off soon.' Dr Croft produced a little box from the pocket of his jacket. Mrs Friend brought a glass of water. Dr Croft handed me a capsule.

'Here, Gordy.'

If I refused it, I would show I didn't trust them and would lose the slight advantage I'd gained. I took the pill. I took the glass from Mrs Friend. While they watched, smiling, I swallowed the pill.

They left me then. Dr Croft was right about the fast action of the drug. Almost immediately I felt thick drowsiness blurring me. The drowsiness made me more conscious than usual of my amnesia. With all the detail fading from my thoughts, there was a great blank left where my name and my memories should be. Gradually a vision of Netti, dim as the image on a myopic's retina, rose to fill the empty space. I had fooled them into believing they had fooled me. I had won the first round. Now if I could get Netti to smuggle Emma up to my room. Or if I could get Netti to tell me the truth about that old woman! ...

They had tried to take everything from me but they hadn't taken Netti.

Netti's red-veined gums ... Netti's white cap ... Netti's sour gin breath ... Netti's hip jutting out ...

I awoke feeling alert and rested. The travelling clock on the bedside table pointed to one. There was sunlight everywhere.

A warm vigorous breeze blew through the open windows, stirring the heavy drapes. It was a wonderful room, gay, uninhabited, part of the summer outside. For a moment I had a pang of longing for Selena. Selena who was summer, who was all a man could want. Selena with the liquid hair and the warm, generous lips.

But the clock said one. One meant lunch. And lunch meant Netti. I quivered with anticipation at the prospect of Netti.

Exactly at one fifteen the door opened. Selena came in. She was wearing a white swimming suit, a scrap of a swimming suit.

She was carrying a tray.

'Your lunch, baby.'

She brought the tray to me and arranged it on the invalid bed-table. She sat down by my side, her blue eyes laughing, the skin of her bare arm, brushing mine, warm from the sun.

'Sweet, darling Gordy. He just sleeps and eats and sleeps and eats without a care in the world.'

She kissed me, her hair tumbling forward, brushing my cheek.

'Where's Netti?' I said.

'Netti? Darling, that dreary Netti. What would you want with her?'

'Nothing,' I said. 'I just wondered where she was.'

'Then, darling, I'm afraid you'll never know.' Selena's smile was sweet as syringa. 'No one will ever know, except maybe a couple of sailors who keep telephone numbers.'

I knew then what she was going to say and I almost hated her.

'Really, she was a frightful girl. Always stealing our liquor. And then, bringing you up a jigger of gin. Gordy, darling, with Mr Moffat coming and everything, you don't imagine we'd put up with that, do you?'

Selena patted my hand. She rose from the bed and strolled to the window, leaning on the sill and gazing out.

'Mimsey was awfully nice to her. Nicer than she deserved. She gave Netti a whole month's salary when she fired her.'

Chapter 10

AFTER lunch Jan brought in the wheel chair. Like everything else produced by the Friends, it was the most luxurious of its kind, self-propelling with deep rubber tyres and gaily chintzed overstuffed upholstery.

Jan was both proud and proprietary about it. He seemed to think it was his toy and that I was just another prop to make the game more amusing. Tenderly, like a little girl putting her favourite doll in a perambulator, he lifted me from the bed and installed me in the chair. He brought a green silk robe and tucked it around my knees. He fussed over me, tidying and straightening my pyjama jacket. He stepped back, surveying me with a huge, white grin. Then he pushed the chair a few feet around the room and burst into a gale of laughter.

I had been entertaining in bed. I was deliriously funny in the wheel chair.

I had thought about asking him if he had taken the lavender-scented handkerchief and, if so, where it was. But the danger, apart from the difficulty of putting the idea across with gestures, discouraged me. He stopped wheeling me around. With my one good arm, I experimented propelling the chair myself. It was easy, but almost immediately Jan called:

'Nein.'

He grabbed the rail at the back with a huge fist and stopped me. His face was dark and sulky.

I had a wheel chair but, apparently, Jan was not going to allow me the potential liberty it offered.

Still smouldering, he pushed me out of the room into a broad sunny corridor. This was my first glimpse of the house that was supposed to be mine. He rolled me into a living-room. It was one of the most spectacular rooms I had ever seen. One entire wall was plate glass, revealing a vast panorama of lonely mountains and a precipitous canyon between.

I had not realized the house was so high up. I had not realized, either, exactly how remote from civilization it was.

We moved through the living-room to a spacious, book-lined library. There was a telephone, I noticed, on a desk in the corner, standing next to a typewriter. The realization of it as a link, however slender, with the outside world was comforting.

French windows opened from the library onto a riotous prospect of flowers. Jan was pushing me towards them when Mrs Friend emerged from an inner door and came, smiling, to me.

'Darling boy, how nice to see you up. And how do you like your house? Sweet, isn't it?'

'Kind of cut off from everywhere, isn't it? Any neighbours?'

Mrs Friend gave her throaty laugh. 'Good heavens no, dear. No one for miles. There used to be an old farmer who had an avocado farm way back in a little canyon behind the house, but your father bought him off. Your father hated neighbours. It was the Napoleon in him, I think. He used to like to get up on high, craggy places and be the monarch of all he surveyed.' She patted my hand. 'The others are at the pool. Is Jan going to wheel you down to join the fun?'

'I guess so,' I said.

Mrs Friend sighed. 'Lucky you. Your poor mother never seems to have a moment's rest. Back to the kitchen I go to order dinner.'

She drifted away. Jan pushed me through the french windows onto a tiled terrace and off it onto a grass path between blossoming hibiscus, oleander, and mimosa. There was no view here, no sense of loneliness, only the bright, almost stifling cosiness of the shrubs and flowers. A turn in the path under a wire arch smothered in blue plumbago brought us suddenly and unexpectedly to the edge of a long, wide-rimmed swimming pool.

It was the swimming pool of your dreams. Screened on all four sides by fluttering eucalyptus trees, it was also bounded by a lower hedge of orange trees. The perfume from the creamy white blossoms was almost oppressive and the ripe oranges glowed like fire among the glossy dark leaves. The water of the pool itself was clear and blue as the sky.

Gay mattresses strewed the broad concrete rim. On one of them Selena in her white swimming suit lounged with Dr Nate Croft. The young doctor, who presumably had no urgent business to attend to, was wearing white trunks. Naked, his body with its soft, dusky skin was as exotic and uncountry-clubbish as his eyes. He lay very near to Selena and his bare arm, I noticed, was lying lightly against hers. Marny was there too. In a brief bra suit of yellow cotton, she sat on the edge of the pool, dangling her long, tanned legs in the water.

The moment they saw me, all three of them came clustering around me, laughing, chattering, commenting on the wheel chair. When Selena had told me that Netti was fired, I had felt at the end of my tether. But the freedom of the wheel chair, restricted as it was, had brought a return of hope. I laughed and kidded back at them with the inward satisfaction that at least my carefreeness was fooling them.

Having delivered me, Jan seemed to feel that his employee duties were fulfilled. Grinning, he stripped off the blue polo shirt and strode to the rim of the pool. He lingered there, lazily flexing the muscles of his chest and arms. His physique was really phenomenal. One glimpse of him and Brünnhilde would have walked out on Siegfried. As I watched him I noticed that Marny was watching him too.

Her lids were half closed and the curly lashes concealed her eyes. But there was a strange expression on her young face, intent, almost greedy.

Jan dived into the pool. His face appeared from the blue water. He was laughing and pushing back the long hair, darker now, the colour of wet sand.

Marny caught me looking at her. Her face quickly assumed its normal, impudent grin.

'The wages of abstinence, Gordy,' she said. 'No drink, no smoke. Let Jan be a lesson to you.'

Jan was playing with a large, red rubber ball now. Tossing it up in the air and catching it, throwing it and diving under it like an exhibitionistic sea-lion. Selena had been standing by me with her hand absently on my shoulder. Suddenly she ran to the pool, dived in and swam to Jan. She was as at home in the water as the big Dutchman. She reached him. She grabbed the ball just before he caught it and squirmed away, laughing a deep, husky laugh. Jan lumbered after her. He caught her leg. The ball slipped from Selena's wet fingers. It bobbed away, floating, bright scarlet, on the water.

Neither of them seemed to notice it. They went on struggling. Both of them were laughing. We could see their sun-tanned limbs, entangled as Selena fought, only half earnestly, to escape. Selena was wearing no cap. The beautiful moulding of her head showed as the wet hair clung around it. She half broke away from Jan and he leaped for her again. As his arms closed around her, I caught a glimpse of her profile. Her eyes were shining and her red lips were parted in a hot, excited smile.

I felt sharp pain in my shoulder. I looked up. Nate Croft was gripping me so fiercely that the knuckles of his hand were white. I glanced up at his face and I knew that he did not have the faintest idea that he was clutching me. His lips were almost as light as his knuckles, and his eyes, fixed on the struggling brown bodies in the pool, were blazing with fury.

I was learning quite a lot about my captors. But this fact was, perhaps, the most revealing. There was no need to wonder any more why a doctor would risk his entire profes-sional career by becoming party to any conspiracy against me. A man who could react that violently to Selena's contact with another male would do anything for her – commit murder if necessary.

Murder! The word brought a chill.

That supposedly playful struggle in the pool had done something queer and heightening to the atmosphere. Even I had been infected by it. Without warning, Nate Croft leaped from my side and dived into the pool. Marny shot after him.

They hurled themselves on Selena and Jan, and the spell was broken. All four of them continued to splash and struggle, but the tension was gone. They were just four people having fun with a red rubber ball.

They were still, however, caught up in the aftermath of that odd quadrilateral emotion. They seemed to have forgotten me. Unobtrusively I started to move the chair back away from the pool. Constantly supervised as I was, I could never make plans in advance. I had to seize opportunity whenever it offered itself. I manoeuvred back to the arch of feathery blue plumbago. Still none of them were noticing. With my one good hand, I steered through the arch and propelled the chair as quickly as I could up the level grass path, onto the terrace and into the library.

My impulse was to search for the old woman. She must be somewhere in that luxurious, rambling bungalow, which was big enough to house a dozen old women. The door leading from the library to the inner corridor was ajar. I started towards it. The rubber wheels of the chair made no sound against the thick leaf-green carpet. Just as I reached the door, I heard footsteps in the passage beyond it. I peered through the crack between the half-open door and the frame and saw Mrs Friend moving serenely down the passage away from me.

With her in the house, I knew any attempt to explore would be hopeless. Disconsolately, I spun the chair around, guiding it at random towards the fireplace. Above it, on the ochre-washed walls, hung four photographs in identical frames. One was a photograph of Selena; one was of Marny; one was of Mrs Friend; and the fourth was of a severe, white-haired man with a bristly, belligerent moustache – presumably Gordon Renton Friend the Second.

I looked at the picture of the man who was supposed to be my father and who had died twenty-nine days before. It was a formidable enough face. I could imagine how utterly different the household must have been with him at the helm.

I felt an odd sympathy with him. Just how much were we tied up together? Mr Moffat was coming tomorrow. I was to recite Mr Friend's *Ode to Aurora*. Did that connect somehow with old Mr Friend? And how? With his life? Or with his death?

My ominous suspicions, which had been partially smothered by the knowledge that Nate hadn't attended Mr Friend at the time of his death, flared up again with renewed violence. Perhaps the Friends *had* murdered the old man and had tricked Dr Leland into signing a death certificate by some typical Friend ruse which they were afraid might not hold up indefinitely. There was, of course, still no evidence to support that theory except a servant's chance remark which had been reported to me second hand. But what other possible explanation could there be for the cat-and-mouse game the Friends were playing with me and for their passionate determination to convince me I was Gordy Friend?

And, whatever their plan, where was the real Gordy? Still off on a genuine bat? Or were they hiding him somewhere until I had paid the price for the murder?

The thought of Gordy made me realize what I should have realized immediately. In the group of family photographs above the mantel, there was no picture of Gordon Renton Friend the Third.

That there should be one was clear. They would not have omitted the only son. I looked at the wall closely and detected nail holes on either side of the photographs of Marny and Selena. There were patches too where the ochre was a shade darker. Unquestionably there had been three photographs and the pictures of Marny and Selena had been moved to give a symmetrical effect.

It wasn't surprising of course, that the Friends had removed Gordy's photograph. Now that I was mobile in the wheel chair, they could not have risked leaving it on the wall. But with a tingle of excitement, I realized that my pretence of trusting them might have paid dividends. Since they weren't expecting me to spy, they probably hadn't destroyed Gordy's picture. It was possible that they hadn't even bothered to hide it, but had just pushed it in a drawer.

I looked around me. The built-in bookshelves of pickled oak took up most of the wall space. The photograph could have been slipped behind any of the rows of books. But first I decided to try the desk where the telephone and typewriter stood. The first drawer contained receipted and uninformative statements, and a box which was filled with bills of various denominations and which presumably was Mrs Friend's petty cash Fort Knox. But as I pulled open the second, a photograph stared up at me.

It was a photograph in a frame which exactly matched the four other photographs on the wall. Taut, I picked it up and looked at it. It was a photograph of a young man with a blond crew haircut, an amused mouth, and straight, ironic eyes which reminded me of Marny's.

The frame and those eyes were almost as good as a signature.

There was no doubt about this, I was sure.

In my hand I was holding a photograph of Gordy Friend.

Chapter 11

MY first thought was: This proves it once and for all. This isn't a picture of me.

Then the propellers, scarcely more than a rustle, stirred in my mind, bringing back some of the old confusion. How did I know whether I looked like that photograph or not? Amnesia had swallowed up all memories of my personal appearance. Since my return to consciousness, I'd had no chance to look at myself. There had been no accessible mirror in the bedroom.

Perhaps I did look like the photograph. Then what? Would that make me Gordy Friend, after all?

A long, bright mirror gleamed on the far wall. I trundled the chair towards it. That was one of the strangest sensations I'd had – moving towards a mirror with absolutely no idea of what reflection I would see in it.

I drew the chair up in front of the mirror. Before I looked

at myself, I deliberately studied the photograph until every detail of it was fixed in my mind. Then I looked at myself.

The big moment was disappointingly inconclusive. The reflection, looking back at me, had the same general type of features as the photograph. From what I could see of it through the bandages, my hair was the same middle shade of blond. I was, I judged, a few years older, and my face was more sure of itself, aggressive. I was almost certain that the picture was not of me, and yet there was enough similarity to leave a shadow of doubt in my mind.

For a moment I forgot the photograph in the simple fascination of studying my own face. I liked it. And in a way it was familiar. I didn't exactly remember it, but it wasn't a stranger's face.

'Peter,' I said to myself.

Somehow the reflection strengthened my memory's weak response to that name. Iris, I tried. Sailor. San Diego. Propellers. Seeing someone off on a plane.

Something white moved into the corner of the mirror. I glanced from my own face and saw Selena's reflection behind mine. She had stepped across the threshold and was standing, hesitantly, by the door. She was still in her swimming suit with her wet hair clinging around her head. She hadn't realized I could see her in the mirror. She was staring straight at me. Her face was wary, alert.

I slipped the photograph of the young man under the green robe which covered my legs.

'Gordy, baby,' called Selena.

I turned the chair as if I'd only just discovered she was there. She was smiling her warm, coaxing smile now. All the wariness was camouflaged. She crossed to me and kissed me on the mouth. Her lips were cool and fresh from the water.

'Darling, we were worried. You suddenly disappeared. We thought something frightful had happened. What on earth are you doing?'

'Looking at myself in the mirror. It's the first time I've seen my face.'

She laughed. 'Baby, it's a face to be looked at with pride, isn't it?'

'It's okay.' I pointed at the photographs over the mantel. 'The old man with the white moustache – is he my father?'

'Of course.' Her hand slid down the back of my neck, caressing it. 'Remember him?'

I shook my head. Her hand moved around to my throat and chin and then up, gently touching my mouth. She was expecting me to kiss her hand and be lost for love of her. I was getting on to Selena now. I wasn't such easy prey, any more.

'Selena,' I said, 'why isn't there a photograph of me with the others?'

Her hand was moving over the bandages on my head now, stroking my hair. 'Darling, don't you remember? You loathed cameras. You'd never have your picture taken.'

I might have known she would have an answer ready for that. She perched herself on the arm of my wheel chair. As she did so, her hip must have hit the corner of the photograph frame, for she glanced down and, slipping her hand under the robe, pulled out the photograph.

For a moment she stared at it, her dark blue eyes narrowing very slightly. Then she laughed and kissed my ear, murmuring:

'Darling, what on earth are you doing with this dreary photo?'

I didn't have Selena's technique in deceit. I hesitated just a fraction too long before I said:

'I just found it. I didn't know what I looked like. I told you. So I carried it over to the mirror to see if it was a picture of me.'

That didn't explain, of course, why I had so obviously been concealing it under the rug or why I had 'just found' something that had been in a drawer. But it was the best I could do.

Casually I said: 'Is it of me, by the way? It's hard to tell with all these bandages.'

She laughed again. 'Baby, don't be absurd. Of course it's not you. I told you you never had your photograph taken. It's your Cousin Benjy. Don't you remember him? Such a dismal boy. Yale loved him though. They gave him all kinds of prizes for meteorology. Now he's doing something gloomy about the weather in China.'

From the tone of her voice I knew I hadn't fooled her and I cursed inwardly. She knew now that my new trusting attitude was a fake. She knew that, in spite of my protestations, I had still been suspicious enough to have sneaked into the house and snooped through drawers for the photograph. I'd lost my only advantage.

From now on they'd be doubly on their guard.

Selena tossed the photograph onto a couch and announced that she had come to wheel me back to the pool. I told her the sun was too hot and that I preferred to stay indoors for a while. I didn't expect her to leave it at that, but she did. She must have been sure that I could do no more damage.

She smiled, kissed me, said: 'Come soon, baby. We miss you,' and left me.

I had refused to go with her not because I had any idea of what to do next but simply because I felt too depressed to keep up a pretence in front of the others. The lavender-scented handkerchief, Netti, and now the photograph – one by one, with an efficiency that was appalling, the Friends had trumped all my aces.

I was left with nothing now to counteract that sensation of impending danger.

The phone on the corner table started to ring. Quickly, before the ring could attract Mrs Friend or anyone else in the house, I rolled the chair over and picked up the receiver. My pulses were racing. I had no plan, only an instinct that any contact with the outside world was desirable. I was more cautious now, though. My latest defeat by Selena had taught me that.

I said into the receiver in a flat, impersonal voice: 'Mr Friend's residence.'

A man's voice replied. It sounded elderly and rather fussed. 'May I speak to Mrs Friend? Mrs Friend Senior?'

'Mrs Friend is out at the pool,' I lied. 'Can I take a message?'

The man coughed. 'I – ah – to whom am I speaking?'

Be careful, I thought.

'This is the butler.' For safety I added: 'The new butler.'

'Oh,' the man paused. 'Yes, perhaps you would give Mrs Friend a message. This is Mr Petherbridge, the – ah – late Mr Friend's lawyer. Please tell Mrs Friend that I will be up tomorrow afternoon with Mr Moffat as arranged unless I hear from her to the contrary.'

'Very well, Mr Petherbridge.'

'Thank you. And – er – how is her son, by the way? What a distressing accident! I trust he will be well enough for – for tomorrow?'

'Yes, Mr Friend seems pretty well considering,' I said. In my precarious role as butler, I dared ask no more than: 'Tomorrow's the day then, sir?'

'Yes, tomorrow.' Mr Petherbridge made a strange gurgling sound that might have been a cough. 'Tomorrow's the ordeal.'

The ordeal.

'Anything else, sir?' I asked.

'No, no. That will be all. If you will be kind enough to have Mrs Friend call me if the plans are changed. But I do not see how they can be.'

There was a click that cut me off remorselessly from contact with Mr Petherbridge, the – ah – late Mr Friend's lawyer.

For a moment I sat staring at the receiver. I was still an invalid emotionally as well as physically. My control over myself was slight and that conversation, so incomprehensible and yet so filled with hints at a plan coming to a head, toppled me over into extreme anxiety. The ordeal – tomorrow. Time then was a crucial factor. I had only a few hours left before – something happened. The trapped feeling was almost more than I could endure. I felt like a fly on a fly-paper.

As I looked at the telephone, a reckless idea came. Netti was gone, but she had left something behind. She had told me that Emma, the old cook, was working for some people called Curtis on Temple Drive.

I picked up the receiver. I said to the operator:

'I want some people called Curtis on Temple Drive. I haven't got the number.'

The wait seemed interminable. At last the operator said: 'George Curtis, 1177 Temple Drive?'

'That's it.'

'Lona 3-1410. You want me to call that number now?'

'Please.'

I heard the soft buzz of the call tone at the other end of the wire. How I would persuade Emma to come to the Friends' house I did not know. I did not know, either, how, once I got her there, I would be able to smuggle her in and use her to expose the conspiracy. But Emma thought Mr Friend had been murdered. Somehow I had to know what had put that idea in her mind.

As I waited, the silent room behind me seemed crowded with invisible enemies. At last the call buzz was cut. A woman's voice said: 'Yes?'

'Is that the Curtis house?'

'Yes.'

'Can I speak to the cook, please?'

'The cook? Why – er – yes. Wait a moment.'

There was a second, gruelling pause. Then another female voice, hoarse and defensive, asked: 'Hello. Who is it?'

'Is that Emma?'

'Who?'

'Is that Emma who used to work for the Friends?'

'Emma?'

'Yes.'

'Oh, I guess you mean the cook. Old with grey hair?'

'Yes, yes,' I said.

There was a pause. Then the voice said: 'She's been gone a couple of weeks. I'm working here now.'

My heart sinking, I said: 'You know where I could get in touch with her?'

94

'Emma? She got sick. She's old, you know. She doesn't work no more.'

'But do you know where she is?'

'She went off to live with her daughter. Where was it now? Wyoming? Wisconsin? One of them States.'

'Then ...'

The wire was cut at the other end. Slowly I let the receiver slip out of my fingers back onto its stand.

'Telephoning, Gordy?'

I looked up. Marny was standing in the doorway. She was leaning against the door frame, a cigarette lolling from her red mouth. Her young eyes, curiously bright, were fixed on my face.

The hopelessness of escape even for a moment from the Friends' watchfulness swept over me. I tried to smile.

'Just a call came in for mother,' I said. 'A Mr Petherbridge.'

I didn't know how much of my disastrous call to Emma's successor she had overheard. She gave no sign either. She moved to my side and put her hands on my shoulders. Suddenly the cynical veneer left her face and she was just a young unaccountably frightened kid. In a strange broken voice, she blurted:

'Is it too awful?'

'Too awful?'

Her lips were trembling.

'You're such a sweet guy. I can't bear watching it much longer.'

'Watching what?'

'What they're doing to you. Selena ... Mimsey ... Nate, all of them. They're fiends. That's what they are – fiends.'

Impulsively she slid onto the arm of the wheel chair. She put her arms around my neck and pressed her cheek against mine. When she spoke again, her voice was choked with sobs.

'I hate them. I've always hated them. They're as bad as Father, worse.' She was kissing my cheeks, my lids, my lips, wildly. 'They'll do anything – anything and never care.'

I was staggered. Was this some new diabolic ruse of the

95

Friend family? Or had I, incredibly, been given an ally when all hope seemed gone? I put my arm around her, drawing her close so that I felt her young breasts pressed against me. She was weeping passionately now. I kissed her hair. She shivered and clung closer.

'Tell me,' I said. 'Marny, baby, tell me. What are they doing to me?'

'I can't ... I can't ... I ...'

She pulled herself out of my grasp. She looked down at me, her face spattered with tears.

'I can't ... I can't ...'

She put her hand up to her mouth. She gave a little whimper. She turned, abruptly, and ran out of the room.

Chapter 12

I HURRIED the wheel chair out onto the porch.

'Marny,' I called. 'Marny, come back.'

She was running down the grass path away from me. She paid no attention. In a moment she was out of sight through the arch which led to the swimming pool.

Fiends. That ominous word echoed in my ears. *Mimsey, Selena, Nate – they're all fiends.*

And it was Marny who had said it, Marny who was in the conspiracy, Marny who knew exactly what they were going to do to me.

'Hello, dear. All alone?'

I looked up. Mrs Friend had come out of the library and was moving towards me. Her massive beauty was opulent as the blossoming flower-beds. She had a wicker garden basket looped on one arm. In her hand she carried a large pair of garden shears. Who did she remind me of? One of the Fates? The Fate who cuts the thread of life?

'How nice, dear. I thought you'd be down with the others by the pool. We can have a little visit together. Let's go around the corner into the patio. It's shady there.'

She started pushing my wheel chair down the terrace, chattering blandly. My nerves were strung very high then. It was almost unendurable having her invisible behind me. I think I half expected her to plunge the scissors into my neck.

'Here we are, dear. So charming here.'

We had entered a little walled patio. Poinsettias and climbing roses in white tubs were massed along the walls. White and green porch chairs were arranged under the shade of a drooping pepper tree. Mrs Friend manoeuvred my chair close to one of the others and sat down. She produced knitting from her garden basket, and her white fingers started a flow of wool across the needles. Everything Mrs Friend did was so unswervingly maternal. That was the most frightening thing about her.

'Well, dear' – she smiled up from the knitting – 'how does it feel in the wheel chair? Overtiring yourself?'

The incidents of the past half-hour had left me limp as a grass stalk. Of all the conspirators, I was sure now that Mrs. Friend was the most formidable. If only I could break her down, the whole edifice here might collapse. But how? She was so sublimely sure of herself and I had nothing – nothing except Mr Petherbridge.

Calmly I said: 'Mr Petherbridge just called.'

'He did, dear?'

'My father's lawyer?'

'Yes, Gordy. I know that, of course. What did dear Mr Petherbridge want?'

'He said to tell you he was coming tomorrow afternoon with Mr Moffat as arranged unless he hears from you.'

She smiled. 'Oh, good. Then I won't have to telephone him.'

Her monumental placidity was exasperating beyond words.

'Why's Mr Petherbridge coming tomorrow?' I asked.

'For the meeting, dear,' she said gently. 'The Clean Living League. He's a member, you know. Your father insisted that he join and your father was a very lucrative client. I'm afraid, as a Clean Living Leaguer, Mr Petherbridge's tongue is a little in his cheek.'

I said: 'Then there's going to be a meeting of the whole league here tomorrow? I thought you said it was just Mr Moffat.'

'Oh, no, dear, the whole league.' Mrs Friend had come to the end of one ball of wool. She took its tail and started to weave it onto the next ball. 'Didn't I make that clear? It's to be a memorial service for your father with Mr Moffat presiding, of course. I suppose service isn't quite the right word. They're not exactly a religious institution. More of a ceremony. Perhaps that's what we should call it.'

'Mr Petherbridge called it an ordeal,' I said.

'And so it is, my dear. You wait and see. So terribly, terribly good we have to be. No liquor, no cigarettes, of course. Not even an ashtray visible. All of us in black. No make-up. And a sort of dismal holy expression. You know, dear. Like this.'

She put the knitting down and twisted her face into an expression of the most lugubrious piety.

'I do hope you'll be able to put on the right face, dear. You must practise. Think of something that smells particularly unattractive, like a dead mouse. That's how I do.' She sighed, 'This is the very last time, Gordy. I've promised myself that. After tomorrow, we're going to eschew the Aurora Clean Living League for ever. My dear, if you knew how I suffered from it. Because they're not good people. You'll realize that when you see them. They're disgusting, revolting hypocrites. Their whole life is one big, fat, smug sham. The times in St Paul when I'd have given my soul to lift my skirt up over my knees and plunge into a can-can in the middle of one of Mr Heber's harangues! I never did, of course,' she added sadly. 'I was always too scared of your dear father.'

Mrs Friend was being charming. I was beginning to learn that she used her charm as a decoy whenever I got near a danger spot. Pulling the conversation back into the path I wanted it to take, I asked:

'And just what am I expected to do tomorrow?'

'You, dear?' A little tawny butterfly settled on Mrs Friend's satiny white bosom. She brushed it off tranquilly,

'Why, nothing, Gordy. Just look respectable and be polite and try to pretend you're not bored. Oh yes, and you can recite the *Ode to Aurora* too.' She glanced at me under her lids. 'Have you learned it all yet?'

'Not all of it.'

'Then we'll all help you tonight. Mr Moffat would love that so because – well, dear, you were always thought of as the damned one of the family, you know. It would give him enormous satisfaction to feel you had been reformed.' She put the knitting down on her comfortable lap. 'You never know, dear. Perhaps the meeting will bring your memory back. Of course you never met Mr Moffat and you never attended one of these California meetings. But you had so much of the same thing in St Paul. Perhaps it'll strike a chord.'

It was a terrific strain never taking what they said at its face value, trying to catch a hint of the truth from an inflexion or an overtone. Now I was thinking: Gordy was the damned one of the family, the one with the bad reputation. If Mr Friend had been murdered and the fact was discovered, Gordy would therefore be the most obvious suspect. And Mr Moffat and Mr Petherbridge had never seen Gordy. Gordy then was the only member of the family who could be represented by a substitute without the ruse being immediately obvious.

Yes, the Friends could have a sporting chance of getting away with the incredible scheme of which I suspected them – if they were daring enough.

And, heaven knew, they were daring.

Fiends. Was that what Marny had meant when she called them *fiends*?

Mrs Friend's sweetness had the effect of scented pillows smothering me. An overwhelming desire to push my way out into the open rose up in me. Surely, whatever resulted, I could be in no worse a situation than I was right now.

'You want a chord struck?' I asked, deliberately challenging her. 'You do want me to get my memory back?'

'Gordy, what a weird thing to say.' She put the knitting down on her lap and made a weary grimace. 'Oh, dear, you're

99

still suspicious of us. I thought so when Selena told me how you'd ferreted that photograph of your Cousin Benjy out of the drawer.'

Selena had already passed on the news. They had a super-efficient organization all right.

'Cousin Benjy?' I said. 'Oh, you mean the whiz from Harvard who's being a botanist in India.' I paused. 'It is India, isn't it?'

Mrs Friend went on knitting serenely. 'Yes, dear.'

I could hardly believe it. At last I had tripped her up. Staring straight at her, I said: 'You didn't get that story quite straight with Selena, did you?'

'Gordy, dear, what do you mean?'

'Selena said this mythical cousin Benjy went to Yale, was a meteorologist and lived in China. You should tell her not to make her lies so elaborate. With four of you working together it must be hard enough keeping the pretence going without having to memorize a lot of odd detail.'

'Really, darling.' Mrs Friend put down her knitting again. She seemed faintly aggrieved. 'What do you mean about lies? Is your Cousin Benjy a meteorologist in China? I'm sure I don't know. He's on your father's side. I've never even met him. Selena's much more apt to be right about it than I.'

'I doubt it,' I said. 'By and large you're much more effective than Selena. Her lie about the old woman, last night, for example. You could have done better than that.'

Whatever the consequences, it was a terrific relief to come out with that at last.

Mrs Friend was staring at me with a surprise that seemed devoid of any alarm.

'The old woman, dear?'

'It's not worth pretending you don't know about her. Selena woke you up last night especially to tell you what happened.'

'My dear Gordy, please tell me what you mean or I'll go mildly crazy.'

'It'll save a lot of time if you get a few simple facts into your head. Selena never fooled me about the old woman, not even after the handkerchief was stolen from me. Netti told me, anyway. I was able to get that much information out of her before you fired her.'

'Gordy, you're insinuating that I fired Netti because ...'

'I'm not insinuating any more. I'm bored with insinuating. I'm telling you that all four of you – Selena, Marny, Dr Croft and you – have been feeding me a pack of lies from the very beginning. I'm perfectly conscious of the fact and I'm not going to be lied to any more.'

'Darling, thank heavens!' Mrs Friend caught up my hand and squeezed it. 'At last you're being frank with me. You can't know how grateful I am. What exactly do you think we're lying about?'

'I don't think. I know.' I wasn't going to mention my suspicions about old Mr Friend's death, of course. That was far too dangerous. 'You're lying about that old woman.'

A sweetly patient smile played around her lips. 'If I knew what you meant about the old woman, dear, perhaps I could explain.'

'The old woman who came into my room last night.' I was smart enough not to add that the old woman had said I wasn't Gordy Friend. 'The old woman Selena said was just a figment of my imagination.'

I glared at her, thinking: *She'll have to break now*. But Mrs Friend had never looked less like breaking.

'Selena said there wasn't an old woman living in the house?' she repeated. 'My dear, how strange. Of course there's an old woman living here.'

I had expected almost anything but that. I said: 'Then why did Selena lie about her?'

'My dear, I can't imagine.' Mrs Friend's voice was soothing. 'Of course I don't know the circumstances. You are still an invalid. Perhaps whatever happened flustered you and Selena thought you'd sleep better if she pretended it was all a dream. But then, you can't expect me to explain Selena's mental processes. Sometimes I wonder whether she has any.'

Once again Mrs Friend had managed to make me feel like a fool. Weakly, I said: 'Who is she then, this old woman?'

'Your grandmother, dear. The poor darling, she's my mother. She's been living with us ever since we came to California. She's quite ancient and rather frail, but she's certainly not a dream.'

'I can see her then?'

'See her?' Mrs Friend's face lit up with a smile of incredulous gratitude. 'My dear, could you really be bothered to? She's always been so devoted to you. And, I'm afraid, you've rather neglected her. Dear, if only you would have a little visit with her, it would make me so happy.'

That was typical of Mrs Friend. You shot an arrow at her and she caught it and then started to croon over it as if it were a beautiful flower you'd presented to her.

But this time, surely, she'd over-reached herself. She thought she was being smart by pretending she wanted me to meet the old woman. But neither she nor anyone else knew that last night the old woman had admitted I wasn't Gordy Friend. With any luck I could turn her latest scheme into a boomerang.

I said: 'How about going to see her right now?'

'That would be lovely.' Mrs Friend stuffed her knitting back into the garden basket and, rising, kissed me sweetly on the cheek. 'Dear, you *are* being a darling boy.'

She started to wheel my chair into the house.

'It's only this, dear, that you're suspicious about?'

'Yes,' I said, lying.

We went down a sunny corridor into a wing I had not explored. We stopped before a closed door. The little contented smile curling her lips, Mrs Friend tapped and called:

'Mother? Mother, dear?'

My fingers, gripping the arms of the wheel chair, were quivering.

'Mother, sweet?' called Mrs Friend again.

'Martha, is that you?' An old, querulous voice sounded scratchily through the door.

'Yes, dear. Can I come in?'

'Come in. Come in.'

Mrs Friend opened the door and pushed my chair into a beautiful lavender and grey bedroom. In a chair by the window, an ancient woman, with a shawl arranged untidily over her shoulders, was sitting looking out at the garden. As Mrs Friend wheeled me nearer, the old woman did not turn. But I could see her profile clearly. I studied the lined, parchment skin, the large eye, sunken in its socket. There was no doubt about it at all.

My 'grandmother', sitting there in the wheel chair by the window, was definitely the old woman who had stood over my bed the night before.

'Mother, dear,' said Mrs Friend. 'Look. I've brought you a surprise.'

'What? A surprise, eh?'

The old woman shifted laboriously in her chair so that she could look at us.

This was the moment.

The old woman peered at the wheel chair and then at me. Slowly the wrinkles around her mouth stretched into a smile of quavering delight.

'Gordy,' she said.

She held out both her thin hands to me. The knotted fingers made greedy clutching motions in the air as if she could not wait to embrace me.

'Gordy,' she cried. 'It's my Gordy. My darling Gordy's come to see his old grandmother.'

Mrs Friend brought the two chairs together. The old fingers were running up my arms. The old lips, dry and parched, nuzzled affectionately against my cheek.

Marny's voice, broken and wild with weeping, seemed to be right there in the room.

I can't bear watching what they're doing to you. They're fiends – all of them ... fiends ...

Chapter 13

MRS FRIEND controlled that 'little visit' with the firm hand of a stage director. She introduced small, safe topics of conversation, sprinkled the old lady and me with smiles and, after five minutes or so, submitted me to another old kiss from 'grandmother' and wheeled me out of the room.

In the sunny corridor, she beamed at me. 'There, darling boy, she's not particularly frightening, is she?'

I could have said: *She isn't, but you are.* I didn't. I didn't say anything. Through her extraordinary talent for intrigue, Mrs Friend had somehow managed to woo the old lady over to her side. She had me trapped now. Saying things couldn't help.

She wheeled me out onto the terrace. Sunshine was good for me, she said. She suggested taking me down to the pool, but at that moment Selena, Nate, and Marny trooped up the grass path through the flower-beds. They crowded around us in their swimming suits, young, handsome, friendly. I looked at Marny mostly. I had no one now except possibly Marny. But there was no sign in her face of her strange breakdown. She was as masked and specious as the others.

'Selena, dear, we've just been to see grandmother.' Mrs Friend's voice was gently chiding. 'Really, what on earth was in your mind when you told Gordy she didn't exist?'

Selena was quick all right. Without the slightest sign of improvisation, she gave a light laugh. 'Wasn't it stupid?'

'Then why did you do it, dear?'

'Oh, it was just that I'd been asleep, Mimsey. I was confused. Gordy was scared. I thought it was easier to reassure him that way. And then, after I'd done it, I knew he was suspicious of us. I thought if he discovered I'd lied a stupid lie it would make it worse. So I asked Marny to back me up.' She caressed Marny's unresponsive arm. 'Didn't I, Marny?'

Marny shrugged.

Selena turned her bright gaze on Nate. 'I explained to Nate

too and he said, as a doctor, that I'd been right, didn't you, Nate?'

'Yes,' said Nate.

Mrs Friend sighed. 'Selena, dearest, I'm afraid you won't go ringing down the centuries for your intellect. Now, be a good girl. Tell Gordy you're sorry.'

'I'm sorry, baby.' Selena kissed me on the forehead. 'Next time an old lady climbs into bed with you, I'll give you her whole life history.'

They seemed to be stuck in the groove of deceit – like Japanese envoys talking good neighbourliness with the drone of their own bombers already audible overhead.

Did they really think they were still deceiving me?

'There.' Mrs Friend smiled dazzlingly. 'Everything's cleared up now, Gordy.'

She started organizing us. Selena, Nate, and Marny were ordered off to change their wet swimming suits. I was turned over to Jan who wheeled me back to my room and, quite unnecessarily, bathed me all over again.

While his hands moved over my skin, I struggled with an idea that was slowly forming in my mind. I had not believed Mrs Friend's threadbare explanation that Mr Petherbridge was coming tomorrow simply as a member of the Aurora Clean Living League. Whatever their over-all policy, I knew they expected something definite from me tomorrow and that definite thing was connected with Mr Friend's poem.

Maybe I could use the poem as a weapon for a counter-attack.

Jan lifted me out of the tub and started to dry me. I said suddenly: 'Why did Mr Friend fire you?'

His hand, gripping the green turkish towel, came to rest on my stomach. He stared from blue, wary eyes.

'You.' I pointed at him. 'Mr Friend say to you – Jan scram?'

For the first time he seemed to grasp my meaning. His eyes cleared. He nodded vigorously, the blond lock slipping over his forehead.

'Why?' I said. 'Why he say Jan – scram? Why?'

He laughed then, a deep, hilarious laugh. It seemed to indicate that he'd been fired for some reason which to him was infinitely entertaining. He was still laughing when he'd dressed me and carried me back to the wheel chair.

Cocktails were being served in the huge living-room when Jan took me there. The family and Dr Croft were lounging in chairs before the vast plate-glass window, chatting, laughing, like any family having a good time.

Mrs Friend permitted me a single cocktail with Nate Croft's sanction as a 'special treat'. Tomorrow was to be a day of gloom, she said. We should all celebrate today.

The celebration was carried over into dinner with champagne which was served in a glass-walled dining-room by a maid I had never seen before. Netti's successor? We were all supposed to be terribly, terribly at our ease. No one was. I frankly sulked. Marny was silent and keyed-up. Selena and Nate – and even Mrs Friend – were much too gay for conviction. They cracked jokes about the Clean Living League; they made preposterous suggestions for shocking Mr Moffat.

They were nervous. That meant things were coming to a head.

The poem was never mentioned at dinner but I was sure it was in all their minds. This mood of forced frivolity was a deliberate prologue to the moment when – oh, so casually and lightly – someone would suggest that it would be frightfully amusing to rehearse me in the *Ode to Aurora*.

When we sat over coffee in the living-room, looking out at the staggering panorama of sky and mountain, Selena left her seat and perched herself on the arm of my wheel chair. It was an uncomfortable position. Only an excess of affection or the simulation of it could have made her take it.

I suspected the latter and I was right. Almost immediately, she squeezed my shoulder, smiled and chanted:

'*In taverns where young people mingle to sway their lascivious hips*. Really, that's divine. I've been saying it over and over to myself all day. Gordy, it'll be sheer bliss having you recite it tomorrow to all those whey-faced virgins. Come on, let's teach you the rest.'

'Yes,' put in Nate, obviously following a cue. 'I'm crazy to hear the poem. Never did, you know.'

Without looking up from her knitting, Mrs Friend said: 'Marny dear, run get the book from Gordy's room.'

Marny tossed back her glossy black hair, glanced at me for a strained, ambiguous moment and then hurried out of the room. Soon she was back. Selena took the book from her and searched through the pages.

Mrs Friend said: 'It's a shame to make a mock of your poor father.' She looked up at me smiling. 'You'll promise to keep a straight face when you recite, won't you, Gordy? It'll mean so much to Mr Moffat.'

Selena found the page. 'Just two more verses, Gordy, dear.'

Nate had left his chair and was standing behind Selena, his hand resting with pretended absence of mind on her bare shoulder. Mrs Friend put her knitting down in her lap. Marny lit a match for a cigarette with a sharp, spurting sound. They were all so conscious of me that I could feel their concentration like fingers on my body.

They were losing their subtlety.

Dreamily Selena started to recite:

> '"Oh, mothers moan sad for their stripling.
> Oh, wives yearn at home for their spouse.
> Both are down in the dark tavern tippling,
> Debauched in their careless carouse.
> Besotted they slump to the floor. Ah,
> Ere they drown in the beer's fatal foam,
> Restore them, reprieve them, Aurora,
> Our Lady of Home."'

Mrs Friend crinkled her nose. 'Really, it's enough to drive Mahomet to drink, isn't it? I'm afraid your father wasn't a very good Swinburne, Gordy.' She smiled at me. 'Now be a good boy, dear. The first line, *Oh, mothers moan sad for their* ...'

Selena was watching me under half-closed lashes. Nate was watching me. So was Marny.

'Come on, dear.' Mrs Friend started to beat a ponderous rhythm in the air with her fingers. '*Oh, mothers moan sad...*'

'No,' I said.

Selena's arm, thrown over my shoulder, stiffened. Nate's mouth went tight. Mrs Friend said:

'No – what, Gordy dear?'

'I'm not going to learn the goddam poem.'

Marny's eyes were bright. Mrs Friend rose and moved towards me.

'Now, dear, don't be pettish. I know it's preposterous. I know it'll be embarrassing for you. But, please...'

I shook my head.

'Why not, dear? Why in heaven's name not?'

She was rattled. For the first time the tranquil smile was so phony you could see right through it. I felt wonderful.

'I won't learn the poem,' I said, 'because this is a free country and I don't want to learn a poem which should have been strangled at birth.'

'But, darling, I told you. For Mr Moffat's sake ...'

'I should care for Mr Moffat.' I paused, gauging the tension. 'Why make a fuss? It doesn't matter whether I read it or not. You said so yourself. A charming gesture you called it. Okay, so there won't be a charming gesture.'

Dr Croft, trying to be the gruff, boys-together doctor, said: 'Gordy, old man, let's not be ornery about it. Your mother wants you to recite it. After all, it's not much to ask.'

I looked at him. It was better, somehow, dealing with a man after all those smothering females. I said: 'I might be persuaded to recite it.'

'Persuaded?' He looked hopeful. 'How, Gordy?'

'If they stopped lying and told me why they really want me to do it.'

'Lying.' Nate echoed the word sharply. 'Gordy, I thought we were through with all these suspicions. I thought ...'

Mrs Friend, still flustered, opened her mouth, but surprisingly Selena spoke in first.

'All right. That's putting it up to us.' She laughed, her husky, amused laugh. 'Why not tell him the truth?'

'Selena!' snapped Mrs Friend.

'Don't you see how stupid we're being? You bawled me out for lying about Grandma. This is much sillier. He doesn't believe us. That's obvious. What's the point of trying to fool him when he won't be fooled?' She leaned down, letting her shining hair brush my cheek. 'Poor Gordy, you must think we're fiends incarnate. And I don't blame you. But it's all so silly, because the truth's so – innocuous. There's no reason in the world why you shouldn't hear it.'

I looked up at her blandly smiling mouth so close to mine. I wished she wasn't so beautiful.

'The truth,' I said, 'is innocuous?'

'Of course.' Selena was watching Mrs Friend. 'I'll tell him?'

I was watching Mrs Friend, too. From the slight puckering around her eyes, I was almost sure that Selena was improvising and that her mother-in-law was uneasy about its outcome.

Tartly she said: 'Do what you think best, Selena.'

Selena nuzzled closer to me. 'Gordy, darling – the poem.' Her voice was caressing, suspect. 'Of course it's important. And you were awfully smart to realize it. We didn't tell you because – well, it was really Mimsey's idea. You see, it's all tied up with your drinking too much. Mimsey's always been worried about it. Then this amnesia came, and she thought maybe, since you'd forgotten everything else, you'd forget your craving for alcohol. She was scared that by telling you the truth about tomorrow – about the poem, it would make you think of yourself as a drunk and spoil your chance of being cured.' She turned to Mrs Friend. 'That's true, isn't it, Mimsey?'

This was being okay with Mimsey. She had quite regained her composure. She had even picked up her knitting and was working the needles.

'Yes, Selena,' she said. 'Gordy, dear, I do so hope you're going to be good about drinking now.'

Nate, also more relaxed, chose the opportunity to put in one of his fancy medical pontifications. 'There's a good chance of it, Gordy, old man. The obliteration of a personality, however temporary, may well also obliterate the craving for alcohol which the maladjustment of that personality induced.'

I glanced at Marny. Marny was the key. There was no expression on her face. She was sitting, flat-eyed, watching Selena.

'Okay,' I said. 'So far so good. You've been lying because you were trying to save me from the beer's fatal foam – you and the Aurora Clean Living League.'

'My dear Gordy, it's not like the League.' Mrs Friend purled or plained or something. 'Of course, none of us mind a little drunkenness now and then. There's no moral attitude, dear. It's just that we don't want you to impair your health.'

'Thank you,' I said. 'Now – give about the poem.'

'It's awfully stupid, baby.' Selena's hand was stroking the short hairs at the back of my neck. 'It's all something dismal from your father's will.'

I looked at Mrs Friend. 'That's why Mr Petherbridge is coming? He's not really a member of the League at all.'

She flushed faintly but said nothing.

'Yes, baby,' said Selena. 'That's why Mr Petherbridge is coming. In fact, that's why Mr Moffat and the Clean Living League are coming too.'

'To hear me recite the *Ode to Aurora*?'

'That,' said Selena, 'and a couple of other things. Oh, it's so absurd. Let's get it over with. Your sainted papa was dreary about drink. Check? You drank. Check? Your father wanted to stop you drinking. Check? So he did this. He made this corny will. You get the money because you're the only son. Sure. But you only get it provided you're cold sober thirty days after his death, sober enough to recite the *Ode to Aurora* before the entire Clean Living League and then, afterwards, sign their abstinence pledge. Mr Petherbridge is coming as a referee. If he finds you living an irreproachable domestic life and if you can recite the poem and sign the pledge, you get the money. It is your father's way of making you teetotal.' She kissed me on the ear. 'There, baby. That's the awful, awful truth we've been so evilly keeping from you.'

I glanced at her. She couldn't have looked more innocent.

I said: 'And if I'm not sober tomorrow and I can't recite the poem and if I won't sign the abstinence pledge?'

She shrugged. 'Then, darling, no money for Gordy. The whole works, great gobs of it, goes to the League to cleanse Southern California and rinse out its mouth with soap.'

They were all looking at me now. Mrs Friend, bright-eyed, said:

'So you see, darling, how terribly, terribly important it is for your own sake for you to learn the poem?'

I stared back. 'Sure,' I said, 'but why are you all so worked up about it? Just out of sweet, spontaneous affection for me?'

'Of course, dear,' said Mrs Friend. 'After all, you recite this poem and you're terribly rich. You don't recite it and you're destitute. I don't want my son to be destitute.'

I looked at Marny. I rather thought that she shook her head infinitesimally.

I went on: 'But your inheritance is all right whatever happens to me? Yours and Marny's?'

'Of course, dear,' said Mrs Friend.

Marny suddenly got up then. She stood, young and tense, silhouetted against the great view of evening mountains.

'Don't believe her,' she said.

Mrs Friend shot her a horrified look. Marny stared back, her young face fierce with contempt.

'For God's sake, now you've started, tell him the truth. What's the matter with you? Do you lie for the sheer fun of it?'

I smiled at her. My ally was crashing through after all.

I said: 'Which means that you all do have a personal interest in this too?'

'Of course we do.'

'Marny!'

Marny tossed back her glossy black hair, ignoring her mother's sharp exclamation. 'They make me sick with their dreary deceits. Okay, Mimsey. Do you want me to say it for you? Gordy drank. Selena couldn't stop him. You couldn't stop him. I couldn't stop him. Father held us all responsible. We didn't struggle with the devil enough, he said. So we're all in the same boat. It was up to us to see he was cured of drinking. Father saw to that all right. Neither you nor me nor Selena get a red cent of the money unless Gordy passes this test in front of the League.'

She swung round to me. 'There's the pretty little story. A true story, for a change.' She dropped down on the sofa, tucking her legs under her. 'Thank God it's out. I don't feel quite so much like throwing up any more.'

I had expected Mrs Friend to show maternal indignation, but she didn't. With a shrug that was almost meek, she said:

'Marny's right, Gordy. I suppose it's just the mother in me. I keep on thinking of you as a little boy in sailor pants with an eye on the cookie jar. Of course, you're grown up and responsible. It's an insult to try to keep the truth from you.'

'So you're not keeping any more truth from me?'

My relief was so great that I wanted to laugh. They were still lying to me, of course. But the thing they were lying about seemed absurdly unimportant now. I had suspected them of such satanic evil. I had convinced myself I was in the clutches of murderers who were planning to foist their guilt upon me. And the real secret behind their charming façade had merely been – this.

Marny with her girlish impetuosities had been exaggerating. They weren't fiends at all. They were just a bunch of very uncomfortable people in a jam.

Mrs Friend was watching me. 'So you will do it, darling, won't you? It's not just for our sakes. It's for your sake too.'

I was amused that I could ever have thought of her as anything more ominous than a handsome woman in a hell of a hole.

'For my sake?' I queried.

'Of course, dear.'

'Don't you mean for Gordy Friend's sake?'

She stiffened. Selena and Nate exchanged a glance. It was all pitifully obvious.

'Gordy, dear,' began Mrs Friend.

'It's really not worth while going on with the lies,' I said. 'Where is Gordy? Off on a bat, I suppose. No, toot is the word, isn't it? How embarrassing of him. The whole Friend fortune at stake and Gordy's off in a dark tavern somewhere, debauched in a careless carouse.'

Dr Croft said crisply: 'This is beyond a joke, old man.'

'You think so? I think it's terribly, terribly amusing.' I grinned at him. 'I suppose you unearthed me in your sanatorium. You certainly delivered the goods, didn't you? One amnesiac, fake Gordy Friend guaranteed to recite the *Ode to Aurora* to Mr Moffat, and win a fortune for the Friends.'

Mrs Friend had risen. Her face was as pale as paper. Selena had slid off the chair arm too. They stood on each side of Dr Croft, facing me. Once those two women, grouped together, watching me, had seemed as formidable as two Fates. They didn't any more.

'How about it?' I said. 'Do we go on playing Guess Who I am? Or do we come clean?'

Suddenly Marny laughed. She got up from the couch. She pushed her way through the others and kissed me enthusiastically.

'You did it,' she cried. 'From the beginning, I knew you'd win. Oh, peace, peace, it's wonderful.'

'Which means, of course, that I'm not Gordy Friend?'

'Of course you're not Gordy,' said Marny. 'Until Nate brought you home from the sanatorium, we'd never any of us seen you before in our lives.'

Chapter 14

MRS FRIEND grabbed Marny's arm with sudden ferocity and swung the girl away from me. For a moment the two of them stood, staring at each other – the leader of the conspiracy and the Judas who had betrayed it.

I'm sure they had forgotten me in their mutual antagonism. I had almost forgotten them, because my whole being was concentrated on adapting myself to this new reality. They had needed Gordy desperately for their inheritance. They couldn't find him. They had invented a false Gordy. It was as simple as that. Now I knew the embarrassing facts about the will, there was no need to ascribe more sinister motives to them.

They were after their money. That was enough to explain everything. Why now should I cling to my far darker suspicions which had never had anything but the flimsiest evidence to support them?

The silence was long enough and tense enough to make me conscious of it. Nate had taken Selena's hand. With a stirring of annoyance, I saw she made no effort to release it. They were both watching Mrs Friend and Marny as if their destinies, somehow, depended upon what happened between the two women.

When Mrs Friend spoke, her voice was gentle. It was not real gentleness though.

She said: 'We've worked so hard. It's been so difficult. Why did you have to do this now?'

'Do what?' challenged Marny. 'Tell him the truth? He's got to be told the truth.'

Mrs Friend shrugged wearily. 'You could at least have left the decision up to someone more responsible.'

'Who's someone more responsible? You?' Marny laughed. 'A wonderful job you've made of it. You with your elaborate web of lies that had us all tangled up before we could look around. He's a clever man. You and Nate have been handling

him like a moron. Five minutes after he returned to consciousness he was beginning to suspect he wasn't Gordy.'

With great difficulty Mrs Friend managed one of her smiles.
'Well, dear, there's not much point in mutual recriminations.
The damage has been done.' She turned the remnants of the
frayed smile on me. 'You must please believe me that we've
been acting for what seemed to be the best.'

'Best for whom?' flared Marny.

Nate Croft moved towards her. Behind the smooth, doctor
front, he was a very angry man. 'Okay, Marny. You've had
your fun making your pretty little scene. Now keep out of
this and leave it to someone who has some conception of the
importance of the situation.'

'The importance?' Marny turned on him savagely. 'The
importance of having the no-good Friend inherit Father's
money on a sham? The importance of keeping Dr Croft's holy
nose clean?'

'Really...!'

'Really.' Marny's lip curled. 'For a doctor, you have an
extraordinary conception of importance. Do you think it's
attractive the way we've been treating this man? He's lost his
memory. The poor guy doesn't know who he is. We try and
make him believe he's someone he isn't. He sees through it.
And yet he's stuck here with a broken arm, a broken leg, completely at our mercy. We've been torturing him. That's what
we've been doing. And you talk smugly about my not realizing the importance of the situation – when you're doing this
to one of your own patients just because you're besotted with
lust for Selena.'

Nate's flush deepened. Selena, who alone seemed as calm
and amused as ever, laughed. 'Marny, darling, try just for
once to keep lust out of your dialogue.'

'If you kept it out of your life, I might keep it out of my
dialogue.' Marny turned to me. Her hand went out hesitantly.
'I couldn't bear watching what they were doing to you. I
wanted to tell you the truth. But I knew I couldn't – not till
it came out naturally, like this in front of them all.'

Mrs Friend said acidly: 'You're developing these lofty sentiments rather late in the day, aren't you?'

'Oh, I'm not trying to white-wash myself.' Marny was still watching me. 'I'm as guilty as they are. We all went into this together. But please, please, try to think that I'm not quite as much of a louse as the others.'

Selena laughed again. 'I'm beginning to see the light. Our little Marny has developed one of her well-known weaknesses for the tortured victim in the wheel chair.' She smiled at me affectionately. 'Watch out, baby. She's not your sister any more, you know.'

Marny flared: 'Shut up, Selena.'

Selena grimaced. 'Oh, dear, I brought lust into the dialogue again.'

I looked at the two girls, Marny who had defied her family and risked a fortune to help me, Selena who from the start had serenely, with absolutely no qualms, made a sucker out of me.

Why was it Selena who still made my pulses beat quickly?

Marny, her straight brown eyes fixed on my face, repeated, 'Do you hate me?'

I grinned at her. 'On the contrary, after the things I've been suspecting, I could take you all, Nate included, in my arms and give you big, juicy busses. How about giving with the facts, though?'

'What is there to tell? You must have guessed almost all of it.' Marny threw a defiant glance at Nate. 'Hold on to your diploma, Nate. Here we go.' She turned back to me.

'The night Father died, Gordy went off on a drunk. You don't know Gordy, but there was nothing unusual about that. He'd been drinking all day. I was the last to see him. He passed me in the hall, saying he was fed up with the family and was going off to Los Angeles. I saw him drive away. I didn't try to stop him, because we didn't know till later that Father was dying and none of us had the slightest idea he was leaving that clause in his will anyway. Afterwards, of course, when we read the will, Gordy mattered terribly. We ransacked L. A. for him. Mother even has detectives out after him.'

'But you haven't found him?'

Selena gave a rueful shrug. 'No, baby. He's probably in Mexico by now. Gordy's drunks usually end up in a Mexican bed with some small town señorita and vermin. There's nothing you can do about him. When he's ready to come back, he'll come back.'

Mrs Friend had sunk into a chair. She looked resigned now and tired – almost old. Only Nate was still standing, alert, hostile.

I said: 'So there you were with no Gordy and everything depending on him. It looked as though the Aurora Clean Living League was going to walk away with the dough uncontested. Then Nate picked me up. Where did he find me?'

Nate shuffled. Marny said: 'In his sanatorium. You were brought in. Some people had found you lying on the side of the road between here and San Diego. You must have been knocked down by a hit-and-run driver. Later, when you'd been operated on and had your arm and leg fixed up, Nate discovered you'd lost your memory. That's what gave him the idea.'

Selena moved from the couch and, pushing past Marny, sat down on the floor at my feet. 'We were pretty desperate then. Only a week to go and no Gordy. Nate called me about you. You seemed to be the answer to prayer. You see, Gordy and I had only been out here a couple of weeks and Gordy'd been drunk most of the time. Neither Mr Moffat nor Mr Petherbridge had ever seen him and, after Father's death, we'd fired all the old snooping servants. There wasn't anyone connected with anything who knew Gordy by sight except Jan. And Jan doesn't count.' She smiled up at me. 'Baby, nobler characters than us would have been seduced by that set-up. All we had to do was to claim you, tuck you in bed, convince you you were our long-lost Gordy. Once you'd been pushed through your routine in front of Mr Petherbridge and the Aurora Clean Living League, the day was ours.'

'Even having your right arm broken fitted so admirably,' Mrs Friend gave a small sigh. 'A left-handed signature on the abstinence pledge couldn't have been proved a forgery.' She scooped up strands of uncooperative hair. 'It was a heroic attempt anyway. Hand us that. And, whatever you feel about us, you must admit that we were pleasant hosts. We did all we could think of to make you comfortable.'

Slowly, I realized, the mood was changing. After Marny's outburst, I had been the outraged victim saved from the unscrupulous plotting. Now, almost imperceptibly, we were drifting back into the Friends' typical atmosphere of amiable chumminess. Marny had been eased into the background. Mrs. Friend was smiling at me almost as if I were a fellow conspirator. Selena's hand, absently it seemed, found mine. The warm pressure of her fingers was as exciting as it had always been – more exciting because I no longer thought of her as an enemy.

I said: 'Very neat so far. But what were you planning to do after I'd got you the money and the real Gordy showed up? Once Mr Petherbridge and Mr Moffat saw the real Gordy the whole conspiracy would be obvious.'

'But they would never have seen the real Gordy, dear.' Mrs Friend sneaked that 'dear' in so deftly that I hardly noticed it. 'You see, we would have left California, sold the house. We none of us particularly like it anyway.'

'And me? What would you have done with me?'

'That we hadn't exactly planned.' Mrs Friend's lips drooped ruefully. 'We thought we'd wait and see what your attitude would be after we'd told you the truth. At least we could have pointed out that we had taken care of all your hospital expenses. And, if you were the type of person who was interested in money ...' She paused, adding: 'You mustn't please feel insulted because we didn't know you at the time. But, if you had been interested in a reward for services rendered, we were prepared to give you a handsome cash present, a very handsome present.'

'And if I'd decided to blackmail you indefinitely? I'd have had a complete hold over you. You realize that?'

'That was a gamble we were prepared to take. After all,

having money and being blackmailed is better than having no money and not being blackmailed. Besides ...' Mrs Friend reached for her knitting. 'We'd been resigned to blackmail anyway. Before Nate produced you, we had been playing with the idea of hiring some unscrupulous character to put on a deliberate masquerade. A man like that would certainly have blackmailed us.' She smiled. 'I don't think, somehow, you would have done anything like that, would you?'

'Of course he wouldn't, Mimsey,' said Selena. 'He's a divine man.'

Mrs Friend's fingers did serene things with the coral wool. 'I suppose we're all criminals really and should feel guilty about it. I'm afraid I don't. Not at all. Your father's ... I mean, my husband's will was immensely stupid and unfair. You must admit that. We have every moral right to the money. And the prospect of it going to the Clean Living League ...' She shivered. 'Wait till you see them tomorrow, dear. Mr Moffat with a couple of million dollars! The very thought curdles my blood.'

There was a moment of silence. Marny, curled on the couch, was scowling at Selena who was still holding my hand. Nate Croft hovered uneasily. It was as if they all realized Mrs Friend had successfully created an effect which they did not want to impair.

In her good time, Mrs Friend's placid gaze came to rest on my face.

'Well, you know the truth now. Marny was right. We should have given up the pretence earlier. Really, what handsprings we've been turning trying to keep you in the dark. I fired that dreary, drunken Netti because I was afraid she was making you suspicious. Selena invented that mythical Cousin – what was his name? – to explain away Gordy's photograph. We bundled poor Peter off to board at the vet's. And, really, the time we've had with Grandmother! You see, because she's so old and a teeny bit wandering, poor dear, we thought it would be safer to keep her out of the conspiracy. We just told her Gordy was back and hoped to keep her in her room until the danger was over. She embarrassed us terribly by creeping into your room that way. Selena was stupid trying to pretend she didn't exist, but she was scared you'd ask to see her and Grandmother would give everything away.'

She sighed. 'We underestimated Grandmother. We should have taken her into our confidence to begin with. This morning when I realized that you were determined to bring on a show-down, I explained the whole situation to her. She grasped it right away. She was thrilled. She simply adored pretending she thought you were Gordy just now.' She shrugged. 'Grandma's turned out to be much more of a law-breaking type than any of us.'

She paused, looking out of the plate glass window at the magnificent view which was blurred in the fading light.

'You know,' she said suddenly, 'this is very pleasant. You can't imagine what a relief it is to be able to speak the truth again – the whole truth.'

Perhaps it was because I had, during the last days, become accustomed to disbelieving Mrs Friend on principle, but there was something about the faint exaggeration of stress upon the words '*the whole truth*' that started suspicion stirring inside me again. The story they had told me was plausible, but after all, all the other lying stories they had fed me from the beginning had sounded plausible too. Was it possible that I was once again falling for a colossal bluff?

'Yes,' murmured Mrs Friend, 'there is great pleasure in telling the truth – particularly for someone like me who is not a liar by nature.' She glanced at me under her lashes. 'Even though, by telling the truth, we have lost all chance, of course, of ever getting the money which I still feel is legitimately ours.'

My suspicions dispersed then because I understood what she was up to. She was faking, but for an immediate and less sinister motive. With her genius for making the best of a bad bargain, she was hoping that I might still prove a sound investment. She had been carefully softening me up with her charm. Discreetly, she had let me know that a large sum of money, as a bribe, was mine for the asking. Now she was waiting for me to say: *Don't worry about tomorrow. I'm so crazy about you all that I'll go ahead with the plan anyway and see the Aurora Clean Living League doesn't walk off with your money.*

When I didn't say anything, she made a little grimace. 'Tell us. Now you know the truth, do you think we're very shameless?'

'Yes, baby.' Selena smiled up at me dazzlingly. 'Are you terribly, terribly shocked?'

I suppose I should have been. After all, even if old Mr Friend's will had been on the whimsical side, they had all of them been unscrupulously prepared to break the law and use me as their stooge. But I wasn't shocked. Although Mrs Friend and Selena had between them less ethical equipment than a gnat, I felt a positive affection for them.

'I'm not shocked,' I said. 'Maybe I'm a criminal type myself, which brings up the one question that really interests me. Okay. I'm not Gordy Friend. Who am I?'

Personal excitement that had nothing to do with the Friends started my nerve ends shivering. Peter ... San Diego ... the propellers ... Iris ... those dim, tantalizing clues stirred in my mind. In a second I'd be a man again with a name and a life.

Mrs Friend put down her knitting. She looked faintly embarrassed.

'I'm sorry, dear. I'm afraid that's one thing we can't tell you.'

'Can't tell me?'

'No, dear. You see, we don't know.'

I turned to Marny who still sat curled up on the edge of the couch. It was always to Marny I turned in times of trouble.

I said: 'Is she speaking the truth?'

Marny nodded slowly.

'That's true,' she said. 'We don't know. None of us know – not even Nate. We haven't the faintest idea who you are.'

Chapter 15

I FELT like a prisoner, almost reprieved, who sees the door of his cell slam again in his face.

'But someone must....'

'I'm afraid that's the way it is.' Dr Croft, who had for so long let the women hold the floor, took control at that point. He watched me from his liquid, unmasculine eyes. 'When you were received at the hospital, there was absolutely no clue to identity on you, no wallet, no papers, nothing except the clothes you were wearing and they seemed to be brand new with no laundry marks.' He paused with a faint smile. 'You must realize that I took a tremendous risk loaning you to the Friends the way I did. I'd never have taken that risk if you'd been someone with a name, an identity who might at any moment have been claimed by relatives.'

'But the people who brought me to the sanatorium?'

'Marny told you. They were motorists who found you lying unconscious at the side of the road. Marny suggested you were a hit-and-run victim. I think it's more likely you were robbed. Perhaps you gave a ride to a hitchhiker who black-jacked you and stole your valuables and your car. The wound on your head's such as might have been made by a blackjack.'

Mrs Friend gave me a sudden, sweet smile. 'Don't worry about it too much, dear. I'm sure your memory will come back soon. Meanwhile think of us as your family.'

'Yes, baby,' said Selena, rubbing her soft cheek caressingly against the back of my hand. 'We simply adore you. We honestly do. We'll adopt you.'

If I'd felt sardonic, I could have pointed out that, since they had kidnapped me, the least they could do was to house and feed me until I found somewhere else to go. But I didn't feel sardonic. It's lonely being a man without a name and without a past. The Friends were the only people I knew. I clung to them.

Nate Croft said: 'Of course, when the right time comes, we'll do everything we can to see that you're restored where you belong.' He looked faintly awkward. 'I must admit that while the – er – little masquerade was on, I did my best to discourage any shreds of genuine memory you showed signs of developing. Of course all that will be changed now. You can rest assured that my services as a psychiatrist are completely at your disposal.'

'Free of charge?' I asked.

He looked even more awkward. 'I don't blame you for feeling antagonism towards me, old man. As a doctor, I have acted in an unorthodox fashion. I'm the first to admit it. My only excuse is that I didn't feel it would do you any serious harm and, believing as I do that Mr Friend's will was outrageously unfair, I thought you might be the means of doing the Friends a great deal of good.'

Nate was as expert as Mrs Friend in finding the favourable interpretation for his own behaviour. In that smooth speech, he had managed to make a shamelessly unethical act sound like a chivalrous attempt to aid ladies in distress.

'Which brings up quite an important point.' Nate's hands were in his pockets now. He was rocking back and forth on his heels – his favourite bedside mannerism. 'Now you've heard the set-up, what's your point of view? About this will, I mean?'

His eyes flicked up to meet mine. Mrs Friend had dropped her knitting. Selena, her cheek still against my hand, moved her head to stare up at me. Even Marny stirred on the couch.

I said: 'You want to know if I approve of Mr Friend leaving that clause in his will?'

'I mean,' said Nate Croft, 'if you'd been Mrs Friend or Selena or Marny – or me for that matter – how would you have behaved?'

I glanced down at Selena for whom Nate was 'besotted with lust' and by whom I was so nearly enchanted myself. I studied Mrs Friend's magnificent maturity and Marny's stripling loveliness.

I said, which was true: 'If I'd been you, Nate, I'd probably have done exactly the same thing – especially if the Clean Living League's as preposterous as they make out.'

'Oh, it is, it is,' said Mrs Friend quickly.

'Then, in that case —' Nate was studying his own manicured thumbnail. It was a gesture intended to show casualness. In fact, it couldn't have been more obviously thought out – 'in that case, maybe, even now, you might feel like ...'

He didn't finish the sentence. There was no need. It was perfectly obvious what he was driving at.

'We would guarantee,' put in Mrs Friend quietly, 'that you'd get into no trouble. Even if the little trick was exposed, we would take the entire blame. I mean, we would swear that you were an amnesia patient whom we'd deceived into genuinely believing he was Gordy. You'd just be the innocent victim. We're doing that for Nate too. We're prepared to swear he never knew Gordy and honestly believed us when we claimed you.'

'At worst it's only a technical breaking of the law,' said Nate. 'If you knew how the whole Friend family had to suffer for years putting up with Mr Friend's impossible tyranny, you'd realize they have every moral right to the money.'

Selena jumped up. She was still holding my hand. She leaned over me, her warm red mouth drooping in a conspiratorial smile.

'Do, baby. Oh, please do. Who cares whether it's moral or not? It's just that it's terrible, terrible fun to have a lot of money and awfully dreary not to have any. Think of Mimsey grilling hamburgers in a hash house and Marny a drab hotel chambermaid and me ... oh, God, what would I be good for? Walking the streets, I suppose.' She looked dreamy. 'Maybe that wouldn't be so unattractive.' She glanced over her shoulder at Mrs Friend. 'Mimsey, do you think maybe it would be fun? I mean, if you could pick only the very best streets to walk?'

Mrs Friend said: 'Selena, don't be frivolous.' She looked at me. 'Well, dear?'

Perhaps an amnesiac is automatically anti-social. Or perhaps it was just because Selena was so beautiful and wasn't lying to me any more and was married to a drunken bum who'd abandoned her at the only moment when he could have helped her. In any case, I knew exactly what I was going to say.

And I said it.

'Sure I'll do it, provided you'll cover me if there's any trouble and help afterwards to find out who I am.'

'Of course we will.' Mrs Friend's face was radiant. 'Darling boy, of course we will.'

Selena traced the curve of my cheek with her finger. 'Angel, you're such an angel. Really, having it be you who is the fairy godfather is the nicest part of it all.'

Nate Croft, now the climax was passed, had reverted to the jealous male. His dusky cheeks flushed with pink, he snapped:

'Selena, don't paw him about.'

'Why not, dear? He's so paw-able.' Selena drifted to Nate then, kissing him absently on the cheek. 'But we're so grateful to you too. You've been absolutely dreamy.'

Mrs Friend had risen and was sitting next to Marny on the couch, squeezing her hand. 'Dear, please forgive me for being so unattractive and snappish. You were right. It's just because you're more honest than we that he's doing this for us.'

'Okay, Mimsey.' Marney pulled her hand away impatiently. 'We've got all that we wanted. You don't have to coo.'

Mrs Friend sighed. 'Such a prickly child I have.' She rose again from the couch and progressing towards me picked up the volume of Mr Friend's poems from the floor. She returned to her own chair, searched through the book and gave a contented little grunt.

'Oh, it's so much nicer this way with everyone trusting each other, understanding each other.'

She patted the book. 'Now, dear, you must be sure to learn the poem perfectly. Mr Moffat is probably down on his knees right this minute praying that you'll fumble or hiccough or do something distinctly drunken and be disqualifiable.'

She looked up. 'Nate, Selena, sit down, dears. It makes me restless, everyone milling around.'

Selena and Nate sat down together on a love seat. Mrs Friend murmured:

'Let's see. Only two more verses. The one we read and the last one. Let's read the last one.'

She peered, seemed to find the print too small for her and fumbled in her work-bag from which she produced a large pair of shell-rimmed glasses. She balanced them on the end of her nose.

'There.'

Emphatically, stressing the rhythm, she read:

'"Oh now is the time when Temptation,
    Like the serpent of yore, must be stunned.
    We must flush every foot of the nation
    Till our quarry is slaughtered and shunned.
    Though our country is stained, pray restore her.
    Up and scour her with spiritual soap.
    Oh scour her and scourge her, Aurora,
    Our Lady of Hope."'

She put the book down on her lap. She peered at us all over her spectacles.

'Your poor father! Never tell a soul but he drank a whole glass of blackberry brandy on our wedding night.'

Magnificently she had asserted herself again. Through the force of her personality, she had turned us all into a harmless little family party cosily sitting around after a good dinner. No one would have dreamed, to look at us, that we were five desperate characters preparing a major conspiracy to break the law.

Suddenly I found myself thinking that if the Friends were this good at deception they might just as well be even better. What if I had let myself be duped again? What if they had cunningly told me only part of the truth and the little comedy in front of Mr Moffat tomorrow was just a prologue to – something else?

I had no reason to think that way, of course. No reason at all.

And yet I could feel the prickle of gooseflesh on my skin.

'Ready, dear?' Mrs Friend's gentle smile had settled on me. Once again she raised her hand and beat a heavy, rather inaccurate rhythm in the air.

'*Oh now is the time when Temptation....*'

Chapter 16

WHEN I had the poem word perfect, Mrs Friend announced that it was time for us all to go to bed so that we should be particularly clear-headed in the morning. Nate, obviously reluctant to leave, was led off to the door by Selena. When they had gone and Mrs Friend had betaken herself to say goodnight to her mother, Marny offered to wheel me to my room.

I didn't need to be wheeled, but I liked the idea of being alone with Marny for a while.

Once we reached the bedroom, she pushed my chair near to one of the silver and gold beds on which she dropped down, her black hair tumbled around her young, cute face. The indignation with which she had fought my battle for me against the family seemed to have left her. She was her cool, sardonic self again.

My groundless suspicions had almost faded but somehow I wanted to be sure that she didn't think I was a sucker.

I smiled at her. 'Well, I've got a lot to thank you for. If it hadn't been for you, they'd never have broken down.'

'You're welcome,' she drawled. 'Any little thing I can do.'

I watched her curiously. 'Why did you say they were fiends this afternoon?'

'Because they are fiends. They weren't treating you like a human being. To them you were just a hunk of flesh they were pushing around for their own advantage. I was sorry for you.' She grimaced. 'I'm being like Mimsey now – making a good story. I wasn't all that Christian. I was scared too. I knew you were getting suspicious. I'd seen you telephoning. I was afraid you might get panicked and call the police and ruin everything. I thought if I dropped the right sort of hint, you'd force the truth out and we'd have a much better chance at the money with you as an ally instead of a victim.'

I grinned. 'Looks like you were smarter than they were.'

'Maybe.'

'And certainly franker.'

Her cool eyes watched me, unwinking. 'After what you've been through, I should think a little frankness would go down well.'

'It does,' I said. 'Then you're not sorry I decided to forgive and forget and help them?'

'Them? Don't be silly. You're helping me as much as them. Of course I'm delighted. I want that money more than I want anything in the world.' One of her straight long legs was dangling over the edge of the bed. She swung it restlessly. 'God, how I want that money. And when I get my share, I'll lam out of this place so fast you won't see me for dust.'

'What have you got against it?'

'Against it?' She stared at me as if I was crazy to ask such a question. 'I've got everything against it. Always, ever since I can remember, home's been the place where you get trampled on. First it was Father. Father – he didn't trample, he oozed. He was like a great, godly slug crawling over my life, turning everything brown around the edges. I was fed wickedness, lusts of the flesh and damnation every day like oatmeal. While I was still wetting my diapers, I was sure I'd committed the sin against the Holy Ghost. Later, when he joined the Clean Living League and went for healthy romps with Mr Moffat in God's sunshine, he was still as bad when he came home. You should have seen me. Until a few weeks ago, I was a little grey frightened mouse, scurrying into the wainscot to hide if anyone raised their voice.' She lit a cigarette, inhaling deeply, her eyes reminiscent. 'The only fun I had was hoping Father would die. For years, every night after

I'd gone to bed, I'd lie awake thinking of him dying.' She laughed. 'That and sex, of course. I was never alone with a man till I was twenty-one and that was only three weeks ago. Boy, what a dirty mind I worked up.'

She stared down at her leg gloomily. 'And then Father did die. For a while I thought Life had Begun. I painted my face. I bought the smartest clothes, the sheerest stockings, I had a cocktail before every meal, I smoked like a blast furnace. I even had a DATE with a MAN. This was it, I thought. Then I started to realize that it was all just as bad as it ever had been – worse really.'

It was quite new for me to think of this girl with her flourished cupid's bow mouth, her brash exhibition of leg and her cynical chatter as a transformation, only three weeks old, from a mousey frightened child under Mr Friend's thumb. Even at their most ominous, the Friends had seemed the epitome of sophistication. This was the first time I saw them as they must really be – three women who had had only a few heady weeks' emancipation from an almost incredible Victorian tyranny.

I asked: 'And why was life just as bad after your father died, Marny?'

She looked up quickly: 'Mimsey and Selena, of course.'

'Mimsey and Selena?'

'Ever hear of the word "stifled"? You try being a woman in the same house with Mimsey and Selena.' She kicked out savagely with her leg. 'It was almost better with Father. At least he wasn't sinister.'

'Sinister?' I reacted instinctively to the word.

'Oh, they don't know they are.' She pulled her legs up onto the bed and sat cross-legged, her hands on her ankles. 'It's just that they're both terrifically forceful characters and all that force was bottled up by Father. Now, with him gone, they're expanding – blossoming like those monstrous South American man-eating plants. They suck everything in, including me. They swallow everyone. Oh, they'd do anything, absolutely anything, however callous. And just because it's fulfilling them, they'll be able to sugar it all over with a pretty word and make it seem oh so charming and sympathetic.'

She was staring at me fixedly now, the glossy hair swinging free around her shoulders. I had the strange feeling that somehow between the lines of what she said there was a warning.

'Tell me,' she asked suddenly. 'Why are you going through with this plan? There's nothing in it for you.'

'There's nothing in it against me, is there?'

'I don't think so.'

'Then why shouldn't I do it out of general chumminess?'

She shook her head. 'You're not doing it for general chumminess. You're doing it for Selena.'

For some reason I felt uncomfortable.

'Of course you are. You're just like all the rest. You're letting her swallow you up. She swallowed Gordy up – what was left of him, poor guy. And she's swallowed Nate.' She gave a bitter laugh. 'Remember I told you I had my first date with a man three weeks ago? That man was Nate. I met him and brought him home. He was supposed to be my beau. No one ever mentions that now, do they? Selena took one look at him and gobbled him like a hippopotamus gobbling water-weed. And you ...'

'Maybe I can take care of myself.'

'You?' Marny laughed again. 'Just wait and see. Any minute now she'll be walking into the room. She'll be so gay and amusing about tomorrow. That's what will happen first. Then she'll start having a pain in her eyes and telling you how awful it was being married to a drunk. Then she'll say Nate's awfully sweet, of course, and she's devoted to him, but what big muscles you have.' Her sarcasm was withering. 'You take care of yourself? Water-weed! That's what you'll be. One big, green mouthful.'

My reaction was curiously mixed. Part of me said: *She's right. Watch out.* Another part strained to leap to Selena's defence. It was checked however by Marny's clear, ironic stare.

She said: 'You think I'm jealous, don't you, because Selena's such a ravishment.'

'Do I?'

'Of course you do.' In a quick change of mood her face was deadly serious. 'Please believe me, for your own sake. She'll be poison to you. She's bad – really bad. It's not just Gordy, Nate. It's every man that comes near her.' She paused and added harshly: 'Jan, even.'

'Jan!'

'Yes, Jan. I saw Selena with Jan just before Father died. I ... Oh, I suppose I shouldn't have told you. It's bitchy. But what difference does it make if only I can make you see?'

A vision of Jan's huge half-naked body swam across my mind. I thought of his gusty peals of laughter when I'd asked him why Mr Friend had fired him. Then the image of him – still laughing – merged with Selena's lithe, suntanned figure, struggling in the pool. Anger, of a violence that startled me, flared up in me.

Marny was still watching me. 'Selena got bored with Gordy. Cynically, without raising her little finger, she let him drink himself into a sudden pulp. She took up with Nate just so she could use him. Soon she'll be bored with him too. Soon she'll throw him on the junk pile. And you're next on the list for liquidation. She can't help it, I guess. It's the way she's made. Without realizing it, she destroys people.'

Because I didn't quite know at what my anger was directed, I focused it on her. 'Aren't you being rather goddam helpful? What's it to you whether I make a fool of myself or not?'

'What's it to me?' She gave a little weary shrug. 'I don't know. Maybe it's because I can't bear to see Selena get away with things. She's got some plan up her sleeve with you. I know she has.'

'Plan?' I was uneasy again. 'What sort of plan?'

She sat there for a moment in silence. Then she shook her head slowly. 'I don't know. But there's something. I can tell it in her eyes.' She leaned forward and touched my hand with a gravity that was almost naïve. 'Don't trust her. Please, promise me you won't trust her.'

It was a funny moment. This was the warning I had half

been expecting. I should have been worrying about it. I should have been worrying too about the vision of Selena that rose, gorgeous and mocking, in my mind. But I didn't worry about either of them. All that seemed to matter was that Marny was looking very young and tired and forlorn. I slid my arm around her, drew her close and kissed her on the lips.

'Thanks for the warning, baby.'

'You won't pay it any attention.'

'Who knows?'

'But you'll see. Sooner or later you'll find out what she's up to and you'll come screaming to me to say how right I was.'

'Okay. That's a bargain. When Selena poisons me, I'll come screaming to you for an emetic.'

I kissed her again. For a moment her lips relaxed against mine; then they went tight and hostile. She wrenched herself free. 'For God's sake stop kissing me.'

'Why, Marny?'

'Because ...' She stared at me, her mouth unsteady. Then she jumped off the bed. 'Oh, God, you make me sick. All men make me sick.' She gave a savage laugh. 'Didn't someone say that before?'

'Marny, baby.'

'Oh, hell, I'll go get Jan to put you to bed. You boys should get together anyway and form a club.'

As she ran to the door, I caught a glimpse of her face. It was white and stricken.

Suddenly I felt like a heel.

Soon Jan came. He was in pyjamas. His blond hair was ruffled and, from the droopiness of his lids, I imagined Marny had waked him up. But he was as amiable as ever. Mechanically, he went through the routine of preparing me for the night. I'd never liked his touching me. That night, with the vision of him and Selena together in my mind, I felt an unbridled desire to lunge my own good fist into his broad suntanned face.

He carried me back to bed as if I were a baby, tucked me

in, smiled with all the friendly sweetness in the world and loped out.

It was only after he'd gone that I faced the truth which I should have faced days before.

Marny was right, of course, about my obsession with Selena. I didn't love her. It was nothing as fragrant and romantic as that. It was worse. Although she had cheated me and lied to me from the start, Selena was in my blood. That's the way it was. For better or worse I was stuck with it.

From the beginning the violence of my reactions to the Friends had really been conditioned by Selena. I had half known it all along but it was as clear to me now as my memory of Selena's dark blue eyes. I had hated the Friends when I thought they were my enemies because I had hated to have Selena as an enemy. That evening I had ignored every instinct of self-preservation and joined their conspiracy simply because, by joining, I could have Selena on my side again. Even now, when vague suspicions of an even vaguer danger ahead preyed on me, I could still be excited because I knew that at any moment Selena would be coming.

The door opened and there she was.

'Hello, darling. Has Marny been warning you against me? I'm sure she has. I saw that predatory gleam in her eyes.'

She came to the bed and sat down. She took my hand in hers and tilted back her head, laughing out of sheer animal spirits.

'I'm sorry I'm so late, baby. I've been having a terrible time with Nate.'

I was happy now. 'What's Nate been up to?'

'Oh, he was seething without my sleeping in here. He said since I wasn't pretending to be your wife any more, I ought to move over into one of those dreary guest bedrooms in the other wing. Really, my dear, he was so stodgy about it. I pointed out that you could hardly become a menace with that cast and, since you'd seen everything there was to see already, it was frightfully hypocritical to go stuffy at this stage of the game.' She leaned over me, kissing me on the mouth. 'Besides, all those proprieties, they're so dismal, aren't they?'

'Terribly dismal.' Her shoulders were bare. I let my hand stray over the warm, smooth skin. Dimly, I thought: *Poor Nate*. But only dimly.

She slipped back against the pillows, wheedling her hand under the nape of my neck. 'Baby, I'm so terribly, terribly glad about tomorrow. You really are an angel. Funny, it all turned out for the best, didn't it? I mean, Gordy'd never have been sober enough to recite that poem himself.' Under their thick lashes, her eyes slid sidewise to glance at me. 'Poor Gordy. I'm devoted to him. Honestly I am. But sometimes – well, it's rather drab being married to a drunk. Can you understand that, baby?'

'I can't understand life ever being drab for you. After all, there's not only Gordy. Nate's crazy about you.'

'Nate.' She gave a little throaty sigh. 'Yes, I suppose he is. He wants me to divorce Gordy and marry him.'

'He does?' I asked sharply.

'That's why he helped us. He didn't want to at all until I pointed out how depressing it would be to marry him if I was penniless. After all, if I was going to divorce Gordy, it was so much more sensible to have Gordy rich, so's I could get a great fat cash settlement, wasn't it?'

She lay back, staring happily up at the ceiling. For a moment the shamelessness of that admission took my breath away. So that was how the Friends had got the invaluable assistance of Nate Croft. Selena had used herself as a lure to induce the young doctor to risk his entire professional career. *Poor Nate*, I thought again. Less dimly this time.

I said: 'So after this is over, you're going to divorce Gordy and marry Nate?'

'Oh, baby, it's so bleak thinking of things way in the future like that. Of course Nate's awfully sweet. But he's a bit of a stuffed shirt. Don't you think he is? Just a bit of a stuffed shirt?'

She rolled over onto her hip so that she faced me. Idly her fingers started playing with the sleeve of my pyjama jacket. She pushed it back, staring down at my arm.

'Baby, such hands. I've always adored them. And the muscles – really, like a stevedore's.'

It amazed me how separate my mind and my emotions had become. Clearly, as if she was in the room right then saying them, my mind remembered Marny's cynical words. She had prophesied almost exactly the sequence of Selena's conversation. But instead of acting as a warning, that knowledge gave me a strange exhilaration.

'Know something, baby?' Selena was stroking the blond hairs on my arm. 'I never enjoyed anything so much as pretending to be your wife. Somehow it was exciting lying all the time. And it's exciting touching you too. Darling, I love touching you.' She leaned one inch closer and kissed me on the mouth. 'You're like something fizzing in my veins. Oh, things are such fun always.'

She drew away from me, reaching up and twisting a lock of my hair out from under the bandages.

'Darling, don't you really know who you are?'

'No.'

'Maybe you're married.'

'Maybe.'

'To a nasty little woman with a stringy neck and curl papers.'

'Could be.'

'Baby, wouldn't it be wonderful if you never got your memory back?'

I stroked her cheek. 'Would it?'

Her eyes were flat, dreamy. 'I think it's that really that makes you exciting. Who are you? Nothing. No identity. No habits. No tabus. Just Man. That's what you are, baby. Man. Oh, don't ever get your memory back.'

'Like me this way?'

She was smiling a swift, enchanting smile. 'That's it, baby. Never get your memory back. I'll divorce Gordy. I'll be rich, stinking rich. You can be rich too because you can hold Gordy up for an enormous cheque too. And we'll go off together and do the most wonderful things. And you'll be part of me. You'll be something I've made. I'll have taught you everything you know.' Her hands fluttered over my chest. 'I'll have taught you everything you know – when the cast comes off.'

My pulses were racing. I couldn't stop my pulses. My blood was racing too so that it was almost a pain. I hadn't forgotten about Nate. I hadn't even forgotten about Jan. I just didn't care.

'Baby.' She whispered that, her lips warm against my ear. 'Baby, tell me. Do you love me?'

'Love?' I gripped her shoulder, drawing her back so I could look at her. 'Love's a rather prissy word to use around you, isn't it?'

'Oh, baby.' She laughed, a deep, husky laugh. 'You and me.'

She jumped off the bed then, her hair tossing around her shoulders. She moved around the bed where I couldn't see her.

'Baby?'

'Yes, Selena.'

'I'm undressing. Turn the other way.'

'I am turned the other way. It's perfectly respectable. I can't see you.'

'I know you can't, you dope. That's what bothers me. Turn around.'

I moved around in the bed. She was standing between me and the window. She undid her dress at the back and let it fall to the ground at her feet.

She was smiling at me, her teeth gleaming white between the red, parted lips.

'You and me, baby,' she said.

Chapter 17

WHEN Jan wakened me the next morning, Selena had disappeared. My first glimpse of the Dutchman was sufficient to remind me that this was The Great Day. His huge body, normally naked except for his scanty swimming trunks, had been forced into a white shirt, with knotted black tie, and a seer-sucker suit. His blond hair had been slicked down too. He looked awkward and unconvincingly holy. He must have been told not to smile, for he maintained a stubborn sobriety as he bathed me and dressed me, as completely as the casts would allow, in an equally dour suit-and-shirt combination with a mourning arm-band of black. I was arranged in the wheel chair with the least colourful of the robes wrapped over my legs and pushed out to the glassed breakfast porch where the others were all assembled.

At a first glance I scarcely recognized the Friend woman. Mrs Friend had always worn black, but her bright lipstick and her rakish upswept hair-do had given the effect of a faintly disreputable goddess in slapdash disguise as a widow. All that was changed. Her face now was devoid of make-up. Her hair was pulled into a tight bun at the nape of her neck. She wore no jewellery and had managed somehow to switch off her magnetism and assume an air of meek, bereaved piety.

Both the girls were in unrelieved black too. I was amazed how it obliterated Marny. She looked the way she'd claimed she'd always looked until her father's death – a little mousey thing ready to scuttle to safety at the first 'boo'. Selena's transformation alone was unsuccessful. In spite of the shape-less black frock, in spite of the preposterous way in which she'd coiled her hair into fat braids around her ears, she still looked bravely voluptuous.

'Darling.' She surveyed me, grinning. 'You're wonderful – that repulsive suit. Try to look a little more constipated. There. Perfect. Gordy Friend – the reformed drunk.'

In spite of her subdued appearance, Mrs Friend was as efficient as ever. Mr Petherbridge, she told me, was arriving before the League convened. It was part of his duties as executor of Mr Friend's will to inspect the house for signs of depravity – bottles of liquor, ashtrays, things like that. He would be coming in an hour.

Mrs Friend whisked us through breakfast and held a con-ference in the living-room where the Clean Living League meeting was to be held. In spite of the room's lavish splendour Mrs Friend had contrived by sheer genius to create an atmosphere of respectable stodginess. There were no ashtrays, of course. Photographs of old Mr Friend himself and of sour-looking relatives had been exhibited clumsily in the least suitable places. A genteel Paisley shawl had been draped over the piano. On it stood a vase stuffed with dead reeds of the type associated with the better boarding houses. Wooden chairs had been arranged in rows to seat the members of the League; and at one end a cluster of chairs around a table indicated where Mr Moffat and the family party would preside.

Mrs Friend made me recite the *Ode to Aurora* three times and even coached me as to the right tone of voice and the correct demeanour for a sheepish ex-sinner who had seen the light.

'We don't have to worry about Mr Petherbridge,' she said. 'He's an old fuss-budget, but I think he's on our side. Mr Moffat's the danger, of course. He'll be crazy for something to go wrong. The slightest slip-up and he'll make a claim. We can't very well afford a law-suit and all the embarrassing things a law-suit might bring out. You realize that?'

The last remark was addressed to me. I nodded. I saw only too well why we couldn't afford a law-suit.

'You'd better know the pattern of these meetings, dear. First there'll be a jolly song. Then Mr Moffat will give a jolly speech about your father. Then you'll recite the poem. Then Mr Moffat will probably launch into a jolly harangue about another lost brother redeemed. Then you'll sign the abstinence pledge. That means you're never to drink again, darling boy. After that, maybe it would be nice if you gave a jolly little speech too. No, maybe you shouldn't. I don't quite trust your sense of humour. We'll skip your jolly speech. Then the meeting'll end with another jolly song, and they'll all troop up to greet you as a fellow member. I've told Mr Moffat they can spend their sunshine hour in the pool so we'll get rid of them from the house after that. Got it?'

'Yes,' I said.

'And don't mention the amnesia, dear. We haven't told Mr Petherbridge or Mr Moffat that Gordy is suffering from amnesia. We thought it might make Mr Moffat suspicious. But since he hasn't the remotest idea you're a fake, he won't try and trip you with awkward questions, I'm quite sure of that.'

'I hope so,' I said. 'Incidentally, are you sure none of the members ever saw Gordy?'

'I don't see how any of them could have, dear. I really don't.' Mrs Friend stared at the two girls. 'Marny, you're all right. Selena' – she sighed – 'I wish there was something you could do with your bosom.'

'I can cut them off,' said Selena.

'No, dear, I don't think that will be necessary.' Mrs Friend took one final, all-observing glance around the room. 'Now I'll get Grandma. She's thrilled at the idea of sitting in on the meeting and I think she'd make a good effect next to Gordy. Gordy with his old grandmother on one side and his wife on the other. Remember, Selena, wifely but not sexy – like St Paul. That's your attitude.'

She made a vague gesture with her hand. 'Oh, dear, I shall feel better when this is over. So tiresome, the whole thing. So very tiresome.'

She went out and came back soon with Grandma, draped in black crepe, spry on her arm. She was settled in a seat next to my wheel chair. She leaned towards me, bringing her own atmosphere of lavender and dust. An ancient lid was slowly lowered and raised over a bright eye.

'This is fun,' she whispered. 'More fun than the radio. More fun than Jack Benny.' She cackled. 'Jack Benny. There's a funny man for you. Didn't have men funny as that in Seattle when I was a girl.'

She was still cackling about the absence of funny men in Seattle in her girlhood when a maid came in to announce Mr Petherbridge.

'Show him in, Susan,' said Mrs Friend.

As the maid departed, a twinge of anxiety came. Was I

sticking my neck in a noose? I looked at Selena. She grinned. I thought of last night and I wasn't nervous any more.

Mr Petherbridge came in behind the maid. From a dramatic point of view, he should have been a tall, ominous character with a steely, penetrating gaze. In fact, Mr Friend's lawyer was tiny and fluttery with a pink bald dome and blue, watery eyes. He looked like one of those butterflies that somehow manage to last through the winter and totter shabbily through the first few days of spring.

Mrs Friend rose. 'Mr Petherbridge.'

'Ah, Mrs Friend.'

Mrs Friend took his hand and led him around. 'I think you know everyone. My mother. Marny. Selena. Gordy ... oh, no, I don't believe you do know Gordy. Mr Petherbridge, this is my son.'

Mr Petherbridge looked at the cast on my right arm, seemed undecided as to whether or not to shake my left hand and then gave up.

'Ah, yes. I heard of your accident. What a merciful escape.'

He smiled awkwardly. In fact, he seemed extremely embarrassed by the whole situation.

Mrs Friend laid her hand on his arm. 'Dear Mr Petherbridge, I know this is uncomfortable for you. Frankly, I think the will's just a teeny, teeny bit silly, don't you? But we must abide by it. You have to inspect the house. Remember? Come on. Let us at least get that over with before our virtuous guests arrive.'

'Virtuous guests.' Mr Petherbridge tittered. 'I must admit I never quite understood your poor husband's enthusiasm for the Clean Living League. Myself, I always enjoy a glass of sherry before dinner, I'm afraid.'

'Mr Petherbridge, you naughty man.' Mrs Friend tapped his sleeve archly. 'Now, let us ransack the house for signs of depravity – you and I.'

She led him out of the room. After a moment's pause Grandma cackled.

'Funnier than Jack Benny,' she said.

None of the rest of us spoke. Jan came in and sat down stiffly on one of the wooden chairs. Soon Mrs Friend and Mr Petherbridge reappeared.

Mrs Friend was looking guardedly pleased. 'There. That's cleared up,' she said. 'Mr Petherbridge feels our house is no more sinful than the average American home, don't you, Mr Petherbridge?'

'Ah, yes, Mrs Friend. Nothing wrong there that I can see. Nothing that would have distressed poor Mr Friend.'

He sat down next to Mrs Friend, his little hands scurrying back and forth over his pin-striped trousers. He was getting more and more nervous. I wondered why.

Splendidly adequate, Mrs Friend kept the conversation simmering until the sound of an automobile was audible from the drive.

'Ah, that will be they. The League. Mr Moffat, I understand, has chartered a bus to bring them all at once. They enjoy doing things in a group. Things are jollier in a group.'

Soon the maid, rather rattled, came in, said: 'They've come, Mrs Friend,' and scuttled out.

People – thirty or forty of them – started streaming into the huge room then. For some reason, I had expected the Clean Living League to be as dour and lugubrious as our own mournful black clothes. I was completely wrong. Most of them, men and women alike, were dressed in white – a discreet gesture, I felt, towards someone else's mourning. But they were far from lugubrious.

Bouncy was the word for them. Although, as they descended upon us, they assumed expressions suitable to greet a bereaved family, they were all bursting with a sort of inner heartiness. I felt that they had come from a jolly good romp somewhere – on the shore, probably, tossing balls to each other and wading and maybe uproariously burying one of the stouter men in the sand and dancing around him.

In spite of their outdoorsiness, however, none of them looked healthy. The men were either fat and middle-aged or young and scrawny with a fine display of pimples. Of the

141

women and girls I didn't see one who would ever be on the receiving end of the drunkest sailor's whistle. They reeked of self-complacency, too. They were obviously thanking Aurora for their own purity which set them loftily above those unfortunates whose romps were vitiated with tobacco and drink and sex. I saw what Mrs Friend had meant the night before. The prospect of these people with several million dollars behind them indeed curdled my blood.

Chattering in respectful undertones, nudging each other in the ribs, carrying on little pure flirtations, they swarmed over the wooden chairs and seated themselves facing our family group.

Until then there had been no sign of Mr Moffat. I suspected he was staging his entrance, and I was right. A moment after the Aurora Clean Living League had finally seated itself, a man's figure appeared at the door, paused there a second and then strode eupeptically through his seated satellites straight up to Mrs Friend.

He grasped her hand, shaking it up and down vigorously. 'Mrs Friend, Mrs Friend. A sad occasion. A very sad occasion. But we know he's still with us, do we not? Part of the sparkling summer light. Part of the lovely garden flowers. Part of the glorious sunset.' He beamed. 'There is no death, Mrs Friend.'

Mr Moffat was unbearably dynamic. Large, youngish, with tightly curled reddish hair and red hairs on his thick wrists, he projected personality as if he was charged with it from a battery concealed beneath his crinkled seersucker suit. He was unbearably chummy too.

He swung to me, picking up my left hand and pumping it. 'And this is Gordy.' He surveyed the casts. 'A crack-up, eh, boy? Well, sometimes we need a real shock to help us Come Through. Ah, alcohol, that weevil-like borer. It's caused many a worse tragedy than a smashed arm, a broken leg. You were lucky, boy. And we're lucky too, for today's a great day, I understand. Today you're Coming Through.'

He leaned over me. From the faint dilatation of his thick nostrils, I could tell he was sniffing for alcohol on my breath.

Coming Through, apparently, was the Aurora Clean Living League's term for conversion.

I smiled weakly. 'I'm Coming Through,' I said.

Mr Moffat slapped me on the back. 'Fine, glorious.' His bright, dirty brown eyes were trying unsuccessfully to register a delight he obviously did not feel at the prospect of my Coming Through. 'Let's be frank, boy. There's a little situation today. Money, boy. A question of the allocation of money.' He bowed at the twittering Mr Petherbridge. 'Let's get this clear, boy. Don't you – or your dear mother – think we care about money. Mr Friend was a fine man, a splendid man, but sometimes he didn't always understand. What is money – when the best things in life are free? The rolling breaker, Gordy. The sunshine over the little kirk on the mountain. The sunlight, boy, in your mother's eyes when you come home to her from your wanderings. Those are the things that brace you. To us, to all of us, it's a millionfold jollier to welcome a new friend who's Come Through than to miss that friend and be a little wealthier in terms of Cash.'

His smile flashed big, irregular teeth. 'We've always been lucky, boy. When times are lean, there's always a good friend ready to put his hand in his jeans for us. Lucre, the old Bible folk called it. Filthy lucre. And that's how I've always thought of it too. We're not going to have filthy lucre come between us and a – pal.'

Having unburdened himself of this disastrous speech, Mr Moffat slapped me on the back again, swung around dramatically to face the crowded chairs, lifted both arms as if he was about to hail the rising sun and cried ringingly:

'At it, boys and girls. Aurora's song.'

One of his raised arms became a conductor's baton. A seedy girl had seated herself at the piano. She played a tremolo octave and, to a man, the group rose and burst into a loud merry song. I caught only snatches of the words – *Aurora* ... *jollity* ... *sunshine* ... *no death* ... *Come Through* ...

Aurora's song concluded, Mr Moffat embarked upon his eulogy of Mr Friend. From it emerged the sharp division

143

between those who had Come Through and those who had not Come Through. Those who had not Come Through were poor misguided sinners doomed to a life of blind debauch on this planet and utter annihilation after death. Those who had Come Through earned the inestimable privilege of Mr Moffat's society both on this earth and, eternally, after death in some jolly Valhalla of Cleanliness.

Mr Friend had definitely Come Through.

I tried to visualize the grim old man I had seen in the photographs frollicking jollily with Mr Moffat's flock and then returning from the romp to excoriate his family's wickedness. The thought made me faintly nauseated. Mr Moffat was extolling Mr Friend's many virtues, ending with his talents as a poet. Suddenly, before I was at all prepared for it, he swung round to me with a flourish reminiscent of a circus ringmaster and cried:

'And now we have the great pleasure of hearing his own very son, who is Coming Through to us, recite what is probably his most inspiring work – his Ode to Aurora.'

A chatter of applause sounded.

Mr Moffat held up his hand. 'But first there's something I'm sure my friend Gordy boy here would want you all to know.' His voice lowered to an awesome whisper. 'Until recently, he was on the Wrong Track – steaming down the Wrong Track. All the weaknesses, the frailties. Alcohol, boys, that weevil-like borer. Even worse, boys. But now, girls, he's seen the red signal. Now he's swung the lever, he's switched tracks. Now, when he recites the Ode' – he paused, raising both hands over his head and clasping them together like a victorious boxing champ – 'now, girls and boys, on this glorious summer day when the very birds sing for joy, he's Coming Through – to me, to you.'

The applause was thunderous. Grandma, at my side suppressed a cackle behind a small handkerchief. I glanced desperately at Selena and then at Mrs Friend. Both of them were sitting quietly with downcast eyes. In a moment of panic, my mind went completely blank. Then Selena half raised her head and winked. I was all right again then.

In fact, I felt so elated that I decided to abandon the meek method of recitation suggested by Mrs Friend and to adopt some of Mr Moffat's rousing swagger.

'"Seven sins lead our sons to Perdition'," I bellowed, '"Seven sins that lure youth like a Whore." ...'

I got my audience. Steadily, accurately, I progressed through the Ode, increasing the passion of my delivery from verse to verse. When I had finished, applause soared. Mr Moffat, a look of undisguised fury in his eyes, swung round and slapped me on the back. Almost before I realized it, he had grabbed a document and a pen. He was thrusting them at me. I glanced at the first line.

I hereby declare that from this day on, I abstain from all uncleanliness, the sordidity of alcohol, the ...

I didn't need to read any more to recognize the abstinence pledge. I held the pen in my left hand over the document. For a moment I hesitated. This was it. Once I signed the forged name, I had irrevocably thrown in my lot with the Friends for better or for worse.

In that second while I hesitated, Selena sprang up as if possessed by a cleanly rapture. Her eyes aglow with evangelical fervour, she clutched my arm.

'Sign it, Gordy boy,' she cried. 'Oh, renounce for ever alcohol, that weevil-like borer.'

Mr Moffat looked taken aback by this unexpected burst of ardour. As I glanced from him to Selena, the need to control an irresistible desire to giggle obliterated every other consideration from my mind. Bowing my head over the document I scrawled a clumsy pretence of the words Gordon Renton Friend III at the foot of the pledge.

Selena sat down with a sigh. Mr Moffat snatched the paper and brandished it.

I had Come Through.

The League was still clapping. With a swoop of the hand, Mr Moffat gave his musical signal. The tremolo octave wabbled from the piano. The League rose and burst into a closing paean to Aurora.

It was all over as quickly, as easily as that. Either Mr Moffat was bowing to the inevitable or he had decided to postpone any legal contentions to the future.

As I looked at him, trying to guess what was in his mind, I had the uneasy suspicion that Mr Moffat was not the type to bow to the inevitable.

Something other than coarse reddish hairs, I felt, was up his sleeve.

It was a feeling I did not like at all.

Chapter 18

'Now, boys and girls,' Mr Moffat was booming to the assembly, 'here is some fun. Mrs Friend has invited us to hold our Sunshine Hour in her glorious swimming pool. We all have our Aurora Swimming Suits?'

A chorus of assent rose.

'Then, boys and girls – to the pool.'

In a clatter of chairs, the League rose and started to swarm around me, heartily greeting their new pal. As one after another gave me a word of cheer, I noticed that two strange men had slipped into the room and were standing uncertainly by the door. One was elderly and stooped with a red-veined nose and white hair. The other was young and very solid with a wary, assertive air which marked him definitely as someone who had not Come Through to Mr Moffat.

While youths and maidens giggled their hopes that I would soon be sufficiently recovered to take an active part in their larks, I saw that Mr Petherbridge had bustled away from Mrs Friend and had joined the two men at the door. The three of them were talking together in low, conspiratorial tones.

Gradully the Aurora Clean Living League was spilling out through the library and the french windows towards the pool.

When the last member had paid his respects, Mr Moffat wrung my hand again.

'Welcome to us, Gordy boy. Welcome. There'll be many a glorious spree ahead for all of us, I'll be bound. Ah, your beautiful mansion – the ideal setting for the League. The ideal setting.' The smile stretched to engulf Mrs Friend who was standing nearby. 'And the filthy lucre?' He gave a rich, false laugh. 'Where do the life earnings of the Father belong but in the lap of his widow and his fatherless children – provided they have been proven worthy?'

The irregular teeth flashed as he completed that faintly ominous remark. Then the shoulders were thrown back. Mr Moffat, much jollier than a man who had just lost several million dollars ought to have been, strode away to supervise the Sunshine Hour. Before he left, his eyes flashed to the two men with Mr Petherbridge and then flicked quickly away as if he was pretending he had not seen them.

I noticed that, but Mrs Friend, apparently, did not. Her face was radiant and she gave my arm a little squeeze.

'We've done it,' she breathed. 'Darling boy, you were wonderful, wonderful. We've done it.'

She hurried after Mr Moffat, presumably to put in a hostess appearance at the pool. Selena and Marny had taken Grandma back to her room and Jan had disappeared. I supposed that I, too, should have wheeled myself to the pool. But the mental image of the Aurora Clean Living ladies in their Aurora swimming suits was too much for me. I stayed where I was.

I had the room to myself now except for Mr Petherbridge and the two strangers who were still grouped by the door. I glanced at them, thinking about Mr Moffat and feeling obscurely uneasy. As if my glance were a signal, the three men started towards me.

Mr Petherbridge seemed almost beside himself with nervousness now. 'Ah, Mr Friend, you – ah – seem to have carried off your duties as stipulated in the will. The terms are plain. You have obeyed them to the letter.'

'Then Mr Moffat can't start anything?' I asked.

'So far as the terms of the will are concerned – ah – no.' Mr Petherbridge's dainty face was almost purple with the embarrassment for which I could still see no cause. 'But ... Mr Friend, before we discuss the matter further, there is something, something, rather distressing ... I wonder if you could spare me and these gentlemen a few moments.'

'Of course,' I said, my nervousness aggravated by his.

'It is awkward. Awkward to say the least.' Mr Petherbridge made a little fluttering gesture towards the older of the two men, the stooped man with the red-veined nose and the white hair. 'This is Dr Leland, Mr Friend. I do not know whether you two have met. Dr Leland is the physician who was attending your father when he – ah – passed on.'

My nervousness was almost panic. Mrs Friend had not planned on Dr Leland.

Dr Leland was watching me from tired, heavy-lidded eyes. After an interminable moment, his hand came out.

'I don't think I've had the pleasure, Mr Friend.'

Relief flooded through me. I took the dry, horny hand.

'And this' – Mr Petherbridge was almost whinnying as he indicated the second man – 'this is Inspector Sargent.'

Inspector! My guilty conscience was like an arresting hand clamped on my shoulder.

Young Inspector Sargent did not take my hand. He was smiling at me, a steady, meaningless smile which kept any revealing expression from his eyes.

'Maybe there's a room that's more private, Mr Friend,' he suggested. 'What we have to say is – well, it's of a confidential nature. '

Mrs Friend wasn't there. No one was there. I was on my own now. Gesturing to the men to follow, I wheeled my chair out of the living-room across the passage into a small sitting-room I had never been in before. The situation was as tough as that. I hardly knew my way about the house that was supposed to be mine. I remembered my anxiety when Mr Petherbridge first arrived that morning. I remembered what I had thought: *Was I putting my neck in the noose?*

Had I already put my neck in that noose?

I thought of Mr Moffat's sidelong glance at the Inspector when he left. Almost certainly this was something to do with Mr Moffat, some wild bid of his to have the will overturned. If I kept steady, everything should be all right.

Inspector Sargent closed the door. The three men grouped themselves around me. I felt quite calm. That was one thing. The potential danger had banished my nervousness.

'Well, gentlemen?' I said.

Mr Petherbridge fluted: 'I think ... ah, that is, I feel Inspector Sargent is the one who ...' The sentence trailed off.

The Inspector had sat down without being invited. He took a notebook and pencil from his pocket. He was still smiling at me.

'Excuse the notebook, Mr Friend. Just regulations.'

'Of course.'

The pencil, gripped in a large, square hand, hovered over the opened book.

'Your name is Gordon Renton Friend the Third?'

'It is.'

'You are, of course, the son of the late Mr Friend who died a month ago in this house?'

'I am.'

I'd said it then. I'd committed myself. There was no turning back.

'I understand that you and your wife arrived here from Pittsburg about two weeks before your father died. Is that correct?'

Now, if ever, was the time to mention the amnesia. It might prove terrifically useful as a protection against unanswerable questions. And yet Mrs Friend had kept it back from Mr Petherbridge. If I suddenly mentioned it now, it would sound highly suspect. I decided to stall until I knew what the Inspector was after.

'Yes,' I said.

The Inspector's grey, uninformative eyes met mine. 'On the day your father died you left for Los Angeles?'

'Yes.'

'To visit?'

Although I had not dared use the amnesia, I could at least blur the issue with alcohol. Gordy's drinking habits were common knowledge, through the will if through nothing else. I couldn't be playing into the Inspector's hands by admitting it.

I grinned. I said: 'I might as well be frank. I'd been drinking. I didn't go to L.A. to visit. I just went – on a bat.'

'I see.' For the first time when we might legitimately have been amused, the Inspector stopped smiling. 'About what time of day did you leave?'

Marny had told me. When was it? 'Sometime in the evening.'

'Before your father was known to be dying?'

'Of course.'

'But you were here during the earlier part of the day?'

'Yes.'

'Did you notice anything at all unusual that might have happened?'

I could feel uneasiness in my stomach – like a rat gnawing a floorboard.

With the same grin that was meant to be carefree, I said: 'Afraid I wouldn't have noticed much of anything. I was quite full of rye.' I hesitated and then asked: 'Why?'

Inspector Sargent closed his notebook and sat with his large hands on his large, muscular thighs.

'This isn't pleasant, Mr Friend. I don't like to have to disturb you with it.' His voice was meant to sound apologetic. It didn't. 'It's just that a certain party's been making – well, what you might call trouble.'

'Mr Moffat?' I asked.

A faint flush diffused his face, making him look suddenly very young. 'To be exact, yes.'

Now he had admitted that Mr Moffat was behind this, I felt a little steadier. Mrs Friend had stated positively that the President of the Clean Living League had had no chance to guess I was an impostor. I was sure enough of myself now to take the offensive.

I said: 'I should think it was pretty obvious that any trouble made by Mr Moffat was on the interested side.'

'Naturally. I realize that there is a large amount of money at stake.' Inspector Sargent was a formal young man. 'But a policeman has to follow up complaints. You appreciate that?'

'I appreciate that.'

'I followed it up,' said the Inspector. 'Since I did not want to disturb the bereaved family unless it was absolutely necessary, I went to the only two men, outside the family, who were in a position to help me.'

He indicated Mr Petherbridge who was quivering and Dr Leland who seemed lost in a gloomy reverie.

'And from what I learned from these two gentlemen,' continued Inspector Sargent, almost sadly, 'I realized that Mr Moffat's complaint could not be dismissed without further investigation.'

The rat was back gnawing the floorboard. I asked: 'And Mr Moffat's complaint?'

'I think,' said Inspector Sargent, 'it would be better to have Mr Petherbridge and Dr Leland tell you first what they told me.'

'Please, Mr Friend, please realize how painful this is to me.' Mr Petherbridge had tumbled breathlessly into the conversation. 'I thought nothing about it, I assure you. It had almost passed from my mind until Inspector Sargent questioned me. But, on the day your poor father died, only a few hours, in fact, before Dr Leland was called in, your poor father telephoned to me. He seemed in a high state of excitement. He made an appointment for me to come around the next morning. He wanted, he said, to change his will. Of course, knowing your father, knowing his rather irascible nature and his constant ...'

Inspector Sargent broke in: 'Now, Dr Leland, maybe you'll tell Mr Friend what you told me.'

For the first time Dr Leland stopped looking gloomy and

showed a more controlled equivalent of Mr Petherbridge's embarrassment.

'It's like this, Friend,' he said. 'I'd been attending your father ever since he came to California. He'd been sick for some time. That was a bad heart he had. That first time when he had an attack and I put him to bed – well, I wouldn't have been surprised to hear any morning that he'd passed on during the night. Understand?'

I nodded, trying not to understand something which was looking a like a thunder cloud in my mind.

'Well, that evening your mother called me, I found Mr Friend in bad shape. His heart beat was rapid, irregular; he had difficulty in breathing; he was in a delirious condition. There were all the symptoms of a serious attack. I stayed with him for several hours, doing what I could. Then sudden cardiac failure supervened and he was dead in a few minutes.'

He paused, the heavy lids drooping over his eyes. 'Now, you're not a doctor, Friend. No point in going into medical details. The point is that on the face of it, there was every reason to suppose your father had had, in the natural course of events, another attack which proved fatal. Knowing his condition, I accepted that diagnosis. I signed the death certificate without the slightest suspicion that anything might be wrong – and I claim that any other doctor in my position would have done the same.'

He paused, once again. It was an ominous pause. 'But, after Inspector Sargent came to me and I started to think, some of the symptoms worried me. And then your father had been improving surprisingly during the few days that preceded his death. There was this, Friend, and that. And now' – he threw out his hands – 'I'm not saying I fell in with this thing the Inspector brought up. I'm not saying that at all. It's just that I am no longer secure in my diagnosis. I'm a big enough man to admit I might have been wrong. I have to admit the possibility that Mr Friend may have died from an overdose of the digitalis I prescribed for him.'

'You see, Mr Friend,' said Inspector Sargent very quietly.

'That is Mr Moffat's complaint. He came to my office yesterday and charged that it was his belief your father had been –
murdered.'

There it was – the noose.

'So you understand, Mr Friend,' the Inspector went on,
'how under the circumstances I am forced to take action on
Mr Moffat's complaint. I'm afraid before we can close the
case there will have to be an autopsy.' He produced a paper
from his pocket and put it down on the arm of his chair. 'I
have brought an exhumation order. It has to be signed by a
member of the family. I thought it would be less painful for
you to sign it than for your mother.'

I searched my mind for a loophole that was not there.
Trying to sound cynical, I said:

'And what if I tell you I think the charge is preposterous
and that I refuse to have my father dug up to satisfy the spite
of Mr Moffat?'

'I would advise you to sign, Mr Friend. After all, a refusal
to sign might indicate that you were uneasy about the results
of the autopsy.'

Inspector Sargent was watching me with steely intensity. I
stared back at him. It was not one of my better moments.

'My right arm's in a cast,' I said. 'It won't be much of a
signature.'

'Anything – a mark – will be sufficient with these two
gentlemen as witnesses.'

Inspector Sargent produced a fountain pen. He brought
the paper over and put it down on the broad arm of my
wheel chair, handing me the pen and indicating the line on
which I was to write. For the second time that day I scribbled
Gordon Renton Friend III with my left hand. Mr Petherbridge and Dr Leland signed too. The Inspector put the
document back in his pocket.

'I know you won't be feeling comfortable in your mind
until the autopsy is over with, Mr Friend. I'll do my best to
rush things through. I should be able to get you the result in
approximately twenty-four hours.'

Mr Petherbridge and Dr Leland had hurried to the door like two housedogs desperately wanting out.

Inspector Sargent shook my left hand and smiled his broad, unfathomable smile.

'Don't worry, Mr Friend. You're probably right. Mr Moffat probably just took a leap in the dark – a last wild gamble on getting that money. If I were you I wouldn't even mention this to the family. You'll only get them nervous. And it would be a shame to get them nervous, if no murder was committed, wouldn't it?'

'Yes,' I said.

He opened the door. Mr Petherbridge and Dr Leland shot out. Inspector Sargent followed.

He closed the door respectfully behind him.

Chapter 19

I PUSHED my wheel chair out into the corridor which was splashed with golden sunshine. The sun always seemed to be shining on the Friends' house. I longed for a thick black fog or a hurricane – anything to mar that gentle, sunny atmosphere of peace and good will.

I made my way into the living-room to find the Friend family alone and at its blandest. Selena had already changed her shapeless black dress for a gay Hawaiian swimming suit. She had freed her hair from the hideous ear coils and it hung loose to her shoulders, shimmering in the sunlight. Marny had changed too. She was curled up on one end of the couch, smoking avidly. Mrs Friend, still meek and widowish, sat at the window with her knitting and a box of chocolates on her broad lap.

They all glanced up casually when I entered. Mrs Friend smiled her maternal smile.

'Hello, dear. The Clean Living League's just finished its sunshine hour and bundled jollily off in its bus. Darling boy, I do think it was rather naughty of you not to come out and say goodbye to poor Mr Moffat. After all, he took his bitter pill with fairly good grace.' She paused, selecting a particularly juicy chocolate. 'By the way, dear, who was that nice-looking boy with Mr Petherbridge and Dr Leland? They scuttled away before I could speak to them.'

Mrs Friend's tranquillity had never seemed more unbearable. I said: 'That nice-looking boy with Mr Petherbridge and Dr Leland was a policeman.'

All three of them stared.

Mrs Friend, her voice carefully at ease, murmured: 'And what did he want?'

'He wanted Gordy Friend to sign an exhumation order.' I let them have it right between the eyes. 'He thinks old Mr Friend was murdered.'

Marny crushed her cigarette into an ashtray. Selena stood up. Even Mrs Friend's reaction was sufficiently strong to make her hand with the candy freeze in midair.

More than anything, I felt tired then.

'You don't have to worry,' I said. 'I played my part as Gordy Friend admirably.' I paused. 'You don't have to bother to look surprised, either.'

'Surprised?' Selena whipped around on me. 'What in heaven's name do you mean?'

'I suspected it from the start. Then I let the famous Friend charm make a sucker out of me again. You've always known Mr Friend was murdered. You've always known it would come out. That's why you imported me.'

'But ...' began Selena.

Mrs Friend flashed her a glance. She got up. She stood massively in front of me, her eyes straight on mine. 'Imported you – for what?'

'To take the rap, of course. Where's Gordy, by the way? I suppose you've hidden him away somewhere until the whole dirty business is over and I've been convicted.'

'You fool,' flared Selena.

'Yes, dear,' Mrs Friend's gaze was still fixing mine. 'If you think that, I'm afraid you are rather a fool.'

With a stately movement of her hand, she beckoned the two girls over. They came on either side of her. The three of them faced me.

Very slowly, Mrs Friend said: 'I know you have every reason not to trust my word. But I'm telling you this because it is true. None of us has the faintest knowledge of this incredible claim that has been made about my husband. None of us has the faintest idea where Gordy is. And you – you were imported, as you so quaintly put it, purely and simply for the reason we told you and for no other.' She paused. 'You believe me?'

'Does it matter whether I do or not?'

'It matters to me because I am fond of you.' She took Selena's hand. 'The girls are fond of you too. I do not want you to think we are – fiends.'

There was that word again.

'Perhaps,' continued Mrs Friend, still scrutinizing my face, 'you may believe me if I appeal to your reason. I know nothing about this murder charge and I am sure it is quite preposterous. But how in the name of reason, even if we wanted to, could we put the blame on you? It is conceivable that we might have been able to get away with it if we had convinced you you really were Gordy. But we have not convinced you. All you would have to tell the police was that you were an amnesia victim whom we had lured here after my husband's death and whom we had exploited in a conspiracy to get the money away from the Clean Living League. Once you'd claimed you weren't Gordy, the police would be able to get any amount of witnesses to prove you were right. The old servants here, for example, who knew the real Gordy. People from Pittsburg where Gordy worked. People from St Paul where Gordy grew up. My dear young man, you would be exonerated before you could say Aurora.'

She was smiling now, that incredibly serene smile of hers.

'As a matter of fact, instead of your being in our clutches, things are quite the reverse.' She had been holding her chocolate all this time. Now she put it in her mouth. She chewed on it. It must have been a nougat filling. 'It looks to me very much as if we were completely at your mercy.'

Mrs Friend, of course, had done it again. There was no flaw in her logic. As always, she had made me feel like an ass.

She was still smiling. So was Selena – radiantly with all the anger burnt out of her. Only Marny still looked wary and on guard.

'So, dear?' queried Mrs Friend.

I shrugged. 'Okay,' I said. 'I'm sorry.'

'That's all right, dear. I'm sure it was a most awkward situation with the policeman. No wonder you were a little rattled.' A vague gesture sent the girls back to their seats. Mrs Friend herself resumed her place on the davenport by the window. 'I hope we are all calm again. I have learned that one is much better off if one does not become excited.' As if to prove her point about the undesirability of getting excited, she picked up her knitting and started the needles going. 'Now dear, tell us quietly exactly what happened.'

I told her quietly exactly what happened. All three of them listened intently. When I had finished, Mrs Friend put down her knitting and smiled.

'You see, dear. How right I was? There's nothing to get excited about at all. It's all obviously a preposterous charge trumped up by Mr Moffat. Not a grain of truth in it. What a revolting man. I wish I hadn't been so pleasant to him. But at least there's one thing good. Whatever scruples I may have had about doing him out of the money have all been swept away – completely swept away.'

Her continued calm seemed now to border upon idiocy.

I said in exasperation: 'You're so goddam eager not to cry "Wolf", you'd look up into a pair of lathering jaws and murmur "Pretty Pussy".'

Mrs Friend laughed. 'What a cute phrase.'

'For God's sake stop being airy. Whether Mr Moffat's accusation is trumped up or not, there's a definite murder charge out against the Friend family – and the Friend family at the moment includes me. The least we can do is to be prepared for whatever happens. If you haven't got the sense to be serious, I'll handle it my own way.'

'Yes,' said Marny suddenly. 'You're right. Of course you're right.'

Selena nodded. 'I guess you are, baby, although the whole thing's utterly out of this world.'

'I'm sure, dear,' murmured Mrs Friend, 'that you will handle it admirably. Men always do these things so much better than women.' She looked up, the faintest trace of amusement in her eyes. 'All right, dear. What do you want us to begin with?'

'You can begin by telling me exactly what happened the day Mr Friend died.'

'Why, nothing happened, dear.'

'At least one thing happened, I know. He fired Jan. Why?'

Mrs Friend blinked. 'I haven't the slightest idea. My husband was rather like the Queen of Hearts. He often had his Off-With-His-Head moods. Probably Jan didn't look jolly enough that morning.'

I glanced at the girls. 'Either of you know?'

Marny was watching Selena. Selena shrugged.

'No, baby. I'd even forgotten that he was fired.' Her glance met Marny's. 'But it's easy enough to find out. Ask him.'

'Yes,' said Mrs Friend, 'if you really want to know – ask him. Marny, dear, run and find him.'

Marny pushed herself off the couch and went out of the room. I had already asked Jan why he was fired and had got nowhere. I wasn't very hopeful, unless the Friends had a better system of communication than I. Soon Marny came back with the Dutchman. He was still in his respectable seersucker suit with his blond hair plastered down.

'You ask him,' I said to Mrs Friend.

She put the question very slowly. Jan seemed to understand it as he had with me. And, as he had done with me, he broke into a gale of laughter. The three women continued to ply him with questions. He reacted with a succession of

158

gestures which were meaningless to me. But Mrs Friend seemed to grasp their significance. She nodded him away. After he'd left, she turned to me.

'Well, that's that.'

'You understood him?'

'Of course, dear. But it doesn't help much. Jan doesn't know why he was fired.'

'He doesn't know?'

'That was what he was trying to convey. And it's reasonable enough. My husband called him in, bawled him out and fired him. Jan didn't understand what it was all about. He just accepted the situation. Jan's always accepting situations and laughing. Really, he is tiresome. You'd think he could bother to learn just a few words of English, wouldn't you?' She blinked again with faint decision. 'Where does the investigation go from here?'

'When Mr Friend died, did he have a nurse?'

Mrs Friend shook her head. 'He'd had one, of course, when he was seriously sick. But he had improved so much that we'd sent her away several days before.'

'Then who took care of him?'

'All of us, dear. Jan fixed him up. The girls and I saw that he got his medicine. None of us sat with him very much, I'm afraid.' She sighed. 'You'd understand that better if you knew Father. He wasn't a very amiable patient.'

'And his medicine was – digitalis?'

Mrs Friend shrugged. 'I really don't know, dear. It was something in drops. So many drops. You mixed it with water.'

'It was digitalis,' said Marny. 'You know perfectly well it was, Mimsey.'

'I forget the difficult names, dear.' Mrs Friend gazed at me. 'Anything else?'

'Who gave Mr Friend his medicine that day?'

'I believe I gave it to him in the morning. He had it twice a day.'

'Who gave it to him in the evening?'

Mrs Friend glanced at Selena. 'Wasn't it you, dear?'

'No,' said Marny, 'it was me. At least I was going to give it to him.'

I echoed: 'Going to give it to him?'

Marny nodded. She looked pale, uneasy – far more aware of the potential danger than Selena and Mrs Friend.

'I went into his room just after dinner. That was when he always took his second lot of medicine. Since he'd fired Jan, one of the maids had brought him his dinner and taken it away. He was in a frightful temper, I supposed the maid had spilt tomato juice on the sheet or something. I offered to give him his medicine but he shouted at me to go away and send Gordy to him.'

'Gordy?'

She nodded. 'I went up to his room. He was pretty tight. I got him some Lavoris, tried to make him as presentable as I could and sent him down to Father.'

'Did your Father say what he wanted Gordy for?'

'No. But whenever he was in a bad temper he always wanted Gordy. He always hoped he'd catch Gordy drunk and have a legitimate excuse for a speech about Satan. I didn't think anything about it.'

'And it was after he'd seen his father that you met him in the hall and he said he was fed up and going to Los Angeles?'

'Matter of fact it was.'

'Did you ask him what had happened?'

'No. I just said: "Is he acting up as usual?" and Gordy tossed out a string of obscenities and went off to the garage.'

'And you?'

'I went back to father to give him his medicine.'

'Did you give it to him?'

'No, Selena was there.'

I turned to Selena. 'That's right?'

'Yes, baby. I was there when Marny came in.'

'And you'd given Mr Friend the medicine?'

She stretched for a cigarette and lit it. 'No, darling, I asked if he wanted it and he said he'd had it.'

I felt a shiver of uneasiness. 'So Gordy'd given it to him?'

'I suppose so.'

I turned back to Marny. 'When was all this?'

'About eight-thirty. It began at eight-thirty and ended somewhere around nine.'

'And your father seemed all right when you and Selena were with him after Gordy'd left?'

'Yes. We didn't stay more than a couple of minutes though.'

I turned to Mrs Friend. 'And when did you discover he was having an attack and send for Dr Leland?'

'Let me see. It must have been around ten-thirty, I'd say. Yes. He usually went to sleep around eleven. I just looked in to see if he wanted anything and – found him.'

It all fitted, of course. I didn't quite know what I was feeling.

'Mr Petherbridge said your father called him and told him he was going to change his will a couple of hours before you called Dr Leland. That means he must have called while Gordy was in the room with him.'

I looked down at my hands and then up quickly. 'See what I mean? Mr Friend was in a bad temper. He called for Gordy. Gordy was drunk. Mr Friend obviously bawled him out. Then Mr Friend called Mr Petherbridge and said he was going to change his will.'

My gaze settled on Mrs Friend. 'Try and laugh that off. Mr Friend threatens to cut Gordy out of his will once and for all. Mr Friend then asks for his medicine. Everyone knows that an overdose of digitalis would be fatal to a man with a bad heart. Gordy leaves the house right away. He says he's going to Los Angeles. He's never seen again.'

I paused, still fixing Mrs Friend with my gaze.

'What's the betting that Gordy never went off on a bat? What's the betting he murdered his father, got cold feet and made a getaway to Mexico?'

I felt dejected and terribly tired.

'If the autopsy shows poisoning, there isn't a policeman in the world who couldn't pin the crime on Gordy Friend in twenty minutes.'

I laughed hollowly. 'And to Inspector Sargent, I'm Gordy Friend. I signed the abstinence pledge. I signed the exhumation order. Even if you didn't plan it that way, it amounts to the same thing.'

I paused. 'I suppose I should be calm about that. After all, one is better off if one does not become excited, is not one?'

Chapter 20

MRS FRIEND'S swift fits of anger always took me by surprise. One came upon her then. She stared at me, her handsome face flushed.

'Really, to accuse my own son of murder – under my own roof. And you – you who haven't even met him.'

'It's not my fault I'm under your own roof,' I said. 'And I'd be delighted if I'd never heard of your own son. But since I happen to be understudying for him at the moment, thanks to you, I at least have the right to speculate as to what he may or may not have done.'

Marny gave a short, humourless laugh. Selena crossed and sat down on the sofa next to Mrs Friend, patting her shoulder. 'Mimsey, darling, don't be stuffy. He's right. We've got to be ready. I don't think Father was murdered any more than you do. But if he was, they're bound to say it was one of us. I certainly didn't murder him. Did you?'

Mrs Friend freed her shoulder with a pettish shrug. 'Don't be silly, Selena.'

Selena glanced at Marny. 'Did you?'

'Sure,' drawled Marny, 'if it makes Mimsey feel any better.'

'You see, Mimsey?' Selena shook back her hair and watched Mrs Friend serenely. 'Who else could it have been but Gordy? After all, he's the one who had the opportunity. And the motive, probably. Of course, I think Gordy's a lamb just the way you do. But, if he'd been off on an ordinary bat, he'd surely have been back by now. And – well, I mean you never can tell what people may do when they're ... What's the polite word for stinking? I never can remember.'

Mrs Friend had become all mother. 'I know,' she said, 'that my Gordy would never deliberately ...'

'Maybe it wasn't deliberate,' suggested Selena. 'Maybe Father asked for his medicine. Gordy was drunk. He didn't count the drops properly. He gave him an overdose by mistake. Then he realized it and got scared and ran away. Gordy always runs away from things.' She turned to me hopefully.

'Maybe,' I said. It was just possible.

Selena laughed almost gaily as if everything had been solved and there was nothing more to worry about.

'There,' she said.

'So we all live happily ever after.' Marny was watching Selena through cigarette smoke, her eyes dark and derisive. 'Since you're so bright, what are we going to do with this poor guy here? We've stuck him with being Gordy. What do we do next? Do what he accused us of doing? Stick him with a murder he didn't commit?'

Selena smiled back sweetly. 'But, of course, dear.'

I stared.

Selena left the couch and, crossing to me, dropped on the carpet at my feet and put her hands on my lap. She smiled up at me radiantly.

'Darling, it's perfectly obvious what we have to do. If you let the policeman know you're not really Gordy Friend now, we'll lose whatever chance we have of getting the money from that repulsive Mr Moffat and we'll all get into the most terrible trouble. I mean, the things we've done, they're frightfully illegal, aren't they? So you'll simply have to go on being Gordy. And then, if the autopsy results are sinister, we'll have to tell the truth and the policeman's bound to suspect you. So you just come out frankly and say that you were drunk and maybe you did give Father an overdose by mistake and ...' she shrugged vaguely ' ... And, well, that isn't something so awful to have done, is it? I mean, they'll understand it was just a mistake.'

'And forgive me with kisses and little crooning sounds of sympathy?'

'Well, won't they, darling? Besides, we'll be frightfully rich. We can give them all big fat cheques and new automobiles and things if need be.'

I could never tell with Selena whether her incredible naïveté was a pose or not.

'I'm sorry,' I said. 'I'm afraid I don't love the Friends quite enough to serve a ten-year manslaughter sentence for them.'

Selena's eyes clouded. 'Is that what they'd do to you?'

'I'd be lucky to get away with ten years.'

She caressed my knee meditatively. 'I'd hate that, I'd simply hate that.' She sighed. 'Then we'll have to think of something else. What shall we think of, baby?'

Dimly, in spite of the grimness of the situation, I realized that the touch of her fingers on my knee was still as exciting as ever. Not that it mattered. Things were far too bad for me to let her make a sucker out of me any more. I knew exactly what I was going to make them 'think of' anyway.

'If the autopsy report's okay,' I said, 'I'll stay on and see this through. If it isn't okay, there's only one thing you can do.'

Selena looked interested. 'What's that?'

'Get me out of here – fast.'

'Get you out?'

'If you know what's good for you.' There was a certain pleasure in being tough with the Friends at last. 'I may not know who I am but I know I'm no sacrificial lamb. If Inspector Sargent thinks Gordy killed your father and starts arresting me as Gordy, I'll come clean with the whole story. Of course it'll put me in a spot but at least I won't be a candidate for the electric chair.'

Selena's eyes widened. 'But what about us? I mean, if you tell, we'd be charged with conspiracy and heaven knows what.'

'That's why I said you'd better get me out of here fast.'

'But ...'

'It's not an ideal solution but there isn't an ideal solution for the sort of jams the Friends think up. You'll have to hide me somewhere where the police won't find me. Then you'll have to put them onto the trail of the real Gordy. Let them find him. And when they have – the rest is up to you.'

Selena said: 'But Inspector Sargent's seen you. If he found Gordy, he'd know he was someone different from the Gordy who'd signed the abstinence pledge.'

'He's only seen me wrapped in bandages. Gordy and I look reasonably alike.' I grinned. 'You and your mother-in-law could convince Einstein the world's flat. Between you, you could certainly persuade the Inspector he had a little eye trouble.'

Selena pouted. 'Really, baby, I think you're being rather selfish.'

'Selfish. For God's sake, haven't I done enough for the Friend family already?'

Marny had been watching us for some time. Suddenly she laughed. 'So you're getting rugged with her at last. I didn't think you had it in you.'

Selena said: 'Shut up, Marny.'

'He's the one you've got to shut up now.' Marny crossed and perched herself affectionately on the arm of my wheel chair. 'I adore this. The worm's finally turned. Keep it up. You're the boss now. Tell them what to do. They'll have to do it.'

I grinned up at her. When I needed her, Marny was always there. 'Know any place you could hide me – till the casts come off?'

'Sure.' Marny glanced down at Selena. 'Selena's passionate doctor has a cabin way up on the mountains. Once we got you there, no one'd find you for weeks.'

'Once you got me there – exactly,' I said. 'A cripple with a couple of broken limbs can't travel under his own steam.'

'That's easy too. We'll have Jan drive you up. In fact, you can keep him to take care of you. You can trust him. If you asked him to bury a body, he'd do it and forget it five minutes afterwards. And if the policeman asks where he is, we can say we've fired him. We still have a right to fire our servants.'

She swung round to face the others. 'Any complaints?'

To my surprise, both Selena and Mrs Friend seemed pleased. Selena said: 'I think that's really rather divinely clever when you think of it.'

Mrs Friend, completely calm again, murmured: 'Yes, dear, all things considered it is the most sensible plan from everyone's point of view.' She smiled at me. 'You'll wait for the autopsy report, of course, dear? If you ran away before you really needed to – I mean before Inspector Sargent was obviously planning to arrest you – you'd make us all seem unnecessarily suspicious.'

'Sure,' I said. 'I'll wait till Sargent's report comes in. But you'd better start getting plans set.'

'Selena will ask Nate. I'm sure he'll understand.' Mrs Friend seemed to have adopted Marny's plan as her own. 'How pleasant to have things settled. Not, of course, that I am worried, because I am sure this entire murder theory is just a figment in the mind of Mr Moffat, that weevil-like borer.' She glanced at her watch. 'Good heavens, it is past time for lunch. I wonder what is keeping them in the kitchen.'

She rose. 'I must investigate. And, Marny, do go and see Grandma. She gets so peevish when's she hungry. Oh dear, do you suppose we'll have to explain all this to Grandma? It's really rather complicated for her, isn't it? But then, since she seems to take to criminality like a duck to water ...'

Her voice trailed off as she moved out of the room. Marny murmured: 'Oh, all right' and hurried out to cope with Grandma.

Selena and I were alone.

She still sat at my feet, letting her hand rove caressingly over my knee. Suddenly she looked up with a grimace.

'Darling, was I hateful just now? I mean, suggesting you stayed and took the blame. You're not still suspicious of us, are you? It wasn't anything. It was just an idea.'

'Not one of your better ones.'

'Baby,' she sighed. 'Isn't this dreary?'

'That's one word for it.'

'I do hope you don't have to go off and hide in that cabin of Nate's. Jan used to drive me up there sometimes for guilty assignations with Nate. It was meant to be romantic. It's incredibly dismal – all trees and views.' Her hand moved to my arm. 'Darling, wouldn't you be awfully bored up there with only Jan and no memory? Wouldn't it be nicer if I came too?'

I smiled at her. 'For a smart girl you're almost feeble-minded, aren't you?'

'Am I, baby?' She laughed. 'I suppose I am.' Her face, warm and heady as a summer afternoon, was suddenly close to mine. 'But, darling, all those things I said last night I meant.'

'What things?'

'About how you excite me. About touching you. It's true. This is different from anything else. I think about you when you're not there. It doesn't matter who murdered who or ... Baby.'

Her lips were torridly on mine. She squirmed up so that she was half sitting on my knees. Her arms weaved around me. I pulled her closer. Her fair, tumbling hair tickled my eyelids. Through the hair I saw something moving in the room. I pushed her hair back, still kissing her.

Dr Nate Croft was standing in the doorway.

He stood very stiffly, staring at us, his eyes blazing in a cold, stricken face.

'Selena!'

Selena twisted away from me, stood up and saw him. She pushed her hair back behind her shoulders and smiled at him cheerfully.

'Hello, Nate, dear.'

Most men, feeling the way he obviously felt, would have done something violent. Dr Croft, apparently, was not the violent type. He dropped into a chair, as if his legs had suddenly melted.

In a pinched voice, he said: 'Does it have to be every man, Selena?'

'What do you mean?' She stared, open-eyed. 'Really, aren't you being rather complicated?'

He looked up, his face haggard and exhausted. That's what happens when you love Selena, I thought.

'This time I thought it'd be safe. I put on the casts. I ... Oh, what difference does it make?'

'Darling, please. So stuffy.'

'Stuffy?' Anger and a sort of weary hopelessness made his voice shake. 'I gambled everything helping you because you said you loved me. Remember? You said you'd divorce Gordy and marry me because you loved me.' A laugh forced its way between his pale lips. 'You'll never marry me, will you?'

Selena moved to him, caressing his arm. 'Darling, it's so silly thinking about things in the future.'

'And if you do, it'll still be every man that comes in sight.' His eyes met mine for the first time. 'It's wonderful. I recommend it. Try it sometime – if you haven't already. Try falling in love with a tramp.'

'Nate!'

He swung round to her. 'That's the word for you, isn't it?'

Selena laughed her deep, full-bosomed laugh. 'It'll do, baby, but I think you could have thought out a nicer one.' She kissed him perfunctorily on the ear. 'Darling, you make such a fuss always. So suspicious. I was only kissing him because he's going away.'

Nate stiffened. 'Going away?'

'Yes, honey. The most exasperating thing's happened. You might as well hear it now and get it over with. The reciting of the poem and everything went wonderfully. We thought we had everything in the bag. Then that dreary Mr Moffat ...'

She told him, with a bald callousness that shocked me, exactly what the dreary Mr Moffat had done. Without giving him a moment to catch his breath, she went on with my theory about Gordy and the plan for getting me out of the house if the autopsy report was bad.

I'd been sorry enough for Nate before. I was almost too sorry for him as I saw his face crumple and his lips start to quiver. I'd taken a lot from the Friends but I had nothing much to lose. Nate had everything to lose. His hopeless desire to make a monogamous wife out of Selena had already lured him into gambling his entire career. Now he was faced with the possibility of exposure as an accomplice in a murder charge. A connexion, however faint, with murder spelled the end of a doctor's existence.

'So you see, baby?' Selena concluded, almost absent-mindedly. 'If the police are objectionable tomorrow, we'll somehow have Jan smuggle him out of the house and up to your cabin. That'll be all right, won't it? I mean, you don't mind his using it?'

'But, Selena,' he stammered, 'if the police find him hiding out in *my* cabin ...'

'And, later, after a few days, when it's time for the casts to come off, you can just run up there and do it for him. Then he'll have to be on his own.'

She slid her arms around him and nestled against him, her lips close to his.

'I know you'll be a darling about it, won't you?'

'Selena ...'

'And you mustn't be selfish, baby.' She caressed his ear. 'After all, you got him into this jam. The least you can do is to help him out of it.'

Mrs Friend came in then. She smiled at me and then at Nate.

'Hello, Nate, dear. Just in time for lunch. How nice.'

'Lunch,' he echoed bleakly. 'How can you talk about lunch when Mr Friend ...'

Mrs Friend lifted her hand. 'Now, dear, I've made the others promise not to talk about it any more. If things should go wrong tomorrow, we have our plans. There's no point in harping upon unpleasantness.'

She crossed to my chair and started to wheel me towards the dining-room. She was humming some vague little tune.

'The only thing now's to be patient until the Inspector comes tomorrow. I'm so glad Nate came to lunch. Cook's thought out a really rather daring aspic....'

Chapter 21

WE ate the rather daring aspic and settled down to be patient. Our plan, unsatisfactory as it was in almost every way, at least had the virtue of simplicity. Nate admitted his mountain cabin was stocked with canned foods. We decided that if the autopsy report indicated murder tomorrow afternoon, we would somehow stall the police from any serious investigation until the next day. As soon after nightfall as was safe, Jan was to smuggle me out of the house to Nate's cabin by way of a disused track which wound from the rear of the Friend house over the desolate, uninhabited mountains. Jan had to be rehearsed in his role. That was all.

Marny and I decided to do it between us. She wheeled me down the corridor past her own room and Mimsey's to the Dutchman's quarters. Then we entered in answer to his call. We found him scrambling off his bed, tying the cord of a blue towel bathrobe around his waist. With the departure of the Clean Living League, he had obviously reverted to his customary nudism.

He grinned at Marny, stared inquiringly at me and tossed the blond hair back from his eyes.

Marny said: 'He understands me if I talk slowly. Let me handle this.'

She put her hand on his huge arm. 'Jan, tomorrow you take him' – she indicated me – 'in car. Okay?'

He nodded, still grinning.

'You take him to mountains – place in mountains where you took Selena. Remember?'

He nodded again.

'When you get there, stay with him all the time. Stay with him.'

The blond lock flopped down again as he nodded.

'And don't tell anyone. Don't say anything. Never, never tell.'

His big bronze hand moved over hers, enveloping it completely.

'Ja,' he said. 'Ja.'

Marny glanced at me. 'He's got it,' she said. 'I'm quite sure.'

'There's only one place in the mountains where he took Selena?'

'Yes. Only Nate's cabin. He drove her up there twice.'

'Okay.'

'Oh, wait a minute.' She turned back to Jan. 'When you drive to mountains – don't go out front drive. Go back way.'

His face clouded.

'Back way. The way behind the house. The old track.'

Jan still frowned his incomprehension.

'Here.' Marny picked up a pencil, found a piece of paper and drew a rough sketch of the house indicating the front drive and the winding track at the back. She showed it to him.

'Not the front way,' she pointed. 'The back way. Go the back way.' She pointed again. 'The way Gordy used to take. Gordy's way.'

Understanding smoothed the wrinkles out of his tanned forehead. He took the pencil from Marny and drew a cross half-way down the back path. He looked at her questioningly.

Marny stared at the cross. 'No, Jan. Not there. Just the back way. Gordy's way. Take the car and ...' She pushed the pencil along the track and then right off the paper, indicating he was to drive me straight off the property. 'To the mountains. To Selena's place. Understand?'

He understood then. It was obvious. He was grinning all over his face, pleased with himself. He was still grinning when Marny and I left.

It was nice to know that someone could find amusement in the situation somewhere.

After our visit with Jan there was nothing left to do but to wait. We spent the rest of the day waiting and, in spite of Mrs Friend's determination to look on the bright side, the hours passed with increasing gloom. The shadow of Gordy as a murderer or at least as a probable murderer hung over me like a pall. Nate had to go back to his sanatorium fairly early. The three Friend women and I managed to get through dinner and an evening of desultory card-playing. But I couldn't keep my mind on four-handed gin-rummy. I saw so many pitfalls ahead, so many things that might happen to make a hash of my very makeshift plans.

Although the Friends were going to try to put the Inspector onto the track of the real Gordy, I was the Gordy he knew and it would be my trail from the house that he would follow first. Sargent would soon know, if he didn't already, that Nate was a friend of the family. If he also discovered he owned the cabin in the mountains, it would be one of the first places he'd search. My plan was really no plan at all. It was merely ignominious flight from a predicament that was impossible to face. And my only real hope for saving my own skin and, incidentally, the Friends, was to remain hidden until the casts were off and then re-establish myself under my own real identity.

But that meant getting my memory back. That's what it would all rest on. My memory.

I looked across the card-table at Selena who was my opponent. Her fair head was bent over her cards; her skin was soft and tanned to the colour of brown sugar. Absurdly, although she had made a wreck of Nate Croft and even now, I was sure, would deliver me as a fall guy to the police without batting an eye if she could get away with it, I knew I was going to miss her. Even an amnesiac knows that Selenas don't happen often.

She caught my eye and grinned.

'I'm ready for bed. I don't know about anyone else.'

Mrs Friend, playing Marny, discarded a card and then picked it up again with a little cluck and discarded another in its place. 'Selena, dear, are you still going to sleep in the same room with this darling boy? It seems rather odd and I don't know that Nate likes it.'

Selena laughed. 'Of course I'm going to, Mimsey. After all, he's so helpless. Even if you did walk out on him, he still needs a nurse.' She turned to me. 'Don't you, baby?'

'Yes,' I said.

'And I'll read you some more of Father's poems to send you to sleep. There's a wonderful one against sex. You'd like to hear that, wouldn't you?'

'Yes,' I said.

Marny shot me a sardonic glance. Mrs Friend said: 'Well, I suppose it doesn't really matter in the long run. Oh, dear, I didn't mean to throw away that jack of clubs. How foolish. It would have made a lovely sequence.'

In spite of the loss of the jack of clubs, Mrs Friend still managed to collect a lovely sequence and ginned, finishing the game. She had won handsomely from all of us. I didn't own any money so I couldn't pay her. But she insisted upon collecting from the girls. Selena went off for her purse, telling me to bring the book of poems when I came. Marny picked up the grey volume of verse and opened it at random.

In a deep, booming voice she recited:

'"Sex, sex, sex
Where the hussy solicits for hire.
Sex, sex, sex
Drags the flower of your youth in the mire...."'

'Oh, god, what a filthy mind Father had.' She tossed the book down on the piano, sending the framed photograph of old Mr Friend lurching over onto its face.

Mrs Friend called: 'Marny, really.'

'Well, he had.' Marny stared at her mother. 'How much do I owe you?'

'Three dollars and seventy-five cents, dear.'

'Okay. I'll get it or I'll never hear the end of it.'

Marny hurried out of the room. Mrs Friend gave me a little rueful smile.

'It's the principle, you know. I've always tried to make the girls realize that a debt is something that must be paid.' She sighed. 'Sometimes I wonder if I'm butting my head against a wall. Excuse me, dear. If I don't watch them, they'll probably just take the money out of my own purse and give it back to me.'

She moved out of the room in pursuit of the girls, absently patting the stray hairs of her upsweep.

It was nice to know that Mrs Friend was instilling a sense of morality into her daughter and daughter-in-law. She should have worked on her son too.

I was very jittery at the prospect of tomorrow. I thought it might be steadying to have Selena read me Mr Friend's atrocious poem. I wheeled myself to the piano and picked the book up. Automatically I restored Mr Friend's picture to its original position. As I did so, the back of the frame, which must have been dislodged by the fall, dropped off and a white envelope slipped out from the space between the frame and the back of the photograph. I picked it up. Typewritten across its front was the word:

Mimsey.

The envelope was unstuck and I saw there was a sheet of paper inside. It wasn't a letter that had come through the mail. Someone in the house must have written it and, for some reason, concealed it in the back of the photograph.

Because I was innately suspicious of everything in the Friend house, I started to take out the sheet of paper. I heard footsteps approaching from the hall. Quickly, I slipped the envelope into the pocket of my seersucker jacket, put the back on the photograph, set it up in its original position and wheeled myself away from the piano.

Mrs Friend came in, clutching dollar bills and change in one hand.

'I got it,' she said triumphantly. 'I sent the girls on up to bed, dear. Shall I wheel you to your room or can you manage by yourself?'

'I can manage myself.'

She moved to my side, smiled at me and picked up my hand in hers.

'You know, dear, I've grown most fond of you. You're almost like my own son.'

'I hope I don't behave like him.'

Her brow puckered. 'Really, I do wish you'd take my word for it, dear. I know there is nothing in Mr Moffat's scurrilous suggestion. Nothing at all. I am glad we have made plans but there is no cause for worry.' She glanced ruefully at the photograph of her husband on the piano. 'He was rather sweet when he was a boy, you know. He had the most divine moustache ... like a young disarming seal ... I shall never forget the night he asked me to marry him. He got down on his knees and then he stretched up somehow and kissed me. The moustache tickled fascinatingly. I'd never been kissed by a lovely big moustache before. Really, I think that's why I married him.'

'Which proves,' I said, 'that he couldn't have been murdered?'

'You!' Mrs Friend slapped archly at my hand. 'It's being cooped up in that wheel chair that makes you so gloomy. I've just remembered. Last year my husband sprained his ankle and he bought the most pretentious pair of crutches. They're put away somewhere in the store-closet off the library. Tomorrow we'll get them out and we'll see if you can't lumber about with one. Won't that be nice?'

She leaned over and kissed me, bringing her heavy, expensive perfume very close.

'You trust me now, don't you?'

I grinned. 'Do I?'

'A very sweet boy,' she said. 'We'll remember you a long time.'

She moved majestically out of the room, still clutching her dollars and cents.

She was right about remembering me a long time. We'd all of us remember each other until we died either in our beds or in the electric chair.

I wheeled myself to the grey and gold bedroom. A sound of hissing water from the bathroom told me that Selena was having a shower. I threw the book of poems on her bed and then, manoeuvring the chair across to my own bed, I pulled the envelope out of my pocket. I knew it must be important. People don't hide notes in the backs of photographs for the sheer whimsey of it. Uneasily I pulled out a single sheet of paper. I unfolded it. I was confronted with a typewritten note.

It said:

Dear Mother: I've thought this out and I've decided there's no use waiting for the autopsy report. It's all going to come out then so why prolong the misery? I thought about running away but how can I? There's only way one out. Please believe me I didn't plan ahead to kill Father. It was only after he bawled me out and called Mr Petherbridge and said he was going to cut me out of the will that the idea came. He even asked for his medicine. It was so easy just to pour half the bottle in. He didn't notice. And then when Dr Leland signed the death certificate I thought I'd got away with it. But I haven't, of course. I never get away with anything. Well, this is it, I guess. I hope you get the money. I think you should. Weather you believe it or not, I did it a bit for you just to make life less impossible for you. Anyhow, good-bye. And don't worry about me. The way I've figured out won't be painful.

The hairs at the back of my neck had started to crawl. Dizzily I glanced at the signature which had been written in pencil, clumsily, the way a right-handed person would sign with his left hand.

It was signed: *Gordy*.

For a few seconds, when I first started to read that diabolic communication, I had thought it was a genuine suicide note from the person who had murdered Mr Friend. I didn't think it for long, of course. With a shiver of horror, the truth overwhelmed me. This note, announcing that the murderer of Mr Friend was preparing to commit suicide, was signed *Gordy* – but it wasn't meant for the real Gordy, the Gordy who had disappeared on the night of the death and had never been heard from again.

It was meant for the false Gordy.

It was a letter to Mrs Friend from *me*, telling her that *I* was going to kill myself.

As I stared blankly, one word kept me hypnotized, one misspelled, tell-tale word.

Weather.

There was, there could be, no doubt as to who had written that note.

I saw then how appallingly right my suspicions had been. While I was still lying unconscious in Nate's sanatorium, the Friends must already have had this destiny prepared for me. They had needed me to trick the Clean Living League and Mr Petherbridge, yes. But that *had* been only the prologue to their plan. They had known that suspicion of Mr Friend's murder would leak out. They *had* known they would need a victim. That had always been the role intended for me. Once again that evening, with a brilliant half truth, Mrs Friend had deceived me. She had made the 'victim' theory sound ludicrous by pointing out how easily I could explain myself away once the police arrested me. But the police had never been intended to arrest me. Before they arrived tomorrow, I was supposed to have committed suicide.

I saw now why Mrs Friend and Selena had fallen in so readily with my and Marny's feeble scheme for hiding me in Nate's cabin. All they cared about was keeping me satisfied at the moment, because they knew I would be dead before any plan could be put into execution.

I had been given the double, the triple, the quadruple cross.

Marny had always been right. There was only one word for the Friends.

They were fiends.

For it was surely *They*. Selena had written the note. The '*weather*' had told me that. But that didn't mean she was in it alone. I could see Mrs Friend finding the note while Inspector Sargent bent over my dead body. I could see her so

177

clearly reading it with dewy eyes and trembling lips, murmuring: 'The poor boy, the poor darling boy.'

The note said I wasn't going to wait for the autopsy report to come in. That meant I was going to kill myself earlier – probably tonight.

The way I've figured out won't be painful.

They had their plan for killing me figured out too. How, when I didn't know what it was, could I combat it?

I sat there in the wheel chair, hideously conscious of the immobilizing cast on my leg.

I was frightened then – really frightened.

Suddenly I became conscious that the sound of the shower in the bathroom had stopped some time before. I put the note in the envelope and slipped it into the pocket of my seersucker suit.

Something Marny had said the day before came back. *'Someday you'll discover what Selena's up to and you'll come screaming to me.'*

Marny....

The bathroom door opened. Selena came out. She had twisted a scarlet towel around her like a toga. One golden shoulder was bare. Her fair hair was piled on top of her head. She looked magnificent as a Roman Empress.

'Hello, baby.' She smiled dazzlingly. 'Here comes your pseudo-wife.'

She wasn't my pseudo-wife, I thought.

She was my executioner.

Chapter 22

SELENA moved into the soft pool of light from the lamp between the beds. She lit two cigarettes from her platinum case and, lolling across my bed, put one of the cigarettes between my lips.

'There.'

For a moment she lay on her back, stretched voluptuously

across the silver and gold spread, smiling up at me. The scarlet towel was the same scarlet as her mouth.

'Our last night.'

She got up then and, tucking her bare legs under her, sat on the edge of the bed, close to my chair. Her soft lips brushed my ear.

'I'd better call Jan and have him put you to bed. I can't get at you in that chair.'

Once I was out of the wheel chair and in bed I was trapped. I smiled back at her. 'Not yet, baby. Sitting up I feel more masculine.'

'You!' She slipped into my lap, twining her arms around my neck. She smelled faintly of bath salts and warm towel. 'Is this hideously uncomfortable?'

'No.'

'Doesn't hurt your bad leg?'

'No.'

She was stroking my cheek.

Risking it, I said: 'Where do you suppose Gordy really is?'

'Oh, Gordy. Don't talk about that dreary Gordy. Who cares?' She was staring into my eyes, her finger tracing the line of my nose. 'Wasn't Nate childish tonight?'

'Was he?'

'I mean making all that fuss. Being so stuffy. Baby?'

'Yes.'

'You're not mad that I kissed him, are you? After all, we do need him, don't we? I had to be nice to him.'

'I don't mind your kissing Nate.'

She pouted. 'I wish you did. I want you to be jealous. I want you to be jealous if any man touches me. Darling, be jealous.'

Her lips slid over my cheek to my mouth and clung to it passionately. Through the glamour of her, I was thinking: *Is this the beginning? Is this the build-up to the 'way that won't be painful?'* I thought of Marny too – Marny lying cool and young in her bed in the other wing, Marny who'd said: *They're fiends.*

'Darling,' Selena's mouth was at my ear now. 'When this is all over, you'll send for me, won't you? You'll write.

You'll tell me where you are. You promised. Didn't you promise?'

'Sure, Selena.'

'Oh, I know you think I'm stupid. You think I'm feeble-minded, don't you? You said so. You'll probably bully me, tread on me. But please say yes.'

'I've said yes.'

'Darling.'

I put my hand around the nape of her neck and drew her head back so that we were looking into each other's eyes.

I said: 'Know your trouble, baby? You're in love with me.'

'Yes, yes. I am. I really think I am.'

Incredibly, as she stared at me, tears glistened on her thick lashes. Her enchantment was as intoxicating as vodka. I wondered how I would be feeling if I'd believed her. She grimaced suddenly.

'God, what a fool I am. I want a drink. I'll get you one too.'

She slid off my lap and hurried out of the room. I felt curiously hollow and shaky. Was it to be this way? With a drink? The old, simple way of the poisoned drink? I wished I was steadier. But it wasn't a situation to inspire steadiness – knowing that a woman you almost loved was planning to murder you.

I was becoming obsessed with the thought of Marny. I needed more than my wits now. I needed an ally. Could I trust Marny? She was a Friend too. But who else was there to trust? I thought of her dark, sardonic eyes. That made me feel a little better.

But a meeting with Marny would have to be clandestine. Selena would not have to know. The tray of medicine, a relic from the days when Mrs Friend posed as a nurse, still stood on the table by my bed. I saw the little phial of red sleeping capsules. I picked it up, took two capsules out and put the phial back. With difficulty I managed with the fingers of my left hand to open the capsules and pour the white powder inside into my palm. I eased the empty capsules into the pocket of my jacket.

Selena came in with the drinks.

I noticed, with satisfaction, that they were straight jiggers of whisky. She crossed to me, smiling. She put one drink down on the table and held the other out to me.

'Drink, baby.'

'Not yet.'

'Why?'

I patted my knee with my cupped hand. 'Get back where you belong first.'

She gave a husky laugh. She put my drink down on the table six inches from hers. She slipped onto my lap. I kept my left arm behind her, my hand swinging free, close to the drinks. Her back was turned to the table. She couldn't see.

She leaned her cheek against mine. The soft, slithery hair was brushing my ear. I emptied the powder into my drink. I swirled it around with my finger. I switched my drink with hers. It couldn't have been easier.

'Darling,' she murmured, 'it'll be so wonderful to get away from here. I hate the Friends really. I've always hated them.' Her hand came up to stroke my hair. 'I only married Gordy because I was broke and I thought he was rich. Such a nasty, sodden man really. And Marny's a little scheming, furtive rat. And Mrs Friend! She's a phony for you, darling. A great fat blousy phony.' She nestled even closer. 'Oh, baby, to get rid of the Friends.'

'Let's drink to that,' I said. 'To get rid of the Friends.'

She laughed and, twisting around, picked up the two drinks. She handed me the one she thought was mine. We raised our glasses. Her dark red lips were parted affectionately. I thought: *If there was poison in that drink, I'm a murderer.*

'Down the hatch,' I said. My voice sounded strange and harsh.

She tilted the glass to her lips and swallowed. So did I.

'Brr, that was strong.' She grimaced and, taking the two empty glasses, put them down on the table. As she eased around, to slip her arm behind my neck again, her face was grave, almost wistful.

'Baby?'

'Yes, Selena.'

'I meant that, you know.'

'Meant what?'

'That I love you.' She gave a funny little laugh. 'Know something? I've never loved anyone before. I'm an awful bitch really. Oh, yes, I am. I know. I was poor, you see.' Her hand was straying over my tie. 'I always thought the world owed me a living. I despised everyone really and used them. And then you came along.'

I was watching her, seeing what would happen. I could feel the skin across my forehead growing tight.

'I came along?' I said.

'With you, it's different. Darling, this is different. I'm not used to it yet. It hurts. Baby, it hurts.' Her eyes, watching mine, were almost pleading. 'Tell me. That is love, isn't it? When it hurts?'

'I'm supposed to know?'

Her lids were drooping as if they were too heavy for her. A dazed quality was creeping into her stares.

'You don't love me, do you? Funny. I've just realized that. You don't love me. That's funny, isn't it?' She laughed. It was a thick, muddled laugh. 'But it doesn't matter. When you love someone, you don't care if they love you. Because you want me. I know that. I'll be like those songs. Darling, won't I be like those songs?'

'What songs, Selena?'

'Songs. You know the songs. He can come home as late as can be ... he's my man ... Cindy Lou belongs to Joe ... can't help ...'

She swayed forward, her lips finding mine and pressing against them.

'Darling, I love you. I love you. I ...'

She was warm and heavy against me. I could feel the weight of her breasts through the scarlet towel. Her bare shoulder brushed against my chin. She was still clinging to my neck. Then I felt the fingers loosen their grip. Her hand trailed around my throat. With a little sigh, she drooped backwards and slid off my lap.

She was lying at my feet. The scarlet towel had folded back. Her hair had broken loose and swirled over the green carpet like gleaming filaments of wire.

She was asleep, not poisoned.

She hadn't tried to murder me and I hadn't murdered her.

I felt a terrific sense of relief.

But what I felt about Selena was too complicated to matter. The danger was the only thing now. I wheeled my chair around her and around the beds to the table where Gordy's gun was kept. I'd feel a lot better with a gun.

I pulled the drawer open. The gun was not there. With a growing sense of futility, I searched every conceivable hiding place in the room, including Selena's tumbled clothes.

I didn't find anything, of course.

It was only too clear now that someone other than Selena had been selected to carry out 'the way that wasn't painful'. It was equally clear that the 'way that wasn't painful' was going to be achieved with Gordy's gun.

Gordy committing suicide with his own gun. What method could be more impressive for Inspector Sargent tomorrow?

I wheeled the chair out of the room into the passage, closing the door behind me. There was no light, but there were many windows and a California moon outside. It was easy to find my way along the heavy carpet without making any noise. I reached the corner that led to the other wing and turned it. Marny's was the first door to the left. Mrs Friend's room was next to it. I'd noticed that when Marny had taken me down to Jan.

I turned the handle of Marny's door noiselessly and pushed the door inward. The room was in darkness. I wheeled the chair in and closed the door as gently behind me. I pushed myself to the bed. Moonlight streamed in through the parted drapes. I could trace the outlines of Marny's face, young and quiet in sleep.

I tapped her shoulder lightly. She did not stir. I tapped

again. I felt her body grow rigid. I knew she was awake and about to scream.

I said: 'It's okay. It's me.'

'You ...' Her voice was uncertain. She twisted over on her side and snapped on a bedside lamp.

The black hair was tousled around her oval face. Without her make-up she looked about fifteen. She stared up at me, her eyes ready to be suspicious. I was just as suspicious of her. A misplaced confidence at this stage of the game would cost me my life.

As we stared at each other, I noticed something lying on the bed beyond her, propped against the wall. It was a large pink wool rabbit with shabby, drooping ears. She'd been lying there in the dark asleep with a toy rabbit! Suddenly, I wasn't suspicious any more.

'Remember our bargain?' I said. 'If Selena poisoned me I was to run screaming to you for an emetic?'

I took the 'suicide' note out of my pocket and tossed it to her. She pulled the sheet of paper out of the envelope and, holding it under the light, pored over it. Slowly she looked up, her face paling.

'You – you found this?'

I told her all about it. I concluded: 'Selena wrote it. I can tell that from the spelling. You said she was up to something. See what it was? I'm supposed to commit suicide tonight and have everything nice and tidy when Sargent shows up with the autopsy report tomorrow.'

She didn't seem to be listening while I told her about what I'd done to Selena and about the missing gun. She just sat there, staring at me, clutching the letter.

Suddenly she dropped the letter and threw her arms around my neck.

'Thank God you found out in time.'

She gave a little sob. Her lips, young and clumsy, were pressed against my cheek.

'And you came to me, didn't you? When you were in trouble, you came to me.'

Chapter 23

SHE clung to me. It was as if a dream she had never really believed in had come true. Behind my anxiety I felt rather proud and rather ashamed. In the last few days my masculinity had been disastrously undermined by Selena and Mrs Friend. Having this young kid trembling against me, frightened for me, brought my self-confidence back. Life seemed to be that way. The people you fell for betrayed you. The people you didn't bother with were there waiting when you needed them.

'Don't worry, baby.' I stroked her thick, black hair. 'I'm not dead yet.'

She stared at up me, her pupils wide with horror. 'But they can't be that bad. They can't.'

'You were the one who called them fiends. Remember? You hadn't guessed about this?'

'Of course not. I knew Selena was up to something, but I never dreamed ...'

'They didn't hint at it?'

'As if they would! You've seen how things are between us. You know they'd never dare hint at anything.' She shivered. 'What are you going to do? Call the police?'

'And get myself arrested for conspiracy against the League? It's not that bad yet.'

'But they'll be trying to kill you.'

'They'll have to catch me off my guard first. And I'm not off my guard.' I grinned at her. 'Besides, I've got an ally now.'

She answered my grin with a pale smile. She was still frightened. I could tell that.

I nodded at the wall. 'Mimsey sleeps in there, doesn't she?'

'Yes.'

'I don't like the idea of her ear clamped against the wall. Put on some clothes. We're moving to the living-room.'

'To do what?'

'Talk.'

Obediently she slid out of bed. Her small feet wriggled into worn felt slippers. A drab grey wrap that looked as old as Marny lay on a chair. She put it on, smiling self-consciously.

'I haven't got used to being glamorous in private yet.'

'I'm glad. I've learned not to trust glamour.'

'But you do trust me?'

'I think I do.'

She looked at me thoughtfully. 'I guess you've got to, haven't you? There's no one else to trust.'

She moved to the door and opened it, glancing down the corridor. She nodded like a conspirator and I wheeled myself out of the room. She ran back, turned out the light and closed the door. Noiselessly she wheeled me down the moonlit passage to the living-room. It looked too big and exposed. We went into the little sitting-room where I had had my fateful talk with Inspector Sargent. Marny turned on one light and shut the door.

'You'd better lock it,' I said, thinking of Gordy's gun.

She did. Then she crossed the room and curled up in a chair, watching me. She had given up trying to be a sophisticated imitation of Selena. She was just a quiet, pretty kid. I liked her a lot better that way.

'Well?' she said.

I'd been doing some thinking. Things were a little straighter in my mind.

'Okay,' I said. 'In the first place we know from the note that Selena knows the autopsy report's going to show poison tomorrow. That means she's known all along that Mr Friend was murdered. When you went back to your father's room after Gordy passed you in the hall, Selena was there, wasn't she?'

'Yes.'

'Then either one of two things happened. Either Selena went in just as Gordy was pouring the overdose and saw him. Or the two of them murdered him together. I think it's more likely they worked it together. Maybe it wasn't premeditated.

Mr Friend had told them he was cutting them out of the will. He called Mr Petherbridge to prove it. He asked for the medicine. They gave him the overdose.'

Thoughts were coming at an almost hectic rate.

'Once they'd done it, they'd have realized the terrific danger. They couldn't be sure Dr Leland would sign a death certificate as heart failure. Obviously. So what would they have done? Gordy, the black sheep, was bound to be the most likely suspect if the murder was discovered. Gordy was famous for going off on drunken bats. Okay. So Gordy was to pretend to go off on a drunken bat. If everything worked well with Dr Leland, he could come back any time. If the murder broke, he'd be hidden somewhere where the police couldn't find him. It was sticking Gordy with all the danger, of course. But that's typical of Selena.'

Marny was watching me in bright-eyed silence.

'As it turned out,' I went on, 'Dr Leland signed the death certificate. Not only that. When the will was read, Selena realized that none of you would get any money unless Gordy came back. It was fairly safe for him to come and he was probably planning to. But, as it happened, Nate found me. Selena realized it was a much better bet to exploit me. I could go through the act with the League. And, if the murder should break after all, I could be made to commit suicide as Gordy. That would make everyone happy. Selena could pick up the money. Gordy would be perfectly safe. They could start off somewhere else under a different name.' I paused. 'Does that make sense?'

'I suppose so,' said Marny. 'It's the sort of devious thing Selena could think up.'

'Okay. Then it comes down to one question. Where's Gordy? Did your mother really put private detectives on him in Los Angeles? Or was that just a little bit of propaganda for my benefit?'

'No. She did. They came to the house. I saw them – two broken-down men with cigars.'

'Then it looks as if Mimsey wasn't in on the scheme. Not

187

then, anyway.' A new thought had come, bringing a tingle of excitement. 'If Gordy had ever been in Los Angeles those boys would have picked up his trail. So he probably wasn't in Los Angeles. And he must have been somewhere where he could keep in contact with Selena. Isn't there only one place he could be? Somewhere near and yet somewhere where no one would dream of looking for him?'

She stared at me blankly. 'You can't mean in the house.'

'No. But I can mean in the grounds. Your mother told me yesterday that there was an old farmhouse way off at the back of the property – a house belonging to some old farmer your father bought off when he took this place. You know it?'

'Of course I know it.'

'It's way back in the middle of nowhere on the track over which Jan was going to take me to Nate's cabin, isn't it?'

'Yes, it's ...'

'And this evening when you were trying to explain to Jan that he was to use the back way to drive me out tomorrow, you kept saying Gordy's way. Remember? And when you said Gordy, Jan drew a cross on the map. Did the cross coincide roughly with the position of the old house?'

Her face was dark with amazement. 'Yes, yes, it did. But how could Jan ...?'

'Someone would have to take food to Gordy,' I said. 'And someone would have to take messages from Selena. You said yourself that Jan would do anything for anyone without asking questions. And, if Selena and Jan were carrying on ...' I broke off awkwardly. 'I'm ready to bet ten to one that Gordy's been hiding in that house all this time.'

Marny jumped up excitedly. 'Then if – if you're right ... what?'

'We'll think about that later. Meanwhile we're going to prove whether I'm right or not. Baby, you're going to drive me down there – now.'

She said explosively: 'Are you crazy? In that cast? You couldn't get out to the car even.'

'A crutch,' I said. 'There's a pair of them in the store-closet off the library. I think I can work it with a crutch.'

'But if he's there, maybe he's got the gun. How could you protect yourself with only one arm and a crutch?'

'It's safer than sitting around here waiting for them to bump me off in their own sweet time, isn't it?'

She took my hand and clung to it. 'Please, please, let me go along. I know the house. I can move awfully quietly. I can creep up the back way. I can tell whether there's anyone there.'

I shook my head. 'This is my danger. I feel badly enough having to ask you to drive me.'

'But...'

'Listen, baby, you want to help me, don't you?'

She nodded passionately: 'Of course. Of course I do.'

'Then do it my way, yes? Run along, put on some clothes, get a crutch and a flashlight. The sooner we start the better.'

She looked so forlorn and worried that I reached up with my left hand, drew her down and kissed her on the cheek.

'Be a good girl. Run along.'

She smiled a sudden, vivid smile. Then she hurried to the door, unlocked it and slipped away.

The pattern had fallen into place so quickly that I was still a little dazed by my own deductions. If Gordy was hiding there, he had probably been elected as executioner. How were they planning it, I wondered. Was Gordy to sneak into our bedroom and stage my suicide in the bed next to Selena's? It would be much easier for Selena to do it herself. I thought of her sitting on my lap, twining her honey-brown arms around me, telling me she loved me. Had she shied off killing me herself? Was there at least that much squeamishness in her?

I glanced round the room for some makeshift weapon of defence! Lying on a desk by the window, I saw a paper knife. I crossed and picked it up. It was more than a paper knife, really. It was a dagger in a leather sheath – a souvenir probably from the Pacific war. I drew the knife out of the sheath and tested its blade on my thumb. It was lethally sharp.

I slipped it into my pocket, feeling a lot easier in my mind.

Marny came back soon. She was wearing a black suit and a white shirt. She carried a flashlight and a single crutch.

I tried it out. After a few minutes I got the hang of it. With the crutch under my left arm and my left leg dragging, I could move forward very slowly. It took a lot of strength but it worked.

Marny watched in dubious silence. Then when I signalled, she helped me back into the wheel chair and took the crutch.

'Okay, baby,' I said. 'Let's get going.'

Marny went ahead. As I followed her into the living-room, she picked up a whisky bottle from the table and pushed it down beside me in the chair.

'Something tells me we may need it.'

She led the way through the library, out onto the terrace and around onto a gravel drive which led to the garages.

In the moonlight it was easy enough to see what we were doing, and, as the garages were at the opposite end from Selena's and Mimsey's rooms, there was little risk of waking them.

Marny backed a car out of the garage. With her help and the crutch I managed to swing myself into the front seat. Marny handed me the whisky, put the crutch in the back, and pushed the wheel chair into the shadows where it wouldn't be noticed if anyone should come to the garage while we were away.

She scrambled into the driver's seat and glanced at me questioningly.

'Okay,' I said.

Marny nosed the car out of the gravel parking circle and down the drive. Neither of us talked as we swerved off the drive onto an old track which led away from the house towards the vast, desolate range of mountains. I was thinking more clearly now. I saw that the danger from Gordy was less real than we had imagined. After all, the whole plan rested upon killing me by stealth in a manner that could be faked to

190

convince Inspector Sargent of suicide tomorrow. That meant he couldn't just shoot me – particularly with Marny there as a witness.

I felt better about having involved her in this enterprise. To begin with, at least, the battle with Gordy would be a battle of wits rather than of weapons.

The track seemed endless. It was one of those sections of Southern California where the moment you've left habitation you might be on another planet. Bare scrub lands stretched on either side of us, and the desert mountains, like the skeletal remains of prehistoric monsters, pressed close around us.

'There's a little canyon tucked away,' said Marny. 'He had an avocado orchard there.'

'We getting near?'

'Yes.'

'Then turn off the headlights.'

She obeyed. For a couple of minutes we drove on by the light of the moon. Then the track swerved to the left.

'It's down here,' she said.

We had reached the mouth of a little canyon. Ahead, gleaming faintly white, I could make out the shape of a building.

'Park here. We don't want him hearing the car.'

'Can you manage that distance on the crutch?'

'I'll have to.'

There was a dense clump of bushes. Marny drove off the road so that the car was concealed behind them. She got out, handed me the crutch and, pulling the keys in their black leather container out of the ignition, clutched them in her hand with the flashlight. I propped the crutch under my armpit and she helped me out. In the moonlight her face was white and tense.

'You're crazy,' she said, 'walking with that crutch. You'll kill yourself.'

I patted her hand. 'Don't worry. Just follow my lead. This is going to be a cinch.'

Together we started laboriously down the track to the house. She supported me on my right side. That helped a lot.

As the white blur got nearer, I could distinguish an old bungalow and another building attached to it.

'A garage,' whispered Marny. 'The back part of the house is a garage.'

No light showed from any of the windows. It was a dead house. It looked as if no human foot had trodden near it for years. We came up to it. A rotting picket fence divided off what had been the yard from the surrounding wilderness. There was a little gate sagging on its hinges and a large area cut in the fence for the driveway to the garage.

'The garage first,' I whispered.

We skirted the gravel of the drive. My crutch made no noise on the rough grass. We reached the garage. The double doors were drawn shut. Cautiously Marny slid them back, marking a space large enough for her to squeeze through. She turned back and eased me in after her.

It was dark inside and the air smelt stale and dusty.

'The flashlight,' I said.

Marny turned on a beam of light. A car was standing in front of us – a new, dark blue sedan, not at all the sort of car to be discarded in an abandoned house. Marny gave a smothered exclamation.

'It's the car he went away in. Gordy's car.'

She ran to the front window and threw the light inside. I followed. The keys were still dangling from the ignition. The car was empty. Marny turned.

'You're right. He must be here – in the house.' Her voice broke. 'What are we going to do?'

'There's no light. He's probably either asleep or drunk. How many doors are there?'

'One in the front. One in the back.'

'How many rooms?'

'Just a kitchen, a sitting-room, and a bedroom. There's an old cot in the bedroom.'

'Know the window?'

She nodded.

'Okay.'

'What are we going to do?'

'Make sure he's there. If he's asleep and we don't wake him – so much the better.'

'And then what?'

'Then,' I said grimly, 'you'll know for certain you've got a murderer for a brother and a murderess for a sister-in-law. Scared?'

Her hand found my arm and pressed it. She turned out the flashlight and started silently out of the garage. I hobbled after her.

She led the way around the garage to the back of the house. In the moonlight I could make out three blind windows and a shadowy door. Marny crept up to the window at the extreme left. Together we peered through it. The moonlight, splashing in, showed me a small, bare room. An old cot with a mattress tossed on it stretched along one wall. No one was sleeping on it. There were no bedclothes. It looked as if no one had gone near it since the house was vacated.

We moved to the kitchen window and then to the last window which gave us a glimpse of the unfurnished living-room. Between them the three windows gave a complete view of the interior. One thing was certain. Neither Gordy Friend nor anyone else was there.

'With the car in the garage he can't have gone anywhere.' Marny shivered. 'Do you suppose he heard us and is out here somewhere hiding?'

'Let's take a look inside.'

She slipped ahead of me. The door groaned as she tugged it open. There was a single step. She had quite a time manoeuvring me up it. Then we were in the kitchen. The air was foul and sour – as if a rat had died.

Marny shone the flashlight around. There was no empty cans, no refuse, no indication that anyone had been living there. The bedroom told the same story. There was a vast spider web that stretched from the ceiling to the leg of the bed where it was anchored.

'No one could have been in this room for a month,' I said.

'Then why the car?' Marny's question was shaky. 'If Gordy hasn't been living here – why the car?'

She twisted away towards the door which led to the living-room, her car keys still clutched in her hand. As I lumbered after her, a new thought was coming – a thought which threw our whole theory out of gear and sent a cold tingle up my spine.

We stood together in the doorway of the living-room staring along the beam from Marny's flashlight into that mouldering, empty shell. The fetid smell was even stronger in here.

The floorboards were sagging and broken. The wood had warped too, making the surface billow.

'Let's get out of here.'

Marny gave a little grunt of disgust and turned, swinging the beam from the torch in an arc.

For one second before it passed back into the bedroom, it illuminated the corner to our right.

'Marny!'

'What?'

'Shine the light back in that corner.'

She obeyed. As the light settled there, I saw my first glance had not deceived me. Two of the loose floor boards were splintered. The light patches where fragments of wood had been broken off showed that the damage was recent. I could even see the splintered-off pieces themselves, scattered over the dusty floor.

'See?' My voice sounded harsh and strange.

'But ...'

'It's got to be you,' I said. 'I'd never make it, goddam it. It's got to be you.'

It was one of those strange moments where we understood each other without saying what we meant. Marny pushed the flashlight into my left hand which was clutched around the handle of the crutch. I kept the beam steady. She ran to the corner. She wrenched at one board. It gave immediately. She tossed it aside. She tugged up another board, and then another. She was working wildly, as if, in some way, violence helped.

I took a few steps towards her. Four floorboards had been wrenched up now. I looked down into the shallow pit she had exposed. She had come back to my side. She was clutching my arm savagely. And she was whimpering.

I had been almost sure of what I would see, but that didn't make it any easier. I didn't look long – only long enough to see that the body of a man was lying there, a man who had been shot through the chest.

Marny's fingers dug into my flesh. The whimper coarsened into a harsh, wracking sob.

'Gordy!' She said, 'Gordy! Gordy!'

I had known that too, of course.

We'd found what we'd come for, all right.

Chapter 24

MARNY was sagging against me. My instinct was to get her out of that charnel room. But I couldn't. She was the one who had to get me out. I hated my own disabilities. After a second or two she was in control again. She slipped her small arm around my waist and together we managed to reach the fresh air and the moonlight. The crutch had worked a sore place under my arm. I leaned back against the wall of the house, propping the crutch at my side.

'Cigarette?' I asked.

Having a specific task to do seemed to make it better for her. She pulled a pack of cigarettes out of the pocket of her jacket, lit two and put one between my lips. The tangy smell of smoke was wonderful after that other smell. But I was still half sick with shock, not because we had found the murdered body of a man I had never met but because the discovery implied something I could hardly bring myself to think about.

In the moonlight Marny's face was deathly white.

I said: 'All right, baby?'

'Yes. I'm all right.'

'I'm terribly sorry – getting you into this.'

'Don't be silly. As if it's anything to do with you.' She paused, making me very conscious of the silence of the dead world around us. Softly she said: 'We were wrong, weren't we? We had it figured all wrong.'

'Not wrong, baby,' I said bitterly. 'Just not enough.'

'Enough?'

'Haven't you got it?' I should have grown used to the idea that Selena's wickedness was without limit; but now that the full truth was obvious, I felt an absurd sense of desolation, as if I had loved her very much. 'First we thought Gordy murdered the old man and Selena broke in on him. Then we thought they both murdered him together. We just didn't go far enough. Selena gave him the overdose and, as she was doing it, Gordy came in. He realized what she had done. You can't trust a drunk with a secret like that – not even if he wants to stick by you. You can never tell what he'll come out with when he's stinking. So ...' I shrugged ' ... she lured him down here and shot him. One murder, two murders.'

'Selena!' Marny's voice was pinched. 'But why would Selena murder Father by herself? He was murdered because he was going to cut someone out of his will. Was he going to cut her out of the will?'

'Don't you see? Mr Friend fired Jan that day. Why? Because he must have seen Jan and Selena together, the way you did. His saintly daughter-in-law carrying on with his model clean-living houseboy, sponsored by Mr Moffat himself. What could have made him madder?'

'And Jan – that's why Jan made the cross? Jan helped her?'

'You said yourself he'd help you bury a body and forget it a couple of hours later. He probably didn't help in the murders. She probably just used him to clean up – to tear up the floor boards, maybe, or to get the car in the garage.'

'But Gordy – without Gordy alive, she couldn't have collected a cent under the will.'

'She didn't know about the clause in the will then. None of you did.' I laughed harshly. 'When Mr Petherbridge read the will the next day, Gordy and her chance for a fortune were both buried down here under the floor. She must have had a bad couple of moments until Nate produced me and saved the day for her.'

'Then – then you don't think Nate and Mimsey knew?'

'I'm sure they didn't. Nate's far too lily-livered to get mixed up with murder, even for Selena. And your mother? She'd never have stood for Gordy being killed, would she?'

'No.' Marny's voice was emphatic. 'Never in a million years.' The tip of her cigarette glowed in the darkness. She said suddenly: 'She did have to kill you, didn't she? Selena. She couldn't pin the blame on the real Gordy, because, even if she could make him look like a suicide, the police doctor would know he'd been killed long before the abstinence pledge was signed and that would expose the whole conspiracy.'

'Sure,' I said. 'My suicide tonight's the only possible way it can end happily ever after for her. You see, she's banking on the fact that you and Mimsey are in this too deep to squawk when Sargent identifies my body as Gordy.' I laughed again. 'Too bad I'm not going to oblige her, isn't it?'

Marny was watching me brightly in the moonlight. 'Does it hurt?'

'Does what hurt?'

'Knowing about Selena.'

'Does it hurt knowing your father and brother are murdered?'

'I'm sorry. It was a terribly stupid question.' She moved closer and slipped her hand into mine. 'Well, boss, what do we do now?'

'We don't have much choice. Tomorrow Inspector Sargent's going to come and tell us that your father was murdered. We might as well save him the expense of waiting for the autopsy report and call him up right now. Let him know there's another corpus delicti for his collection.'

'And tell him about Selena?'

'What do you expect me to do? Commit hari-kari to save her skin? You've certainly got me tabbed as stuck on Selena, haven't you?'

'Weren't you?' She drew her hand quickly out of mine. 'Oh, what difference does it make, anyway?' She dropped the stub of her cigarette and crushed it with her heel. 'It'll come out about the conspiracy against the League, of course. You, me, Mimsey, Nate – we'll all get into trouble.'

'Sure. But maybe with a couple of murders on his hands Sargent won't feel too ornery with us. After all, it isn't as if we got away with anything.' I glanced at her. 'But I guess your glamour days are over. No money now. You'll have to take that job in a hashhouse after all.'

'I don't care,' she said vehemently. 'I'll be so glad to be rid of the whole bunch of them forever. Working in a hash-house suits me fine.'

'You've got guts, haven't you?'

'Me?' She twisted round, staring up at me. 'You're the one with guts. You're the one who's taken the beating.'

She put her hands on my arms and, reaching up, kissed me on the mouth. She gave a little laugh that was almost a sob.

'What a place you picked to lose your memory in.'

Her lips were sweet; her body was young and firm against mine. For a moment she made me forget what a horrible night it was.

'We'd better get started.' She slid away from me. 'You wait. I'll drive the car up.'

'No.'

'Why not? You don't want to walk all that way.'

'I don't have to be nursemaided. I'll walk and like it.'

I slid the crutch under my arm. I knew she thought I was being unreasonably stubborn. I probably was. But hobbling back to the car helped me feel independent. I was tired when we reached it and the skin under my arm was burning. She helped me in, put the crutch in the back and scrambled into the driver's seat.

Her hand felt for the ignition and then dropped back to her lap. She fumbled in the pocket of her suit and glanced uncertainly at me.

'The keys,' she said. 'Did I give them to you?'

198

'No. You had them in your hand when we went to the house. I saw them.'

'Then I must ...'

'You've lost them?'

'When – when we found it, I must have dropped them. I ... I'll have to go back.'

'Into that room?'

'I don't mind. Really I don't.' She gave me a fleeting smile. 'It won't take a minute. Here.' She handed me the whisky bottle. 'Have a drink. You'll need it. I'll be back in a second.'

She slid out of the car and then, turning back, took the bottle from me. 'I'd better have some too.'

She drank, handed me the bottle and hurried away towards the house. I watched her slim, straight figure until it blurred into the featureless moonlight.

She had guts all right, I thought.

Alone I started to think of what was ahead of us. Back at that old house with Gordy's body lying beyond the thin walls, what we had to do had seemed so simple. It didn't seem simple now. I'd have to hand Selena over to Sargent, of course. But the moment I'd done it, that would mean the end of Nate as a doctor, the pauperization of Mimsey and Marny and the probable arrest of all of us. The entire Friend household would crumble like the walls of Jericho.

I tried to think if there was any way of saving something, at least, from the impending wreck. As my thoughts strayed barrenly, I heard a sound that started my pulses tingling. It came behind me from the trail which led from the Friends' house and it was the drone of an approaching car.

The drone grew louder. Since our car was hidden behind the bushes, I had no view of the trail. But soon the car was up to me and the beam from its headlights, filtering between the leafy branches, fanned through the car and passed on. The automobile was headed for the old farmhouse.

In a moment I heard it stop. I heard the click of a door opening and then another click as it closed. I thought I could even hear footsteps on the gravel.

Uneasy thoughts jostled each other. It couldn't conceivably be the police. There was no way in which Inspector Sargent could have guessed about Gordy at this stage of the game. Then, if it wasn't the police, it was ... who? Selena, recovered from the sleeping tablets? Or, much more likely, Jan. I realized then with goading anxiety just what must be happening.

If my body was to be palmed off as Gordy's for the police tomorrow, Selena could never risk a possibility of Sargent's finding a second body so inadequately concealed, in the old farmhouse. And yet, she wouldn't have dared destroy Gordy's body before now because, if the plan with me failed, an attempt to build the real Gordy up as a parricide and suicide would be safer for her than nothing, even though it would expose the conspiracy. But now she was so sure of me that she could afford to destroy Gordy.

But, if she had awakened from her doped sleep, and found me gone, she would have known she couldn't be sure of me. This must have been planned earlier. Probably she had divided the job in two. Her job had been to kill me. Jan's job had been to dispose of Gordy. Not knowing Selena had failed in her task, he was going ahead with his.

As the truth straightened itself out, anxiety for Marny started to crawl through me. I tried to steady myself by reflecting that she must have heard the car too. Even if she had been in the house, she would have had plenty of time to slip out by the back door and hide from any danger. But the minutes passed and she did not return. The anxiety mounted, urged on by wild speculations.

What if she hadn't been able to find the keys and had stayed on searching until it was too late? Or what if she had tried to be smart, to set some trap which had failed?

I told myself that, if I was right and it was Jan, Marny could handle Jan. But could she? Jan as an assistant in double murder was a very different proposition from the grinning, friendly Jan she had known about the house.

My own helplessness galled me, like the skin raw under my

200

arm. I knew it would be folly to hobble after her on the crutch. Instead of helping her, I would be an added burden. But as minutes succeeded minutes, the suspense became unendurable. At length, I twisted around to glance over my shoulder. The crutch was lying there on the back seat. By throwing my arm behind me and leaning back, I was just able to touch it. With a great effort I managed to lean back further. My fingers closed around the crutch. But as I pulled it forward, it slipped out of my grasp and fell on the floor. I struggled to reach it but the back of my seat was too high. With a feeling of frustrated despair, I slumped back against the seat.

Grunting with exasperation and exhaustion, I sat there, gathering my strength for a second attempt. The bottle of whisky lay on the seat at my side. I picked it up and took a large gulp of liquor. It was sheer chance that I did not swallow it immediately. But I didn't. As a small amount of liquid trickled down my throat, my sense of taste was suddenly alerted. I let a little more seep down, testing it. It tasted wrong, thick and bitter. I spat what was left out of the window.

The whisky had been doctored.

In a wave of desperation, I realized what had happened. We had picked the bottle up from a table in the living-room before we left. The whisky had been planted there by Selena. The living-room had been the place she had selected for my 'suicide'. If our scene in the bedroom had worked according to schedule, she would have made no excuse for us to move to the living-room. She would have given me a drink. Once I had passed out, she would have brought the suicide note out from its strategic hiding place behind Mr Friend's picture, put Gordy's gun in my left hand, lifted it to my temple and shot. When the shot attracted the household, she too would probably be found rushing in, aghast, with the others.

That's what might have happened. But, in a fever of anxiety, I realized that what had happened was almost as bad. Marny had taken a drink from the bottle. In the urgency of her return to the farmhouse, she wouldn't have noticed the taste. Marny had not come back because she had been drugged. She would be lying defenceless out there in the darkness somewhere – between the car and that room in which Gordy's body lay in its sordid grave beneath the floor boards.

The extreme emergency must have sharpened my faculties. As I stretched back once again vainly groping for the crutch, an image slid uninvited into my mind. It was an image of Mrs Friend saying, as she had said the day before, how lucky it was for their plan that my right arm was in a cast, so that I could legitimately make a left-handed signature on the abstinence pledge. Lucky! If it hadn't been for that luck, their whole plan would have been doomed to failure. If I'd signed the pledge with my right hand, comparison of my signature with any of Gordy's would have immediately exposed the fraud.

They had been lucky enough to find me. God knows. Wasn't the additional fact that my right arm happened to be in a cast a little too lucky for coincidence? And then suddenly another image came – an image of Nate Croft, white-faced and desperate that afternoon when he had entered the living-room and found Selena kissing me. He had said:

'*Does it have to be every man that comes along? This time I thought I'd be safe, I put on the casts....*'

I put on the casts....

Nate had told me at the beginning that neither my arm nor my leg would hurt. I had accepted his word as a doctor's word. But wasn't it possible that the casts had been as much of a lie as everything else connected with that family? What if Nate had pretended my right arm was broken to assure a left-handed signature? And the cast on the leg? *This time I thought I'd be safe.* I thought of his bitter way of loving Selena, his knowledge of her promiscuity and his passionate desire to keep her faithful. What if he had, unknown to the family, put an unnecessary cast on my leg too to keep me 'safe' from Selena? A chastity belt in reverse.

In the first rush of excitement before I had time to weigh the deduction soberly, I pulled the paper-knife dagger out of my pocket. I tugged up my baggy trouser leg. I started to hack at the plaster. As it began to flake off, I knew I was risking a serious fracture if my hunch was wrong, but I didn't care. The chance of being able to get to Marny overrode everything else.

It didn't take long to crack the cast off completely. Time was too precious for me to work on the arm. All I needed at the moment were two legs and one arm.

I slid out of the car and eased my weight on to my left leg. It felt stiff and weak, but there was no pain. I flexed the knee at the joint. There was still no pain. I took a few steps from the car. I walked shakily, but I could walk.

The excitement welled up, mingled with exasperation. I had held my own against the Friends, but I had let Nate, the jealous lover, outwit me almost to the last minute. If I had been smart enough to have thought of this before, I could have been out of the Friends' danger-infested house days ago.

Fear for Marny blotted out everything else. I picked up the knife and slipped it in my pocket. Warily I moved around the bushes and out on to the trail.

In the moonlight I could see the other car ahead of me, parked immediately in front of the farmhouse. From the square bulkiness of its silhouette, I could tell it was a station wagon. As I moved toward it cautiously, my eyes, accustomed now to the dim light, made out a figure emerging from the front door of the farmhouse. I slipped into the shadow of a bush. I could see no detail, but as the figure moved nearer, approaching the station wagon, I could tell from its height and huskiness that I had been right. It was Jan.

As I watched, the fear for Marny stinging like iodine on a cut, Jan reached the wagon. He moved around to its back. He stopped and seemed to feel inside. Then he turned and I saw that he was carrying a square, dark object in either hand. Without pausing, he started back again to the house.

As quickly and noiselessly as I could with my stiff knee, I moved after him. Marny would almost certainly have taken the same route as we had taken. I kept my eyes skinned but there was no sign of her lying by the track. I reached the picket fence. I tiptoed along the grass which bordered the drive to the garage. Marny wouldn't have gone to the garage. Her only object had been to retrieve the keys from the living-room. Cold sweat breaking out on my forehead, I skirted around the far side of the garage to the back of the house.

There were no trees in what had once been the yard. The moonlight, cruelly bright, shone down, illuminating the whole area. There was no trace of Marny. I ran across the exposed patch to the shadow of the house itself. I inched my way along the wall until I reached the living-room window. Cautiously I moved my head until I could see inside.

The rays of the moon cast a dim light into the room. My eyes rested instinctively on the corner where we had left Gordy's body with the pile of floor boards at its side. To my astonishment, I saw that the boards had been put back into place. There was no sign of Gordy. Then, as my gaze moved to the other side of the room, I made out the huge figure of Jan. He stood by the door from the kitchen. He was bending to place two square objects down on the floor next to a group of four or five similar objects.

In the first second I could not make out what they were. Then, with a flash of recognition, I saw they were cans of gasoline.

And, as I stared, a woman's figure appeared in the doorway behind Jan. Her white hand moved to his arm. He turned, blotting her from view and, from the way he stopped, I could tell that he was kissing her.

They stayed there together clasped in a fierce embrace. I could see the girl's two white hands scurrying to and fro across Jan's great back. And I thought with a hatred that made me dizzy and even blotted out my fears for Marny: *So Selena came with him. He woke her up and she came too.*

Dimly, as I watched them, I thought: *This is the way Nate must have felt all the time. Poor Nate.*

And then, suddenly they were gone. I heard the front door open. There was a brief pause. Then, unexpectedly, I heard the station wagon roar alive and drive away.

It had all happened so quickly that I couldn't make sense

of it. Why should they bring gasoline here and then go away? Marny? Was it something to do with what they'd done to Marny?

As I stood there rigid, I heard the faint sound of feminine footsteps approaching from the kitchen. And I understood then. She had sent Jan away. Jan wasn't a fellow conspirator then. He was only an innocent stooge. That's why the floor boards were back in place. His one function had been to bring the heavy cans of gasoline. And his reward had been that kiss. She was using him just the way she had used Gordy, Nate, and me.

From now on, Selena was working it on her own.

I knew then what I would have to do. I would wait until I saw her again in the living-room. Then I would slip round to the back door. In the shock of seeing her immobilized victim-to-be walking into the room, she would be caught unaware – and caught red-handed.

The shadowy figure appeared once more in the kitchen door. She hesitated a moment. Then she ran to the far corner of the room and started tugging up the floor boards. It was horrible seeing her on her knees, avidly dragging up the boards which would reveal what I knew to be hidden there.

It didn't take her long. In a few moments she stood up and hurried across the room. She picked up one of the heavy cans of gasoline. She half carried, half dragged it to the far corner. I heard a little wrenching sound as she freed the cap. She swung the can up and tilted it. I heard a splashing sound – the sound of the gasoline pouring into the shallow pit beneath the floor.

The plan was diabolically simple. With all that gasoline, one match could destroy the tindery house, Gordy, the car, everything. And at this distance from anywhere, no one would notice the glare. Some day, indefinitely in the future, someone would notice that the old house had burned down at last. And that would be that.

When the can was empty, she dropped it. The fumes of the gasoline must have choked her, for she turned away and headed straight toward the window.

Just before she reached it, I ducked out of sight. But I had seen enough to make the hairs at the back of my neck crawl, enough to make the very ground beneath my feet seem insubstantial.

Because, in moving toward the window, she came directly into the path of the moonlight. I could see her clearly for the first time.

And it wasn't Selena.

It was Marny.

Chapter 25

I LEANED back against the clapboard wall. My thoughts were spinning like a kid's firework. Then, as they steadied, I saw how appallingly I'd let myself distort the truth. I had reconstructed the entire murder design in all its detail. Once again I had been helplessly tricked. I had done exactly what I had been supposed to do. I had fallen into the deadliest of all the traps that had been set for me.

It was so easy to see now that every action, every motive I had ascribed to Selena applied just as well to Marny. Old Mr Friend had found Marny and Jan together. He had called Marny in. He had threatened to cut Marny out of the will. Marny had given him the overdose just as the drunken Gordy walked in. Marny had lured Gordy here to this old house and shot him – and later had used Jan to do whatever dirty work was necessary.

The skein of her cunning was untangled for me then. How had I found the 'suicide note' that evening? Simply because Marny, who knew I was going to take old Mr Friend's poems to my room, had thrown the book down on the piano, knocking over the photograph so that I would find out what was hidden in its back. That, of course, had been the first step in the remorseless plan which was to have ended with me committing suicide in the living-room. She had been able to read my thoughts, as plainly as if they were headlines, before I had even thought them myself. She knew I would be curious and pick up the note. She knew I would read it. She knew that, from the deliberately misspelled 'weather' I would think Selena had written it. She knew that, once I thought that, I would remember my bargain with her and somehow get away from Selena to her.

The device of the letter hidden in the photograph frame had been a risky one. It might not have worked. But her need to lure me out of the protection of Selena's room was so great that she had to take the risk. If that plan had failed, she would have had another one ready.

But I had risen to the first bait; and once I had trundled myself in the chair to Marny as my only ally, the rest seemed simple to her. She had already stolen Gordy's gun. She could have wheeled me into the living-room, offered me a drink from the doped bottle, and, after I had passed out ...

But, by the grace of something, things hadn't happened that way. I'd been smart enough to figure out that Gordy was in the farmhouse and had insisted on coming here to prove it. She couldn't refuse to drive me without arousing my suspicions. So from then on she had to go along with me, improvising.

She'd improvised brilliantly, however. She must have made arrangements earlier for Jan to bring the gasoline, arrangements she'd had no chance to alter. She knew then that even if she strung along with me, she would have to be there in the house alone to receive the Dutchman when he came, so that he wouldn't snoop around and find the body. So she pretended she'd dropped the keys to the car and had gone back for them. She had pretended to take a drink from the doped whisky, which *she* had brought with us, in order to be sure that I would follow her lead and drink too.

Now, while she was meticulously setting about her task of destroying Gordy's body, I was supposed to be lying doped in the car.

Once the fire started, all she had to do was to drive me home, bundle me into the chair, wheel me into the living-room and fake the suicide, note and all. Even if the police made an autopsy and found traces of the sleeping powder, they'd never suspect. After all, I was an invalid and full of sleeping powders anyway.

And, as she had said herself, there was nothing to fear from the rest of the family. Once I was dead, and there was no saving me, Mimsey, Selena, and Nate were too deeply involved in the conspiracy against the League to expose the fact that I wasn't the real Gordy.

Yes. That was brilliant improvising, all right.

I thought of Marny from the beginning – Marny posing as the frank one who only joined the conspiracy under pressure, Marny subtly poisoning my mind against Selena with warnings and lies about Jan, Marny assuming the role of little helper so that I would trust her and, when the time came, go with her like a lamb to the slaughter.

A shiver wracked my body. From inside the room I could hear muffled sounds as Marny dragged a second can of gasoline across the floor. I couldn't bring myself to look in through the window.

Marny had talked about fiends. The shiver tingled up my spine again.

There had only been one fiend in the Friend house after all.

I forced myself to plan, because the danger was still great. It would be hopeless to rush her in the house because she had the gun. She would be able to use it long before I could clinch with her.

Gradually I saw I had one advantage. She didn't know that I had discovered the casts were fakes.

I was supposed to be back in the car, immobile in my casts and doped with the whisky.

Okay. That's where I was supposed to be. That's where I would be.

I slipped away from the house and around the garage to the trail. Silently I made my way back through the cold, desolate moonlight to the car. The flakes of plaster gleamed white on the grass where they had spilled. I tidied them up and tossed them under a bush. I got into the car. I pulled a robe from the back and wrapped it around my legs, concealing the fact that the cast had gone.

I thought of releasing my right arm from the cast and decided against it. I would not be able to hide the fact that the cast was gone, and the added mobility would not be worth the loss of the surprise element. With two legs, one arm, and preparedness, I should be more than a match for her.

I put the whisky bottle ostentatiously on my knee and slumped back against the upholstery with my eyes closed and my mouth open. She would be coming soon. One match would be enough to start the building blazing. She would want to get away quickly then and finish her grisly job in the living-room.

I didn't hear her come. Suddenly, I was conscious of her face at the car window, only a few inches from mine.

For a long moment she stood there, quite still, watching me. Through my lashes, I could see her black, glossy hair, the white oval of her face and her eyes. They were shining with a flat, hard brightness.

'Are you awake?' she whispered.

I made a vague answering grunt as if I was dimly reacting to sound in a doped stupor.

She leaned even closer. I could feel her breath warm and rapid against my cheek. Then she giggled. It was a high, tittering sound like a little girl trying to repress irrepressible mirth in church.

She drew her head back from the windows. I could hear her pattering around the car. The outer door opened. She squeezed into the driver's seat next to me. She giggled again, excitedly, bubblingly. I'd never heard anyone make a sound quite like it before and it curdled my blood.

Her hand, reaching to put the key in the ignition, brushed against my knee. I could feel its hectic warmth even through the robe.

I was thinking rapidly. She had the gun. There were only two places she could be carrying it. In one or the other of the pockets of her jacket. Since she would want it in her right hand, if she had to use it, it was probably in the right hand pocket. And the right hand pocket was on my side.

Lurching a little as if I was moving in my sleep, I turned my head and squinted down. Was there a faint bulge in the black flannel of the pocket?

She had started the engine. She would have to back onto the trail. That would be the moment to act, when her hands were busy.

The car began to lumber backward. I pretended to be thrown against her. Swiftly my left hand grabbed at the pocket.

She screamed, a sudden, sharp scream. Her right hand hurtled down, clawing at the back of my hand with long fingernails. The car stalled. The nails dug deeper. Her other hand made a lunge at my face. I could feel the nails scratching savagely down my cheek. For one second I almost had the gun. Then she wrenched it out of my grasp.

I saw the muzzle pointed at me. I jerked her wrist upward. There was an explosion and then the tinkle of smashed glass. I had hold of her wrist now with my only hand. She was fighting with the seething ferocity of a demon, and screaming – screaming that shrill, rasping scream which wasn't a scream of fear but a scream of rage.

She made a sudden plunge at my eyes with her nails. I ducked and at that moment she shook her wrist free. I grabbed it again in a second. And, the moment I grabbed it, another shot rang out. And a third.

Her screaming stopped as if someone had cut a sound track with a knife. The gun clattered to the floor. Her hands were scrambling wildly. One of them caught my wrist and clung on. I could feel the pressure tightening until it was almost unendurable. Then her body started to slide downwards. Gradually the fingers unwound from my wrist. She was slumped on the floor of the car now. I could see something dark welling up, soaking her white blouse under her left breast. Her head was propped against the seat. Her eyes stared blankly and a little gurgling sound came from her lips.

I bent over her. My hand fumbled for her wrist and felt the pulse. One of the bullets must have got her in the heart. She was dead in less than a minute.

I got out of the car, my head swimming. I walked stumblingly around the bushes to the trail. I stared at the farmhouse. An ominous red light was pulsing beyond the windows. It had begun all right.

Gordy's funeral pyre was lit.

I went back to the car. I hadn't meant it to happen this way. That thin, rasping scream still rang in my ears. Beyond Marny on the floor something gleamed white. I leaned over her and picked it up. It was the suicide note. I put it in my pocket.

I had to get away, far, far away. I knew that. But how? In this car with its splintered windshield and the body of Marny sprawled across the floor?

I didn't really think. I just remembered. I remembered that other car, which Gordy had used, parked in the garage with its key in the ignition. I ran towards the burning building. Flames were tonguing through the windows now, but the conflagration hadn't reached the garage yet. It would, of course. In a few minutes the house, the garage, everything would be swallowed up.

I reached the garage, pushed back the old squeaking double doors and ran to the car parked inside. Clumsily, with my one good hand, I started the engine and backed it out, making it leap down the gravel path well away from the menace of the flames.

I sat for a minute in the front seat, trying to make myself think. I looked in the glove box. There were cigarettes. I lit one and leaned back against the upholstery.

The horror was over, but it had left chaos behind it. Marny had murdered her father and her brother and now Marny was dead, having tried to kill me. But how to explain that to Inspector Sargent without getting myself inextricably committed?

I would have to disappear. I saw that at once. If the police knew there had been two Gordy Friends, it would be fatal for everyone. And I could escape in this car. Gordy was supposed to have vanished in it weeks ago. No one would miss it. I could drive as far away as I liked. What did it matter that I didn't know who I was or where I belonged? That was child's play in comparison with what I would have to face if I remained at the Friend house.

But, even with my embarrassing presence eliminated, what would happen to Selena and Mimsey? Confronted with the disappearance of Marny and the man they thought was Gordy, the police would start a search. Soon they would find the remains of a male body in the burned farmhouse and Marny's body in the second car. Without the information that only I could give, Inspector Sargent would almost certainly arrest Mimsey and Selena not only for Mr Friend's murder but for my murder and Marny's too.

Now that I knew they had been almost as fiendishly victimized as I, my old affection for Mimsey and Selena returned. I couldn't walk out and leave them to face the rap for three murders they hadn't committed.

As I leaned forward to toss my cigarette out of the window, the suicide note made a crinkling noise in my pocket. That little sound gave me an idea. I pulled the letter out and, taking the note from the envelope, read it through in the pulsing light from the burning building.

Yes. After all, there was still a way.

My mind was working very clearly now. I ran back to the other car. Roughly, so I wouldn't have to think about it, I pushed Marny's body to one side. I backed the car onto the trail and drove it past Gordy's car straight into the garage. The house itself was blazing now, and flames were already licking at the garage roof.

I picked the revolver up from the floor of the front seat. I made sure no fragments of plaster had caught in the matting. I pulled the crutch out of the back window.

As I left the garage cones of flame were skittering all over the roof. In a few minutes the garage would be burning as furiously as the house.

I carried the crutch and the revolver around to the back of the house. I could still make out the gaping hole which had been the window of the room where Gordy's body lay. I inched as near to it as I could. The heat was terrific. I tossed the crutch and revolver through the window into the flames.

There were the casts to think of too. I didn't know what happened to plaster of Paris in fire but I was taking no chances. I was sure the cast on my arm was as phony as the cast on my leg. With the dagger, I split the plaster off. I flexed my arm. Like my leg it was stiff but there was no pain. It was obviously sound. I threw the flakes of plaster and the sling through the window. I went back to the spot behind the bushes where Marny had parked the car. I gathered up all the fragments of my leg cast and, bringing them back, threw them into the building too.

I stood a moment, making sure I had taken care of everything. Satisfied, I went to Gordy's car and started driving back to the house. There was only one more thing left to do.

When I reached the house, I parked the car outside the garages and walked to the terrace and through the french windows into the dark library. Jan was the only member of the household at all likely to be awake, and his room was in the other wing. There wasn't much risk of attracting his attention. I groped for the writing lamp on the desk and turned it on. The typewriter stood where it had always stood – by the telephone. There was paper, too.

I slid a piece of paper into the typewriter. I had composed the note on the drive back. I knew exactly what I was going to say. The typewriter had rubber keys. I didn't know whether the police would be able to get fingerprints. I suspected that each finger as it tapped a key would hopelessly blur its print with the print left there before. But once again I was taking no chances. In the note I was going to write, I was posing as a man with his right arm in a cast. So I typed with my left hand only.

And I typed:

Dear Mimsey:
This is terribly important. Tell Sargent. Marny killed Father. I knew it all along. I walked into the room when she was giving him the overdose. I knew with Father dead I'd be rich. Marny made me promise not to tell so I agreed. That's why I went off on a bat. I was scared of being around, of giving it away. I wasn't going to tell but now Sargent suspects, it's different. Marny realized that too. She made me promise to meet her tonight in the library after you'd all gone to sleep. I had to dope Selena with sleeping pills. That was the only way I could get away. Marny was waiting here. She said Sargent would find poison in the body at the autopsy, and it would all come out. She said if I told she'd done it, she'd accuse me of helping her. I said it was hopeless. Sargent would find out the truth anyway. She said maybe I was right and that the only thing to do was to escape while there was a chance. But she wasn't going to leave me behind, knowing what I knew about her. She'd stolen my gun. She brought it out then. She said I had to go with her in the car or she'd shoot me. I pretended to agree. I'm helpless in the casts. But I said I couldn't get into the car without a crutch. I said she must get me a crutch. I pretended they were in the attic instead of the closet so that I'd have more time to write this while she's away. She locked me in here. She'll be back any minute. She says she's going to escape to Mexico and take me with her. I don't believe she's going to take me with her. She mentioned the old farmhouse and looked funny. She has the gun. I think she's going to stop at the old farmhouse and try to kill me. No one would think of looking there. I'm going to stop her. But if I don't, if I'm not back here tomorrow or if I don't call, go to the farmhouse. Please, Mimsey, please. She'll be here in a second, I must stop. I . . .

I picked up a pencil in my left hand and signed a clumsy, scrawling *Gordy* at the foot of the page. I slipped the note under the typewriter with one corner sticking out so that they would be bound to find it in the morning.

That story, compounded of truths, half-truths, and lies, was the best I could do. At least it pinned the crimes on the right person and drew Sargent's attention to the farmhouse. When he searched the ruins and found the remains of Marny in the garage and the remains of Gordy in the house, the note was sufficiently vague to enable him to form his own theory as to whether Marny or Gordy started the fire and whether Marny killed Gordy first or Gordy killed Marny. After the flames had done their work he couldn't possibly tell that Gordy had been dead for a week, and I had arranged my props so that, even if some quirk of the fire left something undestroyed, the right things were in the right places – the crutch and the casts in the room with Gordy's body.

It had been a toss-up whether to leave the revolver with Marny or Gordy. I had chosen Gordy because I thought that made a plausible story. Marny had fatally wounded Gordy. Gordy had managed to get the gun, kill her, and then stumble into the house to die.

Between the lines there was a message for the Friends in the note too. They would realize that I was telling them obliquely that Marny had killed Gordy the day she killed her father and hid his body in the farmhouse. I was letting them know the truth and hinting broadly at the attitude they should take with the police. Unless luck was dead against them, they should be able to clear themselves.

They might even get the money, I thought with a faint twitch of amusement. The police would never know a false Gordy had existed or that the signature on the abstinence pledge was a forgery. Once they believed that Marny had killed her father, there was no legal hitch to Mimsey's and Selena's inheritance. They would have trouble with Mr Moffat, of course. But, between them, Mimsey and Selena were expert trouble girls.

An image of Selena came into my mind. Not one image but a dozen images merged together. I thought of my first staggering glimpse of her. I thought of her bending over me in the moonlight. I thought of her as she had been tonight, her honey-brown arms twined around me, her dark blue eyes looking deep into mine with those unlikely tears smudging her lashes.

'*I love you. I really think I do. This is different. This time it hurts. It must be love when it hurts, mustn't it, baby?*'

I had thought of her as a murderess then, a black-hearted, lying murderess. Now, with a queer pang, I thought:

Maybe she meant it. Maybe for the first time she was on the level.

I wanted to run up the stairs, to see her once more, to slip my arms around her and feel the velvet warmth of her skin against mine.

But I knew that it wasn't to be. If I saw her again, how could I leave her?

And I had to go.

I crossed back to the desk and opened the drawer where Mrs Friend kept her cache of money. I couldn't go out into the world penniless. I took fifty dollars. When Mrs Friend realized what I was doing for her, she would think it cheap at the price.

I turned out the light. There was a bathroom across the hall. I was grimy and dishevelled and there was blood – only a little, luckily – on my sleeve. I washed up. I stuffed the towel in my pocket to be destroyed along with Marny's fake suicide-note. I hurried back to the garage. I got into Gordy's car. I drove away.

I didn't know where I was going. I didn't care.

Just so long as it was – away....

Epilogue

I was in the drab lobby of a cheap little Los Angeles hotel when I read the newspaper. I had been there a week because a cheap hotel in a big city was a good place to hide.

Not that I had much reason to hide any longer. I had read the papers avidly since the sensational murder case at Lona Beach had broken, and things were turning out exactly as I had hoped. Sargent was satisfied that Marny had murdered her father and, although the farmhouse had been so completely destroyed that it was almost impossible to reconstruct what had happened there, fragments of the cast had been found which convinced Sargent that Gordy's body was mine. Mimsey and Selena, who had put on a magnificent show, were almost completely free from suspicion. Even Mr Moffat, in a press interview seething with frustrated fury, had indicated his intention of waiving all claims to the Friend fortune.

My link with Mimsey and Selena through the papers was the only thing that made me feel alive. As my fifty dollars dwindled almost to the vanishing point, my mind remained as blank as ever as to my own identity.

A thousand times a day, I said to myself: *Peter. Iris. A plane. Seeing someone off on a plane.*

But those words that had at once seemed so full of meaning now had association only with the Friends. Selena carrying the black spaniel out of the grey and gold room. Selena bending over the vase of irises, her fair hair shimmering, her red lips parted in a smile.

The future was blank and featureless as a drowned man's face.

It was evening when I bought that particular newspaper. I sat down gloomily in one of the lobby's worn red leather chairs and glanced at the front page for any new Friend story. The photograph of a man at the head of a column of print caught my eye. Wasn't there something dimly familiar about that young, narrow face with the close-set eyes and the flopping mane of black hair? Under the photograph was the caption:

ADMITS TO ASSAULT AND ROBBERY OF
MOVIE STAR'S MATE

Halfheartedly at first, I started to read that the boy, whose name was Louis Crivelli, had been arrested in San Diego for a car hold-up and, under police questioning, had admitted to having bummed a ride from a certain Peter Duluth, slugged him and stolen his car one month before. This, the paper said, only deepened the mystery surrounding the disappearance of Peter Duluth, recently discharged from the Navy and married to the famous movie actress, Iris Duluth. A month ago, having said good-bye to his wife, who had flown with the USO morale unit to entertain the American Army of Occupation in Tokyo, Mr Duluth had left Burbank Airfield and had never been seen again. The police were going to take Crivelli to the spot where he claimed to have abandoned Mr Duluth and were going to start a new search from there. It was believed now that Duluth was probably suffering from amnesia caused by a blow on the head stuck by Crivelli.

At that point I was told to see Column 7, page 3. Halfhearted no longer, I leafed through the paper to page three. Above the continuation of the story on Crivelli, was a photograph, captioned:

LAST PHOTOGRAPH TAKEN OF
PETER DULUTH

An army bomber, its propellers whirring, stood on a huge airfield. In front of it, staring at each other rather foolishly, were a beautiful dark girl and a man.

To me, of course, they weren't just a beautiful girl and a man. Nor was the plane just a plane.

I remembered the plane. I knew the girl. And the man's face was as familiar as my own – for a very good reason.

It was my own.

The sense of relief that rushed through me was indescribable. It wasn't that memory of my whole life came tumbling back in one instant. It wasn't as wholesale as that. It was just that every detail of that moment, caught in the photograph, sprang into life for me. *Seeing someone off on a plane.... Peter.... Iris....* The way the wind from the propellers tugged at Iris's skirt. The feel of the sunshine. Iris's voice: *Peter, darling, miss me.*

I remembered it all as if I had left the airport only ten minutes ago.

'Iris.' I said her name out loud. It was wonderful.

There was more in the paper. At the end of the column I read:

Iris Duluth, who only learned of her husband's disappearance last week, flew back from Japan immediately and arrived at her Beverly Hills home yesterday morning.

That's all I waited for. A phone booth stood in a dreary corner of the lobby. I ran to it. My hands had quite a time getting a nickel into the right slot. The operator looked up Iris Duluth's number and got it. A girl's voice said:

'Hello.'

I was going to ask: *Is this Iris Duluth?* But there was no need. That voice was as much part of me as my own fingers.

'Hiyah, baby,' I said. 'Thought I'd let you know I'll be home in the hour.'

'Peter.' There was a catch in her voice that made my heart turn over. 'Peter, I can't believe it.'

'Neither can I.'

'Darling, I've been half out of my mind. Where are you?'

'Downtown L.A. A cheesy hotel.'

'But what happened?'

'I got conked on the head, I guess.'

'I know that. Of course I know that. And I told you to be careful. I might have known. But none of that matters now.

Peter, darling, half of California's been after you. Where on earth have you been?'

Where had I been? I thought of Selena. Matched up against that voice, her glamour dissolved like a mist. Suddenly Selena seemed sleazy.

'Peter, tell me. Please tell me. Where have you been?'

'Oh, that,' I said.

'I've got to know, darling. There are dozens of reporters plaguing me.'

'Get rid of them – quick.'

'I'll try. But I've got to feed them a sop first – like Cerberus.'

'Who's Cerberus?'

'Something that someone had to feed a sop to.'

I thought of telling her to say I'd been visiting friends. That made a neat half-truth. But I had learned from the Friend family what gaping pitfalls awaited the half-truth monger. For Selena's sake as much as mine I had to lie. The lie had better be simple.

'Tell them,' I said, 'that I don't remember. Suddenly I was wandering about the streets of L.A. That's all I know.'

'All?'

'All. You know. Everything went black.'

'All right. I'll tell them that.' She paused and then added with a trace of anxiety: 'Am I supposed to believe it too?'

I was wondering if I had the price of a taxi or whether I'd have to bum it from her when I got home.

'Try, baby,' I said. 'If it's too much for you, I'll think up something else.'

'Like, maybe, the truth?'

'You never know,' I said. 'If my back's slap up against the wall, I may even tell you the truth.'